I0690309

Published by New Generation Publishing in 2013

www.newgeneration-publishing.com

 **New Generation Publishing**

Also by John von Kesmark

The Rathing Chronicles

The Kytos Project
ISBN 1 84624 047 6

Kytos – The Dark Beyond
ISBN 978 1906221 966

Children's Short Stories

Case File from Charlie Cat Detective Agency
PYBO 1522

Author's websites:

<u>www.thedarkportaltooblivion.com</u>

<u>www.kytos-thedarkbeyond.com</u>

ACKNOWLEDGEMENTS

Many friends and colleagues have been supportive during the writing of this book. I want to express my thanks to each one of you; you all know who you are, and so I raise my glass in a salutation to each one of you – too numerous to mention by name.

Of special note is my wife, Diane and sons Paul and Carl. Their constructive advice has been invaluable and I am indebted to them. Also worthy of mention is my publisher, Daniel Cooke, Managing Director of New Generation Publishing who rendered all possible assistance in ensuring the successful launch of my novel. I am most grateful to him for his support and help, and also to Sam Rennie, Production Administrator of NGP who oversaw the book's production in a most diligent manner. I was off-base for some weeks and Sam not only contended with the technical matters associated with the book's production but he also briefed the artist on the book cover visual concept in an exemplary manner. Thank you, Sam.

Finally, I want to thank my readers for having waited patiently for this third book in The Rathing Chronicles series. The Dark Portal to Oblivion is truly a team effort. To you all, I am most grateful.

John von Kesmark
Old Isleworth, England
2013

"The human psyche is very strange, you know," he said, staring up at the ceiling. "One's train of thought alters radically depending on the circumstances prevailing at the time. Take now, for instance. I know I shall be executed within a day or so. Dying does not frighten me.

"When I was younger, the representative of death was some far distant shadowy image. Because life was so precious to me then, I believed that the soul could not die, that it would continue to exist through the media of reincarnation; it would be the whole basis of evolutionary development. Surely God would not create souls and grant them such an infinitesimally short life span? No. I firmly believed that when one died, one's soul was directed to another plane to await a rebirth in due time.

"In fact, I am now firmly of the opinion that death happens as soon as you step into the dark portal to oblivion; a long black-as-sin tunnel. Then, the soul is no more. The light goes out. A black curtain descends." He smacked down hard on the table with the side of his open hand. "And there is no more. No feeling, no awareness, nothing. Just blackness. A complete and utter void. So that is why I have no fear of death, my dears. Because there is absolutely nothing there to fear. And even if there were, I would be unaware of its presence because I would no longer exist."

THE DARK PORTAL TO OBLIVION

A Thriller

by

John von Kesmark

PROLOGUE

It was a warm June day as the three climbers inched their way towards Uamh an Claonaite, one of the largest caves in Scotland. It was a bleak and remote location. Even though it was a warm day, the climbers felt a distinct chilliness as they approached the cave entrance. They were excited at the prospect of exploring the cave network which had once been the headquarters of General Strŏesser, the Rathing Chief of Staff of Army Group and head of Northern Command at the time the Rathings governed the country. As far as they knew, they were the first humans to visit the cave network since the Americans assisted Great Britain by discharging vast quantities of DTX toxin from their bombers and annihilating the entire mutant clone Rathing and Magar populations.

The climbers – two men and one woman – moved into the cave, their torches playing along the floor and the walls. They saw several items that had once been used by the military garrison scattered along the way; swords, lances, shields and other weapons as well as bowls, cups and various items of crockery. The men and woman had the distinct impression that the earlier occupants had departed in a hurry.

The torch lights picked out what seemed to be large boulders further along the dim cave passageway. They had nearly reached the mound when a sudden realization stopped them in their tracks. These were not rocks but rather the recumbent figures of Rathings who seemed to be asleep.

"God's teeth!" one of the men exclaimed. "They were all supposed to have been killed by the poison!"

"Shh!" the woman whispered. "We mustn't wake them."

The younger of the two men, who had not spoken moved slowly towards the still figures. Perhaps he was a little braver, or more foolish, than the others because he poked one of the bodies with a piton. It did not react to the prod, so he poked it again, this time a little harder.

"It's not asleep," he called out. "I think it's dead."

"Phew! Thank God for that!" The older man cried out in relief.

"I think we should call the police," the woman climber said as she walked out of the cave. Once on the plateau, where the sound reception for mobile phone calls was better, she phoned through to the local police station and reported their find. "It will be a few hours before they get here," she explained to her companions. "What should we do in the meantime?" she asked.

"Might as well continue exploring the cave network," the older of the two men said. "We know those Rathings are dead, so it should be OK."

They continued with their reconnaissance and were amazed at how vast the caves proved to be. It was obvious that the network was artificially extended by the Rathings to house their numerous troops. The three humans examining the cave did know that thousands of human slaves and Droons, an aberrant species of clone enslaved by the Rathings, had once been shipped to Scotland to work on enlarging the cave network. It had taken ten years and the deaths of over two thousand workers before the caves were large enough.

Eventually, one of the men looked at his watch and said, "Guess we should be heading back to meet the local cops when they arrive."

The three climbers returned to the plateau and waited there for another hour before a young constable came puffing up to the plateau. He was sweating and red faced and shaking from exhaustion. It was obvious that rock climbing was not one of his leisure pursuits.

"Thought you'd come by helicopter," the older man remarked, looking with a puzzled expression at the young policeman who now lay prone on his back, gasping for air.

"None... none available until much later. Did.. didn't want to delay getting here."

"Well, you're here now," the man said, "so you'd best go in and have a decko at them."

The constable, seemingly reluctantly, got to his feet and followed the climbers into the cave.

He stood some distance from the bodies and kept bending forward and peering at them. He squatted on his right haunch, then his left. Then stood up and played his torch on the bodies. He moved in all directions but never directly towards the dead Rathings. He studied them for several long minutes but did still not move close to them.

"For Christ's sake!" one of the men shouted in frustration. "The buggers are dead, that's why we called you. Go on. Have a good look. They won't bloody bite you."

The young policeman moved slowly to the bodies and tentatively prodded one of them with his truncheon. "Aye, you're right there. Dead," he announced. "I'm going to have to secure this area until the heavy lifting gear the sergeant's ordered gets here. I have to request you to vacate this location."

3

The three climbers raised their eyebrows in surprise but moved out and onto the plateau. "This isn't a normal crime scene," one of the men said. "So you're being a bit silly acting along conventional lines. Look mate, even if we stayed in the cave, there's bugger all we can do to muck up your 'crime scene'."

"I'm sorry, sir," the policeman said. "We have to follow procedure."

The man shrugged and walked towards his companions. They all sat, leaning against the rock face and silently watched the policeman re-enter the cave.

An hour or so later, they heard the familiar sound of helicopter rotors strimming the sky. Three copters appeared. They were large Sikorskys. It was obvious to the three mountaineers that the rotor blades were too large and too long to allow the craft to land on the narrow plateau without hitting the rock face. The lead pilot also recognized this. The climbers saw him shake his head and then point downwards. They thought he was indicating a return to base. But he did not fly away but rather drop further down. The climbers walked to the precipice and saw the pilot attempt to land on a plateau some ten feet lower down. This plateau was very much wider than the one the three stood on and which led to the cave mouth. Several air-sea rescue personnel spilled out of the helicopter and began unloading some of the heavy lifting equipment. The lead helicopter then flew off, to be immediately replaced by the second craft. The same procedure as the first landing took place, and then again when the third copter replaced the landing space of the second one after it departed.

A total of about twenty men were now congregated on the lower plateau. They quickly assembled some of the equipment. They shouted to the onlookers to stand back as they were about to fire grappling hooks on to the plateau above them. Once this was done, some of the rescuers used their glider (rocket booster) boots to propel themselves to the higher plateau and they began to piece together the various parts of the lifting equipment.

The young policeman came out of the cave, obviously having heard the noise of the new arrivals.

One of the rescuers walked up to the young man. "Are you in charge here?" he asked. The policeman nodded. "Well, we're going to have to take those Rathings down to the next plateau. This one is too narrow for the helicopters to land safely and not hit the rock face with the blades. The one below is larger," he explained.

"Blimey!" the young policeman exclaimed. "That's going to be a bit of a job."

The rescuer smiled. "All in a day's work," he said.

"How are you going to lower them down?" the policeman asked.

"We'll lift them in purse seine nets and ease them over the precipice."

The woman climber, who had been standing nearby, asked, "What's a seine net?"

The rescuer turned to her. He noted her attractive suntanned face and grinned. "This is a strong net made of metal links so it can bear the weight of the creatures. There's a purse line that passes through the rings at the bottom and when pulled draws the rings together."

"You mean like a purse which has a drawstring?" the woman said.

The rescuer gave her an even bigger grin. "Atta girl," he said. "That'll secure the body firmly so it doesn't topple out." He then turned to his crew and began to relay orders.

The men trundled the lifting equipment into the cave. The work was long and hard and dangerous –

especially when they had to lower the heavy weighted dead seven foot four hundred odd pounds Rathing down to the plateau below.

Using a ratchet-armed piece of equipment, they attached the seine net holding one dead Rathing and gently lowered it to the plateau below.

"Wouldn't it be a lot easier if you chucked the carcasses over the precipice and then picked them up at the bottom?" the younger of the two climbers asked a member of the mountain rescue team.

"Look, sir," the rescuer explained. "We're not going through all this palaver out of respect for these creatures. If we did chuck them over the side as you so eloquently put it, how d'you think we could retrieve any bodies that might land on a jutting outcrop? Or get wedged half way up a slope? Trust me, sir. We know what we're doing."

The crew had eventually reached the last few bodies when they were aware of movement below the carcasses. With some difficulty they shifted away one of the dead Rathings and were astonished to see about a dozen squirming bodies of baby Rathings. The little creatures gave high pitched squeaks and some were hissing in annoyance. Baring teeth and teeth chattering signified their anger.

"Blimey O'Reilly!" one of the rescue team exclaimed. "We've got some live ones here."

"They must have been protected from the poison gas by the pile of bodies over them," the woman climber said.

"They're very skinny," one of the rescue team declared.

"Doesn't look like they've eaten for a while," the woman said.

"I'm not too sure about that," one of the rescuers said, pointing at the last remaining dead Rathing which had lain immediately on top of the youngsters. "There's quite a bit of flesh eaten away from this one."

"Aha! Cannibalism in the Rathing world," a rescuer said jokingly.

"If you were near starving to death under some meat, you'd have more than a nibble," the woman said angrily. "The poor creatures needed to survive."

"I'm going to have to call my sergeant," the constable said and moved out of the cave.

The constable told the sergeant about the live baby Rathings. The sergeant called his Inspector who, in turn, felt he had to refer this to higher authority. He was eventually connected to a member of the Scottish parliament who then contacted the Home Office in London. A few hours later, the Inspector received a call from a senior Government minister in London.

"Look here, Inspector," the minister said firmly. "It is essential that this discovery is kept under wraps. If any story about the re-emergence of Rathings reaches the public the panic will be incalculable. Fear and the image of Rathings once again assuming power would grip the entire populace. Once the live baby Rathings are down here, we will have them destroyed," he lied. Then he said, "Now, this is what you will do."

"Yes, sir," the Inspector answered.

"You will gather in your office all those involved in this operation and you will contract them under the Government's Official Secrets Act. You must include yourself."

"Is there any official wording for this, sir?"

"Of course there is, man. But we don't have time for all that malarkey. Just cobble up a few official sounding terms – such as 'my attention has been drawn to the provisions of the Official Secrets Act ... and I am hereby aware of the serious consequences that may follow any breach of these provisions... I shall be guilty

7

of a misdemeanor'. You know that sort of thing. Have you got that?"

"Yes, Minister. I think so. Do I have to include the mountain rescue team, sir?"

"Of course, man. I said 'all those involved'".

It took two days to complete the removal of the Rathings. The rescue team had come well prepared. They had bags of sandwiches, flasks of coffee and even a roll of toilet paper. Everyone bedded down in the cave as comfortably as they could manage.

When the clearance task was finished and everyone returned to the village, the police inspector summoned everyone to the Station and the Official Secrets Act was invoked.

Large trucks loaded the dead Rathings and drove them to Gretorex Hall, an Elizabethan manor house in Hertfordshire. There, several at a time were placed in large incinerators. The stench of burning flesh and fur was so great that complaints were received from nearby homes.

The baby Rathings were also driven to Gretorex Hall but there, they were housed in cages in the basement hospital, given a small amount of nourishment and slowly nursed back to health. Certain senior people in a Government department had other plans for the small Rathings.

None of the truck drivers were required to attend the Inspector's Official Secret Acts ceremony as they were all Government employees and had signed the Act when they were first employed some years before.

*****

Three days after the mission at Uamh an Claonaite was completed, the young police constable was killed in a road traffic accident.

8

On the same day, the police sergeant was killed when his cottage caught fire following an explosion which the authorities said was due to a gas leak.

The three climber's bodies were found at the foot of Glencoe's highest peak. It was assumed they had been killed falling 1000 feet down Bidean Nam Bian.

The police Inspector was found hanged in his garage. The Coroner's verdict was suicide whilst his mind was unbalanced. The Inspector's wife assured the Inquiry that her husband had no worries and he and his wife and children led a happy life. The Coroner did say, however, that some people were very good at disguising their inner turmoil and he had no option other than reach the verdict he issued.

The mountain rescue team all disappeared about three weeks after their mission was completed. They never turned up for work and were never heard of again.

The Scottish parliamentarian whom the police inspector had contacted with news of the presence of the baby Rathings blew his brains out in his office, shortly after holding a meeting with an unexpected visitor from London.

ONE

Friday 26 November 2094 : night

The man looked down at the young female Rathing's body. She was completely naked and lay on her back. Unlike the rest of her body which was covered in a very light brown shade of rat fur, her small breasts were hairless – a sure sign of her young age. A further indication of her youth was the fact that her facial features had not yet fully assumed the normal rodent-like expression. Her face still bore strong resemblance to her human genes, although her ears were certainly those of a rodent and her nose was just beginning to protrude and resemble a very tiny snout. There was no question that she was dead. Her eyes were still open and her terrified expression had remodelled her once lively impression into an ugly questioning accusatory look. He could not bear to look at her face. He threw a towel over it.

The man wore a blue waist length pyjama top and pyjama shorts. His bare legs were very pale, hairless and very thin. His feet, big, gnarled and ugly, were bare. His expression was cold, his lips almost as pale as were his alabaster white legs. He moved apathetically towards the drinks cabinet and poured himself a large cognac. He noticed that his hands were shaking. He lit a Black Sobranie cigarette, the packet of twenty bought from his black market contact for £50. He took a generous gulp of his drink and swore under his breath. "Shit! Shit! Shit!" He sat on the edge of a richly carved armchair upholstered in black crocodile leather and leant forward with his elbows resting on his knees. Cigarette ash dropped onto the navy blue Aubusson Persian rug but he paid no heed to it. Instead, he took another heavy drag on his cigarette and a further generous mouthful of cognac. After some five minutes, he went to the telephone and keyed in a number known to only a select number of people.

"O'Connor?" he said. "I am in need of your help. I'm afraid there's been a total fuck up and I've got a dead Rathing lying on my bed."

He listened whilst the other spoke.

He replied to an obvious question: "Yes. I know. The question now is we've got to get rid of the body, hide it. Would you handle that for me? Good man. An hour? That's fine. And O'Connor? Thanks a lot."

*****

O'Connor, a short, thickset muscular man with a shaven head looked down at the Rathing's body. The gentle expression in his grey-green eyes that he'd held when studying the dead Rathing now turned hard and cold when he looked at the man in the pyjama suit. "How did this happen?" he asked.

"D'you want a drink?" the pyjama suited man asked.

O'Connor shook his head. "Well?" he prompted.

"I, I got her sent up from the experimental hospital."

"Why was that?"

"Well, I wondered what it would be like to have sex with a young female Rathing."

You sad bastard, O'Connor thought. "So what happened?" he asked.

"You don't really need to know all the facts," the pyjama suited man said arrogantly. "Your job is to get rid of the body."

12

"If my job is to clear up your mess, I need to know the facts."

"Oh, all right," the other man said petulantly. "If you must."

"I must," O'Connor's voice was now as cold and hard as was his expression.

"Within a few minutes of her being brought in she started acting up. Prowling around the bedroom, being very agitated. I calmed her down, gave her a bath and assured her I meant no harm and had a gift for her. When she'd relaxed sufficiently I quickly gave her an injection of Propofol. She went absolutely crazy when she felt the needle jab."

I shouldn't wonder, O'Connor thought. "What's Propofol?" he asked.

"It's a short acting and controlled sedation. It puts the injected individual into a semi-hypnotic state, still being aware of what is being done to them but unable to fight against it."

"Which means you could rape this creature whilst she could do nothing about it." O'Connor clapped his hands silently, mockery portrayed in every movement, and said sarcastically. "Congratulations! So how come she died?"

"Propofol should be administered by an Anaesthetist, who, of course, I am not. I was given a phial by one of the doctors and told to be very careful in using it. I can only assume that microbial contamination caused serious infection. It is obvious that she had a septic shock. She had a high fever, cold hands and feet and a weak, rapid pulse. She was also vomiting and had diarrhoea."

"And all because you wanted a fuck a Rathing," O'Connor snarled angrily. "You've done a great job, Grey Goose." O'Connor had used for the first time the man's code name. "Give me your car and garage

13

keys," O'Connor said, stretching out his hand towards the pyjama-suited man. Once he'd been handed them, he turned to the man he'd called Grey Goose and said, "I'll let you have them back in two days. I'll leave you to clear away the vomit and shit on your bed sheets. Oh, and you'd better get rid of that stink of cigarette before a nosey neighbour smells it and reports you to the police Behaviour Force."

He lifted the Rathing and laid her on the carpet.

"Not, not on the Aubusson!" Grey Goose protested, stepping forward.

O'Connor ignored the man's protestations. He looked at him and raised an eyebrow. He continued to lay out the dead Rathing on the carpet which he then rolled and lifted onto his shoulder. He walked out of the apartment without saying goodnight.

He put the rolled up carpet into his jeep, then opened the garage doors, went in and drove out Grey Goose's Bentley, which he parked in one of the reserved parking bays of the apartment block. He then drove his jeep into the garage and laid and unrolled the carpet before gathering a number of large stones and small boulders from the garden area and which he placed on the carpet alongside the body. Some of the Rathing's hair had fallen across her face; he delicately moved the hair to one side, and touched her face very gently, smiling at her. She looked so young and innocent, a mere child, and he felt a sudden revulsion at the thought of what the man who had killed her had done to her beforehand. At that moment he wished he had never got involved with these people.

He then rolled up the carpet, which now was bulky due to the presence of the stones. He moved to the side wall of the garage and took hold of a big, heavy chain that lay on a shelf. He wrapped the chain around the rolled up carpet. He then took a couple of padlocks and fixed them to the chain. He locked the garage door from the inside. He got into the passenger seat of his jeep and settled back, prepared to spend the night in his vehicle.

Patrick O'Connor had completed the first step of his assignment. He would now sleep before undertaking the long nine hour or so drive to the Lake District. He had timed his departure so as to ensure he arrived at Lake Coniston at about ten o'clock at night. What he had to do, he wanted to carry out in the dark and away from curious eyes.

TWO

Because of the continually falling snow, it took Patrick O'Connor much longer than he had expected to reach Windermere. But it was winter; it was cold, snowing and dark and he doubted anyone would be venturing out and about at that time of night. He drove on to Lake Coniston and to Lowthaite Landing. He was pleased that the Council had recently resurfaced the area, as it made driving near the river bank much easier.

He got out of the jeep. He put on a beanie hat and tightened his coat around him. He walked along the river bank, the heavy torch in his hand lighting up the area. He eventually located the dinghy he was looking for. He untied the rope that anchored it to a mooring and pulled it along the shoreline until it was close to his parked jeep. He then tied the dinghy's rope to a heavy tree branch.

O'Connor then opened the boot of the jeep and heaved out the rolled up carpet. He carried the carpet to the dinghy and carefully placed it in the boat. He lowered himself slowly onto the dinghy's bench seat and fixed the oars into the rowlocks. Throughout these manoeuvres, he kept looking around furtively to see if he was being observed.

The oars kissed the water and the dinghy glided smoothly to the centre of the lake. O'Connor stopped rowing. He sat bent and looking down at his feet for a good five minutes before stirring himself and moving the rolled up carpet towards the boat's prow. He again

16

looked around carefully to see if there were any obvious observers. But it was pitch black; he was satisfied that he seemed to be on his own. He gently rolled the carpet over the side into the water. It sunk immediately.

O'Connor stood up in the boat. He pulled off his beanie hat and bent his head. He stood in the dinghy, swaying with the water's movement, seemingly oblivious to the heavy white curtain of snowflakes that floated around him. Although he had put on extra warm clothing, anticipating that the weather would be considerably colder than in London, the raw, biting temperature chilled his bones. He appeared to say a prayer. He ended by saying "Peace be with you, young Rathing." He made the sign of the cross. He put back on his beanie hat and remained standing, looking at the pitch black water that lapped against his dinghy. It did not occur to O'Connor that his pious action might be considered somewhat incongruous. He was a devout Catholic and believed that all of God's creatures deserved recognition, especially in death - even though this creature's forefather had been artificially created in a laboratory.

He quietly sat on the dinghy's bench seat for some five minutes. Then he rowed quickly back to shore, the oars digging into and slapping the water. O'Connor got into his jeep and prepared to make his return journey.

THREE

The warble of the telephone woke Penny. She cursed loudly, pulled the heavy winter duvet over her head and buried herself more deeply into her bed. The telephone maintained its incessant call for attention, interrupting the Sunday morning silence. Penny eventually stretched out her hand and lifted the receiver.

"Yes?!" she snapped.

"Good morning, Penelope," said a deep, mellifluous voice. "I trust you answer your phone more politely at the office when a client calls, as opposed to your uncle."

Penny groaned and cursed silently. This is my home, not my damned office, she thought. And for God's sake, don't call me Penelope. "Uncle William!" she cried. "What an unexpected surprise."

Sir William Henderson gave a laugh, which to Penny sounded contrived and far from genuine.

"I need to see you with some urgency. I have a job for you. Can you meet me at eleven o'clock?"

"Tonight?"

"No, Penelope. This morning."

Penny looked at her bedside clock. The time showed 9.40.

"It, it doesn't give me much time to get ready," she mumbled.

"Aren't you out of bed yet?" Sir William demanded.

Penny ignored his question. "Can we make it eleven thirty?" she asked.

"Yes," her uncle replied. "But not at my office in Whitehall. Have you a tablet or other writing material handy?"

Penny nodded then realized that that acknowledgement could hardly satisfy her uncle. "Yes," she said hurriedly.

"Right. Take this down. Caledonia Road. Greek café called Apostolo's. Eleven thirty. Got that?"

"Yes." Penny wondered how she could get from her flat in Teddington to Caledonia Road by bicycle by eleven thirty.

"Get a cab," Sir William ordered, as if reading her thoughts. "I'll pay for it. And for your return." He cut off the connection.

Penny threw herself back on her pillow and closed her eyes. Not even a goodbye from good old Uncle William, she thought. Typical. She knew that her uncle William, her father's brother was a bachelor – seemingly unloved and unwanted? But she thought he might have cared to be more polite to a girl. Goodbye was not a word that made you beholden to the recipient.

God, she wished Peter was still with her. She missed him dreadfully now five years since his death. She missed not cuddling against his warm body on cold mornings. She missed his cheery morning smile as he brought them both a cup of coffee to savour before getting up. She was fed up with having solitary meals, with watching television alone or with the occasional solo cinema visit. And she greatly missed their love-making. She recalled his gentle kisses and caresses. How he touched her before she felt his hard muscled body press against hers and how he entered her, slowly at first then more forcefully. There was a slight stirring in her groin. Her hands moved down to her pudenda and her eager fingers explored herself, gently at first then rubbing more vigorously. She gave a gentle moan, and then suddenly sat upright. Stop it, she demanded of herself. Now's not the time. You've got to get going.

Penny got out of bed and shuffled to the bathroom. As she brushed her teeth she gave a quick glance at herself in the mirror. Her natural blonde hair, pixie style cut, framed her face, still slightly tanned. Her blue eyes had that sleepy look about them but certainly did not detract from the very attractive image reflected in the mirror. She leant forward and studied the skin around her eyes and mouth. She was pleased to note that there was no trace – faint or otherwise – of ageing lines. You're wearing reasonably well for twenty eight she muttered satisfactorily. She showered quickly then stepped into the body dryer cubicle where she was bathed in a blanket of warm air, drying the whole of her body. She then carefully considered what she should wear. Penny was rarely summoned to see her bachelor uncle. The Hon. Sir William Henderson was a senior government official – Minister of State for Internal Affairs and he had a sumptuous office in Whitehall, which made his choice of meeting at a Greek café in Caledonia Road rather strange. He had said he had a job for her which she felt excited about. A government assignment was certainly a step up from tracing errant wives or checking up on the habits of wayward husbands. God knows, the Private Investigations office she and Peter had established, badly needed the money. She had found it increasingly difficult to run the agency on her own since Peter's death. But she had studiously refused to hire anyone. No one could replace Peter and, anyway, she did not have the money to pay wages to a staff member.

As she would not be cycling to the meeting, she decided to wear something smart, so she choose a black cashmere polo neck, black trousers and a red blazer jacket. She certainly sensed that she was smart enough to have a business meeting with a government official. A glance from the window at the light feathering of falling snow convinced her that it would be sensible to wear her black boots. She went downstairs and threw on her Mac and grabbed her slim briefcase, which was empty. She decided to leave her case. Instead, she reached for her coat and umbrella. She closed the door of her flat and was half way down the garden path when she realized she hadn't had any breakfast, or even a coffee. Ah well, she thought, I should at least be able to get a coffee at Apostolo's café.

The cab journey took under an hour, which was pretty good going as the Sunday traffic had been quite light and the snow hadn't settled yet. Penny got to the café at 11.10. Sir William had not arrived. A balding, fat little man scuttled towards her on her entrance. "Good morning, Madam. Please to take a seat – wherever you like." So she sat at a window table and ordered a skinny latte. She debated about having some toast but decided against it. She thought that greeting her uncle with a mouthful of toast crumbs on her lips might not give the best first impression.

The tables were plastic with plastic tablecloths patterned in red and white squares. The chairs were plastic but in myriad colours – some red, some blue, a few green and most yellow. Brown linoleum covered the floor. A few prints of the Acropolis, Parthenon and other Greek city scenes decorated the yellow painted walls. The colour design and materials were most certainly not of the 2090s but more reminiscent of a workman's café in the late 1900s or early 2000s. Yet the place was impeccably clean.

She watched out of the window at the few people who passed by. Most of them wore glider boots and they skimmed by a few inches above the pavement.

21

Penny thought how useful the boots were as it prevented the wearer from sloshing through the melting snow or sliding on ice patches. She thought that perhaps she should use hers a bit more often.

FOUR

At precisely 11.28 a black chauffeur-driven Bentley drew up outside the café. The uniformed driver jumped out and opened the rear door of the car. He was hatless, a tall, well-built, muscular man with blond hair. Penny thought he looked like an ex-wrestler. Penny saw her uncle emerge, his usual haughty expression etched on his face. His black leather shoes were so highly polished that Penny could have sworn he would see not only his own reflection in them but also the winter clouds scudding above him. He noticed Penny sitting by the window and he raised his bowler hat in salutation. She thought how quaintly old fashioned he was; few people wore hats nowadays, and even fewer sported bowler hats.

Apostolo – so Penny assumed – rushed to the door as soon as he had seen Sir William arrive. The Greek bowed as he opened the door. "Sir William," he muttered obsequiously, "It is an honour and a pleasure to see you again." Sir William gave the Greek a strained smile. "Apostolo," he acknowledged.

To see you again, Penny said to herself. This must be a regular haunt of Uncle William's. Strange. Hardly the kind of workmen's cafe you'd expect to see him in.

"Your usual, sir?" Apostolo asked.

"Please."

Sir William removed his hat but not his expensive looking overcoat. He was of medium height, somewhat thick set, with a strong, sharp featured angular face and

23

gray hair, perfectly cut and swept abundantly above his ears.

"You still trundling around on a bicycle?" he asked as he sat down.

Penny nodded. "Yes, Uncle."

"Damned dangerous in London traffic, I would think. And this is hardly the weather for cycling. That's why I told you to get a taxi."

"Near six thousand or so daily London cyclists would not agree with you. Numbers shot up after the famous London 2012 Olympics."

"That was in another life - some eighty plus years ago. Road deaths are still regularly posted."

Penny knew one could never win an argument with her uncle.

"You should get yourself a car. A little run-around."

She shrugged. "I can't afford a car. Apart from the actual cost of the vehicle there's all the extras – petrol, insurance, road tax, service costs, replacement parts and so on and so on."

"Surely Peter had some pension arrangements or death insurance policy in hand?"

"He was twenty five when he died. He hadn't reached the stage of setting up pension plans. And no, no death policy."

"Harrumph!" Sir William grunted. "Look here. If you'd like to borrow some money I can lend you some. I don't like to think of you struggling."

Penny shook her head vigorously. "Thank you Uncle but, no, I don't wish to borrow money. I am not struggling. I live quite well but don't have so much more than I need to waste it on a car purchase. I am very happy with my bike. But I appreciate your considerate offer. Anyway, on the subject of cars, have you any idea what the daily cost is of that wonderful looking Bentley of yours parked outside?"

Sir William gave her a weak smile. "It's not mine. It's the government's car. In any case, I didn't arrange this meeting in order to discuss car costs."

"So what did you want to see me about? You said something about having a job for me."

"Let us wait for my coffee, which I see wending its way towards us." Do you want something to eat?"

Penny shook her head. "No thanks."

The Greek cafe owner placed a small square shaped cup before Sir William. "Thank you. And Apostolo, would you be good enough to take out a coffee and a bun of some description to my driver?"

"Of course, sir," Apostolo bowed.

"I believe he has a double espresso with warm milk on the side."

Apostolo bowed again and moved towards his kitchen.

"It always pays to look after the little people," Sir William explained.

Penny bristled.

Her attention was drawn to the thick looking black coffee before her uncle. She leaned forward to study it more closely. "What on earth is that?"

"Kopi Tubruk; an Indonesian style coffee, very similar to Turkish or Greek, but very thick."

"It looks hideous," Penny scowled, leaning forward again and giving it a further study.

"Care to try it?"

Penny shook her head. "No thanks, uncle. So what's this job?"

Sir William took a sip of his coffee. "You are no doubt familiar with the current rumour of the re-appearance of Rathings."

"I have heard some whispers," Penny admitted.

"Naturally, it's complete nonsense. We have firm evidence that all Rathings were annihilated when the Americans very kindly came to our aid and bombarded them with poison toxin."

"Wasn't it called DTX?" Penny asked.

Her uncle ignored her question. "If this kind of gossip continues unabated, the consequences would be catastrophic. It is only a few years since we were liberated from the yoke of repression that we suffered under Rathing rule. The fear of the general populace imagining such a return of rule would give rise to all kinds of mayhem. Riots would follow on the heels of panic. The resultant outcome would be calamitous. It is the Government's firm resolve to prove to the populace that this rumour is without foundation."

Penny nodded. "And may I ask where do I come in on this?"

"We, the Government, want to have a report from an independent source confirming that the Rathings have not re-emerged, that they were all killed by the toxin, and that this rumour has been started by those whose sole objective is to create alarm, hysteria. They are simply being mischievous.

"This is an internal matter and it therefore falls within the responsibility of my department to deal with."

"And you wish me to prepare and submit this report?"

"In a nutshell."

"Uncle. May I ask why you don't have this looked into by MI5 or MI6 or whatever Intelligence department you use?"

Sir William smiled. "And have people say it's a government cover up? No, my dear, many would suspect that we had instructed our Intelligence service on what to report. That's why I said we want a report from an independent source.

"You have been operating a private investigations agency, initially with Peter, and I regard you as suitably qualified to investigate this matter. Admittedly, your agency is not a member of any official body – the IPI or ABI - but as such is not essential and I know about you and Peter when he was alive, about how dedicated you are, I have no hesitation in assigning you to this case."

"I am very happy, of course, that you thought of me but there are many larger, more established private investigators in London. May I ask why you did not contact any of them, Uncle?"

"Because you are my niece and I know that I can trust you to keep this case confidential. At this stage, confidentiality is very important to the Government. It is for that reason that I am assigning this case to you."

"I see. Well thank you again, Uncle."

"I presume you want to make a note of these, but have obviously not brought with you any writing material."

Penny now wished that she had brought her briefcase. She said nothing.

"Apostolo," Sir William summoned. "Some paper and a pen if you please."

Once she had the paper and pen Penny waited for more information; she had so far received no information which needed noting down.

"There is some urgency. However, it should not take you too long to undertake this task. You won't need to go into any in-depth investigation; we already know the facts. Make a few soundings then submit your report on your company letterhead which we can show to the Opposition party and to the press and television people. Once the Media circulate this piece

27

of information, it will ease the minds of the public. This investigation should not take you more than a week or so.

"I assume you are able to take on this task immediately?" Sir William asked whilst studying his fingernails.

Penny was rather excited at the prospect. "Yes, Uncle."

"You will be paid handsomely."

"I'll get on to it straightaway, Uncle. And thank you Uncle."

"I shall assign someone from my Ministry to work with you on this case, to assist you. He will advise you on the steps involved when working for the Government. Due to procedural methods in Government work being very strict, you will have to refer to the person I am sending of any meetings or contacts you intend to make. He will be representing me therefore you will have to obtain his agreement before you take any action. I trust that will be acceptable to you. But as I said earlier, you need not go to any lengths investigating the veracity or otherwise of these rumours. You could, in fact, just knock off a report without going to all that trouble of making too many in-depth checks."

Penny shook her head. "No. Sorry, uncle but a good agency doesn't work like that. My report will be based on evidence gleamed in the course of my enquiries.

"Uncle. Would you grant me a moment to put to you a hypothetical scenario?"

"If you must," Sir William grunted ungraciously.

"Imagine if you will that in this imaginary scenario I am a senior Minister in a Government. I want to show people – it doesn't matter whom – that a field of peas are actually carrots. What's the best way to go about it? Firstly, I contact a business services company that offers in their services a mail address facility and a phone number. So I sign up for this virtual office. With the vast resources at my disposal I register a company name – let's call is Joe Bloggs Agency. I then have the letterheads printed, incorporating my newly acquired mail address and phone number. I then word process a report stating that I (that is Joe Bloggs Agency) have done an in-depth investigation and have concluded that the field of peas *are* in fact carrots and I advertise this piece of fake investigation to all those whom I want to receive it."

"Is there much more to this ridiculous fantasy story of yours?" Sir William interrupted.

"No, uncle. I am practically finished. What you suggested a few moments ago is tantamount to what I have just described. If you want the kind of report you just suggested, why don't you do what my hypothetical principal just did?"

"You sometimes really do amaze me, Penelope. In the first place, that is not the kind of thing we would do. That is a scam of sorts and no self-respecting organization would entertain such deception. And most certainly this Government and I would never consider such underhand action. Furthermore, if anyone decided to check up on the worthiness of such a report, they would soon learn that your Joe Bloggs Agency is not really a bona fide firm. So you, as this fictional Government Minister, would have destroyed the very thing you were trying to achieve, you'd be laughed out of court and possibly swept into prison. Frankly, Penelope, I take some exception to your suggestion that I am proposing some sort of swindle. My suggestion was made to simply try and save you time. No more than that."

"I'm sorry, uncle, if I misunderstood your intention. There was no criticism implied."

Sir William's scowl slowly disappeared. "Good." He shrugged. "I must have your report very, very quickly, so I'll make my point again. Don't spend too much time on your enquiries.

"Your contact will be a young fellow called Pelllow. I'm not sure of his first name. I shall arrange for him to visit you at your office tomorrow. Your office is still in Putney, I assume?"

Penny wrote 'Pellow' on her piece of paper. "Yes, uncle." She was not sure whether she liked the conditions her uncle had just stipulated. She was far from overjoyed at the thought of having to obtain someone else's permission before doing something. She decided to say nothing at this stage but wait and see how it went.

Sir William smiled at Penny. "Oh, incidentally, as you will have been engaged by the Ministry and not by me, personally, I think from now on whilst on this assignment you should address me as Sir William. There is no need for family familiarization in this instance. You will also be required to sign the Official Secrets Act and I shall arrange for this to be conducted within the next few days. "

Penny nodded. "I understand, Uncle. Er, I mean Sir William."

Sir William leant back with a satisfied smile. "Good. I shall give you a lift back as far as Whitehall. You shall have to make your own way home from there." He drew his wallet from his inside jacket pocket. "I said I'd pay for your taxis." He extracted three twenty pound notes and placed them on the table.

"That's far too much, Uncle," Penny protested. "I don't want to take more of your money than is necessary."

30

Sir William smiled again. "It is not my money. It is the Governments, who can stretch to an outlay of sixty pounds. Shall we go?" He rose.

"Shouldn't we pay first for the coffees?" Penny asked.

"I have an account here."

"You come here often then? Well, I did think it rather out of the way and in a strange location for you."

"Apostolo serves the best range of coffees in town. Besides which, this kind of location is far removed from prying eyes."

Penny was still a little puzzled. "But why so far out of town, Uncle? I mean Sir William."

"The chances of our being seen here in Caledonia Road are far more remote than if I'd arranged to meet at, say, Megabucks in Regent Street or in Kensington High Street, if indeed there is any such an abomination in either of those locations.

"I shall arrange for this chap Pellow to call on you tomorrow. Come on, let's go."

FIVE

Despite it being a Sunday, Sir William Henderson had summoned in his secretary, Miss Annette Pilgrim and she was in the Ministry's Whitehall office awaiting Sir William's return from his meeting with Penny. Pilgrim was tall, grey haired, impeccably dressed and one of the most intelligent women in the Ministry. Sir William, on his arrival, walked through Miss Pilgrim's office en route to his own, greeting her with a perfunctory "Good afternoon."

Once seated at his desk, Sir William buzzed through to Miss Pilgrim. "Were you able to contact Mr. Pellow and instruct him to come in this morning?" he asked.

"Yes sir. He is already in."

"Then please have him come and see me immediately."

"Yes sir. Oh, and Sir William. Do you wish for coffee?"

"No thank you, Miss Pilgrim."

"I also have a message for you, sir. One of Our Leader's aides called. The Chancellor wishes to talk with you soon as possible."

Sir William grunted. "You may try and connect me to him after I have finished my meeting with Mr. Pellow."

Sir William busied himself at his desk until the arrival of a casually dressed, good looking young man.

"Ah, Pellow! Good morning to you. Sorry to have dragged you in on a Sunday."

"Not at all, sir."

"I regret to say that there is something of a panic on. The Government – the Chancellor in particular – is becoming very agitated with the increasing rumours about the re-emergence of some Rathings. This kind of tittle tattle must be scotched before it grows out of hand. It has been decided to have the matter scrutinized and reported on by a firm of private investigators. I want you to work closely with this firm and report to me what action is being taken. Do you follow me?"

The young man nodded. "I do, sir."

"Do sit down, Pellow. You make the place look untidy standing there," Sir William grumbled.

Pellow sat on one of the visitor's chairs opposite Sir William's desk.

"This Investigations firm happens to be run by my niece," Sir William continued. You still follow me?"

"Yes sir. May I ask a question?"

"It is?"

"Is there not some rule about not appointing family members to Government contracts?"

Sir William gave a cold smile. "You are quite correct, Pellow. I am, however, ignoring that particular ruling in this instance for the very reason of the necessity for us to achieve the result I desire. I know that my niece would submit a report she believes to be true, based on the information which we steer her way. For reasons which are obvious, I do not wish this matter to be investigated too closely. To be brutally frank, Pellow, I don't think my niece is experienced enough to delve too deeply into this issue. Therefore, I am confident that her findings will be very much in line with what I want to see. All I want to have is a piece of paper on the letterhead of a bona fide investigations agency for us to show to the Opposition and the Media. That piece of paper must be in line with what I want to see, and I believe that my niece can be manoeuvred diplomatically in order to produce the right findings. She has been told that we are concerned about the rumours of Rathings having been seen.

"Besides which, I have had my intention cleared by the Chancellor and the Department Minister responsible for the appointment of outside contractors."

Pellow nodded. "I understand, sir."

Sir William leaned forward and moved into a straight line the objects on his desk. Neither man spoke whilst the older one aligned each item in precise order. When seemingly satisfied, Sir William leant back in his chair.

"Furthermore, my niece's fee will be considerably less than larger firms would levy.

"Now, you may be wondering why I called you in today, it being a Sunday."

"Not at all, sir."

My niece is Mrs. Penelope Campbell. She is a young woman with, as I've already said, limited investigative experience. She has not before handled any Government contracts and she may well be unaware of the way we do things. I therefore intend to assign you to oversee the running of this assignment. I have informed her that she must clear with you first any contacts she proposes to make and to get your approval."

Pellow nodded but said nothing.

"I want to make it quite clear that you are to report to me the actions she is taking or proposing to take; preferably before she takes such action and once she has had your approval."

Pellow nodded. "Clearly, sir."

"I want you to visit her at her office in Putney tomorrow morning. I have already had a meeting with her this morning and told her of your participation, so she will be expecting you." Sir William handed to Pellow a piece of paper. "I have written her address on there."

Pellow pulled out from his smart, expensive-looking denim jacket a slim black EID card and flashed it across the paper so as to instantly record the details in his card memory.

"I also have this for you to give to Miss Pilgrim," Sir William continued, handing over another piece of paper. "It is the wording to be printed onto fifty business cards for Mrs. Campbell. Have Miss Pilgrim arrange their printing and you are to ensure you collect them and deliver them to Mrs. Campbell when you see her tomorrow."

Pellow took the paper and held it in his hand.

"I shall arrange for Miss Pilgrim to have a cheque drawn out in Mrs. Campbell's favour as her agency's fee. You will collect this from Miss Pilgrim later today and give it to Mrs. Campbell. You will also tell Mrs. Campbell that she is entitled to claim reasonable expenses. Have you got all that, Pellow?"

"Yes, sir."

"Good. Now, do you have any questions?"

Pellow shook his head. "No, sir. Everything is perfectly clear."

Sir William smiled. "Good. Then I shan't detain you any longer." He reached for his phone to indicate that the meeting was finished.

Pellow got up and walked out of the office.

A few moments later, Miss Pilgrim buzzed through and said, "Sir William. I am about to connect you with the Chancellor".

Sir William hurriedly picked up his phone. He heard himself being connected.

"Henderson," the Chancellor snarled. "What are you doing about this damned rumour of Rathings wandering about?"

"It's well in hand, sir. I had an early meeting this morning and have appointed the investigative body to check out the - in my opinion – the false rumours, and to submit a report to you."

"I am not interested in your opinion, Henderson," The Chancellor snapped. "Whether you believe that the rumours are false or are not is immaterial. I want an independent answer. This is an internal matter which falls within your ministerial jurisdiction. I want this matter resolved without delay. Do I make myself clear?"

"Perfectly, Chancellor."

SIX

After Penny was dropped off in Whitehall by her uncle she took a taxi to her flat. En route, she used her mobile to instruct the central heating system in her flat to switch itself on.

She walked in and took off her coat and her boots in the hall before going into the kitchen where she made herself a mug of hot chocolate. Cradling the mug in her cupped hands to warm them, she moved into the lounge. Penny flopped down into her favourite armchair and pulled off her socks. She picked up her landline phone and keyed in a number. Whilst the ringing tone tried to connect she wriggled her toes and waggled her ankles to help circulation. A strong feeling of contentment wrapped itself around her.

"Bill?" she said when connection was made. "Hi! It's Penny. Penny Campbell. Oh, I'm fine, thanks, Bill. How are you? Good, good. And Ellie? That's lovely to hear. And how are the children? I know, I'm sorry I've only seen you a couple of times since Peter's funeral but, well, you know..." she left unsaid any further excuses What? Tonight? Are you sure? Well, of course, I'd love to. No, I'll make my own way over – by taxi if it's still snowing or bike if it's eased off. Seven thirty? That would be great." She watched her wriggling toes for a few seconds then she asked. "Tell me, Bill, are you still editor of The Globe? Oh good. I called you because I think I'll need your advice. Perhaps we can talk about it tonight? Lovely. Thanks, Bill. Look forward to seeing you all this evening."

She disconnected and lay back in her chair, a satisfied grin spread over her face. She wriggled her toes briefly one more time, then got up, went to the kitchen and took a bottle of wine out of a cupboard which she put into a plastic bag. She next went to the bathroom and run a hot bath. She stripped, studied in the large mirror her slim figure and the bikini outlined tan from the summer, before sinking into the warm vanilla and honeysuckle scented foam bath.

At half past six Penny went out of the flat and got on her bike. She much preferred using her own transport, especially as it had stopped snowing, rather than relying on taxis.

When she reached Barnes, she found easily Bill and Ellie's large detached house. The light was on in the garden and she recognized Bill's old, but expensive Van den Plas car in the drive.

She leaned her bike on the wall in the porch-way and rang the door bell. It opened and she saw a tall, young man-boy standing in the entrance and grinning at her. "Hi Auntie Penny," he said, opening his arms to embrace her. "Great to see you."

"Adam?" she queried. "No. You can't be Adam. Who *is* this tall, good looking young man?"

"It's me, Adam," the young man said, displaying perfect white teeth in an even wider grin.

He and Penny were hugging each other when Penny heard Bill's voice call out "Is that young Penny at the door?" Bill came ambling out into the hallway. He was a big man, with a tendency to being slightly overweight. His blonde hair was tousled. He wore jeans and a food splattered cook's apron circled his ample girth. "Penny!" He called out. "Hello stranger."

Penny released Adam and went into Bill's open arms. "I'm so sorry, Bill, for not being in touch sooner."

"Nonsense!" Bill objected. "If anything, I should apologise for not contacting you."

"Hey Dad! Now that apologies have been exchanged," Adam said jokingly, "shall we go in and see mum?"

As Penny entered the drawing room, her attention was immediately drawn to the enormous fireplace in which several logs blazed away. There was no main centre light switched on but several table lamps cast subdued lighting. Penny immediately saw Ellie, tall, blonde and elegant, standing by the fire. "Darling, Penny," Ellie said, quickly walking forward and embracing Penny. "How very lovely to see you. My dear girl, you look gorgeous as usual."

"And you, Ellie, are as lovely and elegant as ever," Penny said warmly.

Ellie gave Penny a kiss on both cheeks then turning to the two young children aged about ten or so who stood beside her, she said, "You remember Pavo and Alicia, of course."

"Gosh! They have grown a bit since the last time I saw them."

The young boy stepped forward and extended his hand towards Penny. There could be no doubt that he was Bill's son. He had the same unruly blond hair and round face. "Hello, Aunt Penny. I'm Pavo and I'm ten."

Penny shook his hand then leant forward and whispered, "Am I permitted to give you a hug, Pavo?"

The boy nodded, smiled and said, "Yes please."

Penny squeezed him and kissed his cheek. She then turned and looked at the very beautiful girl who stood next to Ellie. "And you are, of course, Alicia," Penny said.

The girl gave a small curtsy and whispered shyly, "Helo, Auntie Penny."

Penny walked over to her and gave her a hug. "Hello, little angel. I can see you are going to be as beautiful as your mother."

Ellie then said, "You've already met Adam this evening. He was very keen to open the door for you." Ellie waved Adam forward.

Penny was now able to study Adam more carefully. He looked nothing like Bill, although he had a passing resemblance to Ellie. He was tall and slim and dark complexioned. Penny guessed he was about 16 or 17 years of age. Penny knew that Adam was born to Ellie after she had been practically raped by her boyfriend, Ashok. This happened when they together with Bill were hiding from the Rathings in a cave at Rumrunner Cove in Cornwall. Ashok, Bill and Ellie had ventured on to Rumrunner Cove when they were teenagers as it was Ashok's intention to return to the past through a Time Gate and try to persuade the scientist who created the clones to stop his experiment. Ashok had remained at Rumrunner and joined a band of mercenary humans fighting the Rathings; Ellie and Bill had later learned that Ashok had been killed in a skirmish. On Bill and Ellie's return to their home village, Ellie learned that she was pregnant. Bill had long been in love with Ellie but he had never indicated this as she was the girl friend of one of his best mates. He asked her to marry him. To explain Adam's birth, they concocted a story that Ellie and Ashok had got married secretly at Rumrunner Cove by an officiating priest who was with the band of mercenaries fighting the Rathings. Adam knew that his biological father was Anglo-Indian but he looked on Bill as his Dad, as did Bill regard Adam as his son.

Bill and Ellie's marriage was not one of convenience. They both loved each other and were sublimely happy. Penny was very conscious of the family's happiness and love that was evident in the room's atmosphere. Penny was suddenly aware how empty and sterile her own life seemed when compared to the comforting warmth exuded by those around her. What a lovely, lovely family she thought.

Adam came over with two glasses of wine that Bill had poured out. "For you, Mum," He handed Ellie a glass of red wine. "And for you, Auntie." He handed Penny a glass of white wine.

Bill had returned to the kitchen to finish his dinner preparation. Adam volunteered to put his younger brother and sister to bed so as to allow Ellie and Penny time to chat.

The two little children gave Ellie and Penny good night kisses and then rushed into the kitchen to kiss their father goodnight.

"Come, sit beside me," Ellie patted the sofa seat next to where she sat. When Penny was seated, Ellie leant over towards her and whispered, "Tell me all your news. Are you seeing anyone at the moment?"

Penny shook her head. She took a sip of her wine. "I've had the odd dinner date or theatre visit but other than that I am leading a Nun's life. Otherwise, life goes on in its usual -"

"Oh my dear," Ellie interrupted softly. "I am so sorry the way things have turned out for you. Still, you must remain confident."

Penny gave a small laugh. "Oh, Ellie, I do try to be confident but ...well, I must confess that there are times when I miss Peter very much."

Ellie patted Penny's hand. "I know, Penny. I can well understand."

They heard the phone ring, which Bill answered in the kitchen.

Bill marched into the drawing room. "Dinner's ready, ladies. We'll eat at the kitchen table. No standing on cere -."

"Who was that on the phone, darling?" Ellie asked anxiously.

"Adam's friend, Tom. They're picking him up shortly. On their way to the snooker club."

"On a night like this?" Ellie said in a surprised voice.

"You were young once," Bill laughed. "And not so long ago. We didn't think twice about swimming with Ashok in the middle of the night in icy water across the point at - ."

"Ah, but we wore condritherms," Ellie reminded Bill.

"And you were about the same age as Adam is," Bill countered.

Just then Adam entered and said with a smile, "Did I hear my name mentioned?"

"Just about your going out tonight, darling," Ellie said. "Will you be all right?"

"Fine thanks, Mum. And I have put on *my* condritherms." It was obvious from his comment that he'd heard more of the conversation than he'd originally let on. He went over to his mother and kissed her, then kissed Penny. He walked over to where Bill stood and kissed his cheek. "See you later, Dad. I'll be home before midnight. "We're just having a few games of snooker at the Club." He went to the drawing room door. "See you later – and hopefully before you go home, Aunt Penny."

After Adam had left Penny, Ellie and Bill sat down to dinner. Bill served up large plates full of chicken casserole in a rich sauce, with chunks of freshly baked bread to mop up the juices and vegetables in side dishes. He poured out generous glasses of wine.

After dinner and whilst relaxing over coffee and brandies, Penny raised the subject with Bill which she had been keen to discuss.

"I've got some good news to tell you two," she announced. "Oh, and I forgot – I've brought you a small present of a vintage burgundy. It's in the hall. I know how much you love good wine, Bill."

Bill and Ellie smiled at Penny.

"Thanks, Pumpkin," Bill said. "If Ellie keeps behaving, I'll let her sample a sip or two."

"Well, go on, Penny" Ellie said. "Don't keep us in suspense about this good news you have."

"I've got a Government contract job."

"So, who did you have to sleep with to get...ouch" Bill exclaimed when Ellie kicked him under the table. "I'm sorry," he mumbled.

"It's from Uncle William."

"The Government's Minister of Internal Affairs?!" Bill exclaimed. "My, your Gumshoe business is coming up in the world!"

"Bill, you're not funny!" Ellie scolded angrily. "That's not a very nice way to refer to Penny's business."

"Oh, I don't mind, Ellie," Penny said with a laugh, to hide her embarrassment. But she felt a little hurt at the way the world perceived her line of work, and especially hearing it from Bill.

"I'm sorry, Penny. I was joking."

"So what's this Government contract you've got?" Ellie said quickly in an attempt to ease the situation.

"Uncle has asked me to look into the rumour about the re-emergence of Rathings and submit a report on my findings."

"What's there to look into?" Bill said.

"If it's true or not."

"And how d'you propose to do that?" Bill asked, filling his balloon glass with two inches of cognac.

"By asking intelligent, informed people their opinion."

"Are you seriously putting us up in that category, Penny? Intelligent *and* informed!"

"Yes, I am, Bill." Penny was becoming somewhat agitated at Bill's flippant attitude.

"Bill, do be serious please," Ellie frowned.

"Yes. I am serious, Bill" Penny answered Bill. "And I need to receive serious and considered opinion."

"Have you an opinion yourself on this subject?" Bill asked.

"My opinion is of no concern. My report must be based on facts I obtain."

"You won't get any facts, Penny," Bill said, as he swirled his brandy glass around. "There are no facts or evidence to this story."

"As a newspaperman I thought you might have some inkling on the veracity of this rumour."

"No, I don't. But let me spell out some facts, if I may."

"Of course," Penny smiled at him.

"Firstly, please don't forget that I was a prisoner of a Rathing Overlord when I was a young lad. I witnessed at first hand their cruel nature. I was punished but not tortured like some other prisoners were. I ... I saw others killed for simply talking to another prisoner – for breaking the Overlord's rule by speaking in the presence of a guard." At this stage, Ellie leaned over and took Bill's hand and held it tight.

44

Bill continued. "Every single human in this country experienced unmitigated upset, no, distress and abject fear of the Rathings. I must therefore question why anyone should be sick enough to conjure up a false scenario by claiming having witnessed the presence of Rathings somewhere up in Scotland. It achieves nothing."

"It frightens people," Penny said.

"True," Bill agreed. "But then one must ask what purpose is served in frightening people?" He stood up, picked up the percolator and rinsed it out before putting in it fresh coffee grounds. He filled it with water and switched it on. "For what it's worth, I believe that there is more than a grain of truth in the story – *but I have no evidence to support my suspicions.*"

"Where is this Scottish place they've been seen at?" Penny asked.

"It's called Uamh an Claonaite."

"How does one get the evidence, darling?" Ellie asked.

"The rumour maintains that some Rathings have been seen in a somewhat remote area in Scotland – supported by evidence that an army contingent of humans cleared out all villagers in the vicinity on the pretext of there being unexploded bombs, or something like that," Bill said, as he watched the percolator make its usual slurping sound to indicate it was brewing the coffee grounds.

"Where exactly is this place?" Penny asked.

"In some remote, outlandish part of Scotland. So, short of going up there, I can't immediately see where else you'll get evidence."

"You surely must, Bill," Penny pressed him for more information. "After all, you run a newspaper; part of the great information media."

"My paper is not interested in rumour mongering. My Scottish correspondents have sniffed around but found nothing of any particular note. I am sorry I can't be of further help, Penny."

"But you think it might be true," Penny remarked.

"A personal opinion. Not that of a newspaper editor."

Penny thanked Bill for his honest appraisal. She then said she'd have to make tracks home.

Bill, who was standing at the kitchen window, said, "I think you may have a job there. There's a snow blizzard dancing merrily outside at this moment."

Ellie just said "I hope Adam is alright and will be home soon," when they heard a car drive up and stop in the street at the entrance to their drive.

"That'll be Tom dropping him off," Bill said.

A few seconds later they heard the front door opening and Adam marched in, snow clinging to his hair and clothes.

"Aha! The Snowman cometh!" Bill said jokingly.

"And that's just from the gate to the front door," Adam laughed. "Cor! It's Eskimo weather out there."

"If you plan on cycling home you'll cycle as far as the gate and then get snowbound," Bill said.

"You're staying here tonight," Ellie stated. "It won't take me a minute to get the guest bedroom made up."

"So you stay here tonight," Bill said.

"I really couldn't..." Penny objected before Adam interrupted her. "If you try and go by bike, I'd say – with due respect, Auntie – that you're round the twist. And any taxi or minicab will take two days before they get here to pick you up."

Penny laughed. "What can I do when faced by a concentrated family attack? OK, I give in – reluctantly.

But thank you so much. I do really appreciate your kindness."

SEVEN

Penny was in her office early the next morning. Her new assignment excited her, especially more so after hearing Bill admit that he believed there might be a grain of truth in the rumour about Rathings.

She felt very grateful to her uncle for his kindness in selecting her, even though she thought it quite curious. She had seen him on only two occasions at family gatherings since Peter's death, which made this encounter all the more unusual. Still, Uncle William was a strange man and she soon stopped trying to fathom out why he had chosen her for this job.

She checked her file of outstanding cases. Three. All non-urgent. She reckoned they could be tackled after dealing with her uncle's assignment.

She was going through her mail, which were mostly bills when the door bell rang. She walked to the intercom. "Yes? Who is it?"

"Pellow. Alistair Pellow from the Ministry of Internal Affairs. I am to see a Mrs. Campbell."

"Yes. Come up." Penny pushed the button to release the downstairs door lock. She thought her visitor had a nice voice, well modulated, rounded and pleasant, definitely Oxbridge but far from sounding self-important.

The office door opened and a young man walked in. Penny quickly appraised the person she was to work with on this assignment. She thought he was in his early to mid-thirties, of medium height and with the physique of a rugby prop forward. His brown hair was cut short. His smiling dark brown eyes looked at her with keen interest. His features were boldly handsome, enhanced in some surprising way, by a nose obviously broken some time ago.

He had on a smartly cut black woollen overcoat which had a sprinkling of snow on its shoulders. Over his crisp white shirt he sported a tie, an obvious college, university or military tie, Penny wasn't sure which. He carried a slim-line briefcase.

"Hello," he said. "Is Mrs. Campbell in?"

Penny smiled. "Yes, she is."

"Would you mind telling her that Alistair Pellow is here? We have an appointment."

"She already knows. Would you like a coffee?"

"Yes please."

Penny walked to the coffee percolator, chose one of the unchipped, better mugs, and poured out the coffee. "Milk? Sugar?"

Alistair looked at her from behind. Her light grey skirt stretched tightly as she leaned over the coffee table and emphasized her pert bottom. He could not help but admire her well shaped calves leading to slim ankles and her firm, natural figure. He tried to visualize her naked and was pleased with the image conjured up.

"Third time of asking. Milk and sugar?" Penny stood facing him with the mug of coffee in her hand and a questioning if amused smile which made her already pretty face even prettier.

For a sudden second Alistair almost thought she had read his imagined perception of her being naked and he felt himself reddening. Oh, sorry," he said. "I was miles away. Just one sugar please. No milk, thanks."

Penny handed him his coffee.

"Is Mrs. Campbell through there?"

"I hardly think so," Penny teased. "Through there is the stationery cupboard."

Alistair raised an eyebrow. "I see," he said in a puzzled voice. That was the only door in the small room, other than the entrance door. "I thought you said she is in."

Penny decided to play fair. "She is. I'm Penny Campbell."

Alistair put down his mug of coffee. "My God! I'm sorry," he exclaimed. "I thought you were a member of staff."

"I don't have one. Neither do I have a receptionist, a switchboard operator, typist, cleaner or, as you have just seen, an office coffee maker. This strictly a one-man band operation."

"Perhaps a one-woman operation might be more correct?" Alistair said with a grin. "Well, it's nice to meet you Mrs. Campbell." He gave a slight bow of his head.

"Penny, please," she said putting her hand forward.

They shook hands and Alistair liked the softness and coolness of her hand. Lucky sod, Mr. Campbell, Alistair thought. The girl was quite petite, about 5'3" or 5'4" Alistair reckoned as he glanced at her breasts which were not large but were firm and nicely shaped beneath the blue sweater that she wore.

"Penny," he smiled. "I'm Alistair. Alistair Pellow."

"I know. Sir William told me yesterday he'd be sending you here."

Alistair bent down and opened his briefcase. "I have an envelope to give you." He handed her a brown envelope, from which she drew out a compliment slip and a cheque. The compliment slip had the House of Commons logo on the top and printed beneath it 'From the Desk of the Hon. Sir William Henderson, GCVO,

JP, MP. Minister of State for Internal Affairs.' Her uncle's scribbled wording read:

You can rely on Pellow to give you every assistance. He is very capable and highly thought of. W.H.

She gave a gasp of surprise when she saw the cheque amount. £20,000. My God, she whispered. That's a fortune!

"That cheque is your fee charge for handling this assignment," Alistair explained. "You are entitled to submit a claim for reasonable expenses.

"Oh, I've got some business cards we prepared for you," Alistair said, taking out his wallet and extracting from it a white business card. He handed it to Penny. "I've got a box of them for you in my case."

Penny looked at the card. "Who did this?" she demanded angrily.

"I'm sorry?" Alistair looked puzzled. "It was printed in-house."

"No. Who decided to call me Penelope Campbell, Investigations Officer? Whose idea was this?"

"Sir William's," Alistair replied.

"Damned cheek. I am Penny and always will be. I haven't been called Penelope since I was in Reception Class at school. I will not accept this antediluvian attitude of Sir William. How dare he presume?"

"I rather imagine he thought Penelope added more gravitas to your position as Investigations Officer."

An awkward silence hovered for a short while in the room. Alistair was a little surprised at Penny's outburst over what he regarded as a trifling matter. To break the silence, he eventually suggested that perhaps she would like to tell him her plans.

"Why?" she asked archly.

"So I can know what you'd like me to do. Have you an idea when you propose to start?"

"I have started already."

"So early this morning?"

"No. Last night. I had a meeting with the editor of The Globe."

"I thought Sir William had told you to clear things with me first."

Penny began to get annoyed. "Look, Alistair. I was informed by Sir William that you would be assigned to assist me, to advise on how certain things proceed when working for the Government. I don't refer to you before I do anything and I have no intention of doing so. As far as I am concerned, you are here to advise me on Government procedures when the investigation reaches that stage. I hope you're clear on that."

"Sorry." Alistair held up his hands in a placatory manner, palms facing her. "I didn't say that very well. What I meant is that Sir William is concerned if news of your investigation leaks out to the Media. Your meeting with this newspaper chap should really have been discussed first with me."

"He is not a 'newspaper chap'. He is a senior executive in a newspaper group who happens to be a personal friend."

"I'm sorry, but it could be awkward if his paper makes any mention of the Government's role in this business – though from what you say, I am sure such won't happen. On this occasion."

Penny had become so irritated by now that she felt she needed to get out of the office. She had never before in her working life had to clear first any project before going ahead with it. Even when Peter was alive and they worked together, they consulted each other but not for either of them to gain permission to go ahead with their intentions. She was damned if she was going to now have to answer to Alistair before doing anything. She felt she needed to clear her head, to cool down. She moved to the door. "I am going out for a short while. If the phone rings or anyone calls, would you mind telling them you are office sitting, make a note of who they are and tell them I'll be in touch." With that, she stormed out of the room.

She went down the stairs and into the street. It was still snowing and she was annoyed that in her haste to exit the office she did not take a coat or umbrella. She decided to rush to the small café two doors down. She ordered a Skinny Latte and went and sat at a table at the rear of the place. There was nobody else in the café. She sat at her table, inwardly boiling with anger. She decided that she would have to have a word with her Uncle and tell him that she did not want to have anyone from the Ministry holding her hand. If her Uncle was to be adamant, then she would drop the assignment.

She ordered another coffee. She began to take stock of her life. The happy family atmosphere with Bill and Ellie and their children the previous night made her realize that her life, rather existence - because she did not believe she enjoyed 'a life' – was empty and quite pointless. Of course, she needed a job because she needed to earn money, but she wondered whether she might not gain more satisfaction becoming an employee in some corporation instead of struggling to pay her business overheads from minimal returns. It had been fun and challenging when she and Peter had worked together building up their business. But the spark had been extinguished after Peter's death and she found the daily drudge of working on her own debilitating and unexciting. She thought that there must surely be better ways of earning a living than tracing peripatetic husbands or wayward wives, which constituted the bulk of her business nowadays.

She looked at her watch and realized that she had been away from her office for nearly an hour. Right, she thought determinedly. Time to sort out young Mister Pelllow.

Alistair was on his mobile phone when she entered. He cut the call and said, with a smile "Hi! All right?"

She nodded. "Yes thank you," she replied curtly.

Alistair said, "Look, whilst you've been out I thought I'd help. I've fixed up for us to see the head of the Department of Genetics at the University of Cambridge. Meeting's arranged to tomorrow morning. He's an old friend of my family and owes me a big favour. He will be most helpful to you in answering any questions on the Rathings as he's quite an authority on molecular function and so on. And he studied the makeup of the DTX toxin the American used to kill the Rathings, Magars and Droons."

Penny sat at her desk. "Thank you, Alistair. However, by the same token as you expect me to clear things with you first, I would have thought it only courteous for you to do so with me before taking unilateral action."

Alistair gave a laugh of embarrassment. "Oops! You're quite right. In my anxiety to help, I forgot that I should have asked you first if you were in favour of such a meeting."

"What time is this meeting?"

"Eleven o'clock. I can drive us there. It would take an hour to ninety minutes to get there. I could pick you up at your place."

"Thank you." Penny took one of the visiting cards Alistair had brought, and the scribbled her address and phone numbers on the back. "I've noted my details on the back," she said as she handed him the card.

Alistair flashed the details on his EID card. Penny was curious when she noted the slim-line black case. "Is that an Electronic Identity Device you have there?" she asked. Alistair nodded.

"Yes."

"Gosh, I've never seen one so very slim," Penny said.

"It's a prototype manufactured by Adelo Electronics. Not on the market yet."

"It looks really quite amazing," Penny remarked.

"I can get you one if you like," Alistair said.

"How, if it's a prototype and not yet on the market?"

"My Dad owns the company that made it. He can get me one."

"It sounds super," Penny said then she shrugged as she thought it unwise to be beholden to Alistair in any way. "But I'm not sure. Thank you for your offer but perhaps we could take a raincheck on that?"

"As you like," Alistair remarked. "Let me know if you change your mind. Anyway, how if I pick you up at nine thirty?"

"That will be fine. Phone me as you're arriving and I'll go downstairs to meet you. It can be murder finding a parking space at that time of the morning."

Penny then said, "Alistair, as we have a meeting with your friend tomorrow, I don't propose to do any more work on this assignment today but instead clear up some work I already have in hand. So, I really shan't need you any more today."

"You're sure I can't be of further help?"

"Positive. Thank you."

"OK then," Alistair said as he collected his coat and briefcase. "See you tomorrow."

Penny nodded. "Yes. Goodbye, Alistair."

EIGHT

Penny's phone rang at 9.20 the following morning. "'Morning. I'm just approaching your street," Alistair announced.

"OK. I'll be down," Penny replied.

She stood outside her apartment block looking out for Alistair. The thin patina of snow had disguised the starkness of the red-brick walls of the building recently erected. The snow's attendance gave the impression that someone had whitewashed away the severity of the brick building and given it a gentler, placid demeanour. Paper bags, discarded cellophane wrappers, fluffets of other rubbish were tossed about by an angry snow blizzard that had bestirred itself from its overnight slumbered stillness. The street was a vista of whiteness. The weather seemed eager to make life uncomfortable for the people who were going about their normal business.

Penny heard a car toot and turned to see Alistair waving at her from a low-slung metallic grey sports coupé that was the most stylish vehicle she'd seen for a long time. He opened the car doors that rose upwards like two bat wings and quickly got out help her in. She looked at the vehicle in amazement. "This is yours?"

"Yep." He smiled. "Like it?"

"I know nothing about cars," Penny admitted. "But this is certainly some vehicle. It must have cost a fortune."

"A bit," Alistair admitted. "But not bought from my salary. It was a birthday present a couple of years back."

"From wife or girlfriend?"

Alistair laughed. "Neither. I am happily unattached. My parents thirty first birthdays present to me."

"I see," Penny said. "Your family is obviously loaded." She gasped. "Sorry. There I go with my big mouth. I really should learn to think before I speak. That was very rude of me."

"Not at all. As I think I mentioned to you yesterday, my father happens to be Chairman of Adelo Electronics. And my mother is a consultant surgeon. I guess they're reasonably comfortably off and could afford this."

"Wowser!" Penny exclaimed. She looked hard at the bat wing doors. "Does this thing fly as well?"

"Like a dream."

She looked at the car again. "What is it?"

"A car."

"I know that, silly. I mean what type?"

"A McLaren F12," Alistair said proudly. "An advancement on the F1 manufactured at the turn of the century. She's got a top speed of three hundred and eighty six kilometres per hour or two hundred and forty miles per hour in old money. And she reaches one hundred kilometres an hour in three point two seconds."

"A bit fast for travel in town," Penny noted loudly. "You can hardly move a few metres without having to stop because of traffic."

"Ah, but I often drive to Italy and Europe and some stretches of road over there are perfect for this beauty."

"In any case," Penny said with a smile. "You could never get to do your top speed on the motorway in this country as all traffic speed is automatically controlled by Central Computer."

"Ah! Speed control is employed by Central Computer on all cars except emergency vehicles; ambulances, fire engines, and police cars and Government vehicles."

"So you'll be speed controlled."

"No. I am registered with Central Computer as a Government car."

"I see," Penny said in a seemingly disinterested voice, although she was impressed by Alistair's explanation.

There was no question that the car was low slung and Penny had some initial difficulty getting in. But once settled she relaxed in the unquestioned luxury of the car. Alistair put the car in gear and moved off, pressing the throttle to the floor so that the engine growled noisily several times. She doubted there was any need to make that raucous noise, but then recognized that many young men needed to show off their sexual prowess and masculinity through their toys. And obviously, Alistair was no exception. She recalled Peter sometimes doing very much the same thing but not as demonstrably as Alistair and in a Ford Fiesta as opposed to this McLaren whatever number.

Alistair had activated the heating system when they had first got into the car and the temperature was now a pleasant, comforting degree. Penny felt safe in the snug, warm car cocooned from the harsh weather conditions outside.

Alistair fiddled about on the dashboard. "Let's have some music. Jazz, Blues, Classical or Modern?"

"Classical would be nice."

"Wagner OK?"

"A bit heavy for me, I'm sorry."

Alistair laughed. "Philistine! Let me think. Chopin. Bet you're a Chopin girl."

"I find Chopin most relaxing," Penny affirmed.

The strains of Chopin's Concerto No.2 in F Minor filled the car and Penny lay back in her seat. "This piece is one of my favourites," she whispered.

"I'm glad," Alistair said. "I too like this very much."

The journey took an interminable time. Traffic, creeping hesitantly, held them up at practically every corner. Heavy flakes of snow now decided to join in the game of inevitably slowing down the movement of vehicles. The music had stopped playing for some time and Penny sensed that Alistair was becoming restless at the slow pace of things. He gunned the car forward several times, when he ought not to, with the result that he had to apply the brakes every short one minute distance due to traffic hold ups.

"Amazing braking system, don't you think?" he said proudly.

"Yes, isn't it," Penny replied out of politeness.

"D'you realise that beneath this beautiful chassis lies a six point one litre engine V twelve manufactured by BMW?"

"Really? Amazing!" Penny said, hoping she would not have to listen to a detailed account of the car's technical assets, which hardly interested her, for the entire journey.

They finally reached Cambridge.

"Time for a coffee, I think, before our meeting," Alistair said.

"What is the name of this person we are meeting?" Penny asked.

"Oh, sorry. I thought I'd told you. His name is Professor Branko Antonijevic. Charming old boy."

"What is he? A Serb?"

"Was. He's now British."

They passed a small coffee shop. Alistair pulled in to the kerb and parked the car opposite the café. They went in and ordered coffees.

"Want to eat anything?" Alistair asked.

Penny shook her head. "No thanks. Too soon after breakfast."

"So tell me, Penny. What qualifications or experience must one have to be a private detective? Had you been in the police beforehand?"

"Alistair, perhaps I should tell you the difference between a private detective and a private investigator. I am not a private detective. I am an investigator. Private Investigators are more involved in personal investigations such as matrimonial disputes. Infidelity, tracing missing people. A Private Detective is more associated with criminal investigations. I don't do that. I do P.I. work."

"Sorry. I really never appreciated that there is a difference. So, were you with the police?"

"No I was not. Many people believe that Private Investigators are ex-police, but this is a myth. You don't have to have been in the police."

"So why did you become an investigator?"

"My husband was and he encouraged me to join his firm."

"Is he no longer working with you, then?"

Penny shook her head. She did not reply immediately. Then she said, "No, he is no longer with the Company."

Alistair had a vague sense that Penny no longer wished to continue along that conversational line.

Alistair looked at his watch. "Well, I guess we'd better make tracks."

NINE

After their coffee, they walked to the Department of Genetics. Alistair spoke to a young girl at the main reception desk, who directed them to the lifts.

"Third floor. The Prof's PA will meet us at the lift," Alistair said as he joined Penny who had waited for him to finish talking to the receptionist.

The elevator rose quickly and smoothly. The doors opened. They saw an attractive, smartly dressed middle-aged woman waiting for them. "Mister Pellow?" she enquired politely.

"Yes," Alistair smiled. "And this is Mrs. Campbell."

"Good morning," the woman said. "Would you please follow me this way," she indicated towards a corridor.

They walked down the corridor and came to a door which the woman opened. The room was very well furnished and had a rich blue carpet. Penny thought it was probably the woman's office because of the familiar way she stood at the desk and the handbag Penny saw on a small table next to the desk. She walked up to a desk and spoke into an intercom. "Professor Antonijevic, your guests have arrived," she said. "Yes. I shall do so." She turned to Penny and Alistair. "Would you care for a coffee?" she asked.

They thanked her but declined. She went to another door, knocked and opened it. She indicated to them to enter.

As they walked in, a small, elderly man rose from behind a desk which was strewn with papers and files. His hair was long, white and seemingly unwashed. He wore a shabby brown cardigan over an old sports shirt. His trousers were corduroys. The man obviously disliked modern clothing and seemingly much preferred a dress style of many years gone by.

"Alistair, my boy," he greeted with open arms.

"'Morning, Branko. It's good to see you again," Alistair clapped the Professor's back as he was held in an embrace by the old man. "May I introduce Mrs. Campbell?" Alistair said as he extricated himself from the embrace.

The Professor turned to Penny and took her hand. "A pleasure, dragi dama," he said in his native tongue. A good morning to you, dear Madame." He bent his head over her extended hand, his pursed lips hovering an inch above her hand. "So you are the privatni javnim okuplljanjima," he said in Serbian; "the private detective – Mrs. Perry Mason. Although you are far littler and far prettier than that fat American who plays the part on television in old movies."

"Hello, Professor,"

Alistair said, "I think it best if Mrs. Campbell were to explain to you the reason for our visit, which I mentioned briefly in my phone call to you."

Professor Antonijevic smiled at Penny. "Please to proceed, Mrs. Campbell."

"Do you mind very much if I record our conversation? It's far easier to refer to afterwards."

"Not at all Mrs. Perry Mason," the old man said with a grin.

Penny placed a small recorder on the desk and switched it on. "Good morning Professor Antnisesevick..." she stumbled over the correct pronunciation of his name.

The Professor laughed at her apparent discomfort. "Please do not worry. It is not an easy name for you English to pronounce. Call me Branko. Everybody does."

Penny smiled and said thank you. She deleted her preliminary attempt and began again. "Good morning Professor Branko. You are no doubt aware of the rumour of Rathings having been seen again in the country. The Government has appointed me to investigate the veracity of such rumours. Mister Pellow very kindly asked you to help me in my research, and for this assistance by you I am grateful."

"I have, of course, heard this rumour. But you know, young lady, rumours are like butterflies. They flit around seemingly aimlessly but in truth, trying to find somewhere to settle. Yet whereas the butterfly has substance, the rumour does not. It is like a religious faith, built on nothing more concrete than a belief in something, especially without proof. Religious faith is developed through indoctrination; followed blindly, never or rarely questioned. Rumour, like faith, is a transient being which, like the butterfly, is looking for somewhere to settle. And when a rumour settles in someone's mind and then travels to their mouth, it has found its home. But rumour is a whisper in the dark. Rumour is not a fact.

"But I deal in facts. My specialty is genetic oncology. I work on cellular component, molecular function, and biological process. So I am hardly in a position to comment on this rumour. I do not know if it is true that Rathings have re-emerged. Neither do I know if Rathings have not re-emerged. There could well be Rathings present in the country. Also, it is unlikely that any Rathings survived the attack on them of the DTX toxin. I cannot prove or disprove a fantasy..."

Alistair interrupted. "You will remember what we spoke about, Branko."

"All too well, my friend," Antonijevic replied testily. "Please to not interrupt."

Alistair raised his hands in a gesture of resigned acquiescence.

Penny noted the furtive look exchanged between the two men and recognized the tone of annoyance in the Professor's retort.

"Let me show you something," Professor Antonijevic said as he rooted around in one of his desk drawers. He brought out a brown folder that held a sheaf of papers. "I have here the results of my analysis of the DTX toxin from a small container we came across, one presumably dropped mistakenly from one of the American aircraft. But before I go on I must ask a question of you." He looked at Alistair.

"Of course, Branko. And what is that?"

"The high and mighty ones up there," he raised an index finger and jabbed it several times in the direction of the ceiling, "Those who are in charge here and have their executive offices up there, they have suggested to me on several times that perhaps I should leave here early. 'Take early retirement, Branko,' they say. 'Enjoy doing the things you like instead of work all the time. Cultivate your garden and learn to relax in it. The fools! Do they not know that I enjoy doing this work? And they did not even bother to check up that I live in a flat and do not have a garden. Also, they do not want me to make any statements to newspaper men on my research. So, I do not want anything I say to you today to be in any newspaper. If that happens I am in the hot soup. I want your assurance – no mention in newspapers. Please."

Alistair smiled. "You have my assurance, Branko. Whatever you say will be contained only in Mrs. Campbell's report to the Government."

The Professor nodded. "Good." He opened the folder and rummaged through the papers it contained. "These are the notes of my analysis of the toxin DTX. Included in its makeup is a powerful component which allows the poison toxin a long period of activity. This means that the poison retains its active functions for a long time after dispersal. On tests we conducted with the sample we obtained, it was evident that the toxin hung around for some several weeks. On that basis, and from assurances received from the Americans, it would be unlikely that any Rathings survived the attack." The old man shrugged. "Of course, I cannot state categorically that none survived, but on balance, it would seem unlikely. There you have it." He turned to Alistair. "Was that alright? Is that what you wanted?"

Alistair looked somewhat embarrassed and said quickly, "It's not what I want, Branko. It is what Mrs. Campbell needs that matters."

Penny felt a little uneasy. Something wasn't quite right in the way this had been dealt with. The Professor's explanation appeared too pat, too perfect, as if it had been rehearsed. His earlier broken English had assumed a cogent smoothness, a quality of speech she had not expected. And she was puzzled as to his asking Alistair if that was what Alistair wanted. What was meant by that comment?

Penny smiled at the old man. "Thank you, Professor. You have been most kind. I very much appreciate your honest appraisal of the situation and your most detailed explanation. This is of great assistance to me."

After some pleasant chit chat, they bade farewell to Antonijevic and walked to Alistair's car.

The return journey to London was much quicker. Alistair was in a buoyant mood.

"I think that went very well," he said. "Hope you'll find it useful to incorporate into your report."

"I'm sure I will," Penny replied.

She still felt unsettled by the underhand look exchanged between the two men and even more so by the Professor asking Alistair if what he had said was what Alistair wanted. What did he mean by that? What had Alistair said to the Professor when they spoke on the telephone?

Penny was sorely tempted to ask Alistair what that comment might have implied. But she constrained herself from raising the subject. She remembered her father saying to her – 'Never let it be known what you are thinking, Penny. Never tell the other person your thoughts. By doing so, you lower your guard and you allow them the opportunity to make a countermove. Always keep your thoughts to yourself.' It was a rule, a doctrine she'd always kept.

"You seem a bit subdued," Alistair said. "I should have imagined you'd be over the moon. Being able to quote such an eminent person in your report will go a long way to your findings achieving credence."

Penny shrugged. "I suppose so," she said.

"So what's bugging you?" Alistair persisted.

"Nothing. It's just that I'm puzzled as to why the Professor asked you – not me – but asked you if that he'd said is what you wanted. What could he have meant by that?"

Even as she asked her question, Penny felt like kicking herself for breaking the rule. You must learn more self-control, she reprimanded herself.

"Oh, I don't think anything was implied," Alistair said. "Don't forget that Branko is a foreigner and his command of English may not be perfect."

66

"Oh, I thought his explanation was perfect," Penny countered. "I would say word perfect. Almost rehearsed."

There I go again, Penny swore to herself. Control, control, control yourself. Keep to your rule, for God's sake!

"I don't understand what you're getting at," Alistair said as he gunned the accelerator of the car and entered the motorway.

"Oh, nothing," Penny replied. Then she forced a smile and said, "I really am most grateful to you for having arranged this meeting. It really has been a great help."

Yet despite her polite words of thanks, Penny had the sensation that Alistair was slightly annoyed.

"Oh, incidentally. As you seem to require knowing what I plan to do before I do it, I think I should mention that I plan to phone a contact I have in Scotland. She might know something about the Rathing rumour."

"What? In Scotland?"

Penny nodded. She said "That's right. She runs a private investigations agency in Edinburgh."

"Called?" Alistair said, trying very hard to sound nonchalant.

"High and Low Scotland; you know, for Highland and Lowland Scotland."

"Cute," Alistair said with a smile.

They eventually reached Putney. Alistair pulled up outside her office.

"I'll let you off here and find somewhere to park," he said shortly. He didn't bother helping her to get out of the car.

"Thank you," she said.

She let herself into her office. The scene that greeted her was one of chaos. Desk drawers had been pulled out and they alongside scattered papers, as did the coffee percolator, strings of ground coffee creating an ugly pattern on the carpet. She stood rooted to the spot. She then saw a large white piece of card. On it was written in red paint block letters:

DROP THE JOB - OR ELSE!

She reached for the phone and immediately keyed in the number of the local police station. She reported the break in and was told that a police officer would be calling round later that afternoon.

Why? She asked herself. Who could do this?

She heard Alistair coming up the stairs.

"God!" he laughed, talking as he walked up the short flight of stairs and along the landing outside her office before he'd entered... "I'd swear the cars are giving birth out there. There's hardly a space left." He walked in and saw Penny and the disordered scene around her. "Bloody hell!" he exclaimed. "What's happened here? Penny are you alright?"

She nodded.

"Why should anyone want to do this?" Penny cried.

"Probably young lads with nothing better to do." Alistair said.

"And leave a note like this?" Penny pointed at the white piece of card with red lettering.

Alistair walked over to the desk on which the card stood. "What's this then? Oh, I hadn't noticed it." He read the note. He was silent for a while and then said. "I don't like the look of this."

"What job am I to drop? I can only assume it is the one from my Uncle."

"Unless you have any other high profile cases?"

She shook her head. "A handful of others. All low key."

"Guess it must be the Government job," Alistair said. "I don't like this," he said again. "Anything missing?" he asked.

"I don't know. I haven't had time to check."

"Well the computer's still here, as is the photocopier," Alistair remarked.

Alistair picked up the coffee percolator, looked around for the coffee grounds, and started on the coffee making ritual.

"I've got something stronger in there," Penny snuffled, pointing towards the stationery cupboard door.

Alistair tried to cheer her up. "Ah, a secret drinker, are you Mrs. Campbell?"

She shook her head. "No. I have one important client who likes a 'drop of the old nectar' he calls it. I only bring it out when he comes in to discuss his case."

"Then I'm sure he won't mind us having a drop of the old nectar, in view of the circumstances," Alistair said as he opened the stationery cupboard door. "Aha!" he exclaimed, holding up a bottle of Chivas Regal. "An excellent old nectar. Did you choose this? A bit of an expert in whiskies, eh?"

"No," Penny said. "It was Peter's choice. He loved whisky."

"Peter?" Alistair raised an eyebrow.

"My late husband."

"Oh, I'm sorry. I didn't know his name," Alistair apologised.

"Why should you?"

"Did you say late husband?"

Alistair had found two glasses and poured generous tots in each.

"When did your husband die, if I may ask?"

"Five years ago. He was killed in a car crash together with his parents whom he'd collected from Heathrow airport. It was on the A316, just a few miles from home."

Alistair then realized what Penny had meant in the café when she said her husband was no longer with the Company. "I'm so sorry to hear about your loss, Penny. Sir William told me nothing about your husband's death or that you are a widow. All I was told was to see a Mrs. Campbell and I assumed there was a Mister Campbell in the background. I am truly sorry."

"Thank you," Penny gave a weak smile.

Alistair said, "I suggest you get on to the police, Penny."

"I've done so. They'll send someone round later. Perhaps we should clear up first," she said.

"No, don't," Alistair said quickly "Let the police see it in its present state when they come round."

"OK," Penny answered.

TEN

On this cold November morning, a solitary figure walked in the grounds of Gretorex Hall, an Elizabethan manor house in Hertfordshire. The house was laid out in the shape of an'E' for Elizabeth as were many mansions so designed at the time by suitors in the hope of impressing the virgin queen.

A film of early morning mist wafted sensuously over the lawns and hedges and the early morning caw cawing salutation of crows and rooks offered an accompanying chorus. A light carpet of yesterday's snow lay on the lawn and the footpaths. The trees stood like silent mourners, their branches like raised limbs wearing ghostly shrouds of clinging snow. Thankfully, it had stopped snowing in the early morning hours.

The wandering figure was that of a gentleman, a doctor, whose code name bestowed on him by his gathered colleagues most of whom were already in the Hall, was Septimus Forceps. For the most part, he had been wondering on the lawns close to the building although, had he so wished, he could have journeyed in over 111 acres of herbaceous borders, sunken gardens and a fountain court. He passed various ponds. He stood at one of them for some time but saw no fish and therefore presumed they were hibernating, as they normally did at this time of the year.

He walked back towards the building. It was a spectacularly beautiful house, built out of tawny-coloured stone with curved gables.

The man was wisely heavily wrapped in a greatcoat with a scarf about his neck and a woolen balaclava hood clamped firmly on his head. He also had on a pair of thick woolen gloves and wore a heavy pair of snow boots. He gave a final look at the dark marmalade-coloured barns and outbuildings in front of the bank of trees that hid the two tennis courts before walking on the gravel path that led to the front door of the large, imposing house. The man was looking forward to breakfast and warmth, neither of which was available in the entrance hall, which was as icily cold as it was outside. Tendrils of mist had crept in from the garden and now danced in the cold air. He stamped his feet heavily on the floor mat to wipe off the thin film of snow from his boots. The man then stuffed his gloves into the coat pocket then took off his coat, scarf and balaclava which he hung on a free standing coast hanger already laden with other clothing. He pushed open the door that led to the breakfast room and was delighted to feel the warmth welcome him. He walked to the large fireplace which was ablaze and stood before it rubbing his hands.

"Good morning, gentlemen," he greeted the already seated breakfasters.

There was a chorus of returned morning greetings.

"Is it indeed a good one?" another rejoined. "Freezing and unfriendly."

"Nonsense," Septimus laughed. "It is bracing and healthy." He walked to the long sideboard on which breakfast dishes stretched out. He placed a slice of toast on a plate and spooned a small amount of scrambled egg on top of the toast. He was tempted to help himself to a kipper but decided against it; kippers had a habit of repeating on him.

He sat at the table and poured himself a coffee from a silver coffee jug. He took no milk or sugar.

The fifteen men present – ranging from middle age to old - chatted pleasantly amongst themselves. Their expensively tailored suits reflected their wealth and important social standing. They were all powerful men, establishment figures in the arts, sciences, church, law and business. They talked quietly among themselves until one short, rotund member of the coterie rose and gently tapped his pen against the crystal drinking glass in front of him, in a request for attention. The conversations ceased immediately. "Gentlemen," he said. "I have been asked to chair this meeting in the absence of our commanding officer, Blue Eyes. I wish to thank you all for attending at such short notice. As it appears that we have all finished our breakfasts, may I ask that we adjourn next door for our meeting."

The men rose and walked into an adjoining room which was extremely large but with no furniture other than a long table and chairs around it. The men sat around the table that looked like a boardroom table, but wasn't. It was a banqueting table that twelve very strong young men had moved some years ago from the dining room to the large room where they all now sat.

Several logs burned in an enormous fireplace yet only a small amount of heat was evident. The men assumed that perhaps the fire had been lit only a short while before they had entered the room.

The rotund member, whose code name was Purple Pill, stood to address the group.

"It is my sad duty to inform you that one of our members discovered that his intended partner for the night – a young female Rathing - had died in his bedroom due to a drug error. The body has been disposed of and is unlikely to be found."

A few of those present whispered uneasily amongst themselves.

73

"Did I hear you correctly?" a very elderly, white haired man seated at the head of the table asked. He was Lord Gretorex, owner of the house and accorded the position of President of the group and the code name Bald Eagle.

"Regrettably, that is correct," Purple Pill replied.

Lord Gretorex raised a trembling hand. "I have some observations to make."

Purple Pill, smiled at the doyen of the group. "Of course, Bald Eagle."

Lord Gretorex nodded and continued. "You have just stated that one of our members was responsible for the death of a young Rathing. The phrase 'one of our members' is not good enough. You also said it was in his bedroom, which can only mean one thing. In the pursuit of enjoying the pleasures of exploring young bodies we do no harm to those who entertain us. Although why anyone should desire to sexually conjoin with a creature that is no more than a rodent, admittedly with some human element in their makeup, is quite beyond me.

"However, to act in such an unthinking manner as to cause a Rathing's death is a gross dereliction of responsibility, especially as we need all such creatures for the upcoming battle with the Government's army."

Purple Pill looked down at the table and said nothing in immediate reply. He then said, "I do not think it would be in order to disclose the person's name."

"Well, I do," Gretorex snapped.

"I'm sorry, Bald Eagle, but some things should be treated confidentially and ..."

"In that case, we should put this to the vote and have a show of hands. We could be faced with untold problems. This member's action affects all of us. It is therefore only right that all of us should know who it is. All those in favour of my request."

Lord Gretorex looked round the table. One hesitant arm raised itself slowly, followed by another and another until all hands were raised.

Purple Pill shrugged. "I see that the motion is carried."

"So who is it?"

"It is Grey Goose."

Everyone looked around the table and noted Grey Goose's absence. "I'm afraid that Grey Goose is in New York on his bank's business," Purple Pill advised.

"I think the blighter should be drummed out of the regiment. I am going to propose at the next Committee meeting that his membership of The Group be rescinded."

There were a few muttered 'hear hears. Some members, however, did not seem to be overly happy at the way things had gone.

ELEVEN

Purple Pill was rather subdued when he spoke again. "Now I wish to introduce two new members to our group." He smiled at two men who sat next to each other. "Both have been recommended by our honourable friend, October Moon. First, let me introduce Cello. Come, please stand, Cello so all can see you," Purple Pill invited. "And next is Algebra." Both new members stood and bowed. "As you will note, gentlemen, we only use code names – never birth names. This ensures we maintain our confidentiality at all times.

"I have no doubt that your Sponsor, October Moon has explained our group's objectives but I should wish to reiterate key points. Firstly, we all share a common desire to establish a new regime in the country. When the Rathings controlled us, the population faced the uncertainty of life. Now we face the uncertainty of a future. We have long realized that it was difficult for the present Government to rationalize our country's management after the long period of Rathing control. Because of the harsh regime imposed by the Rathings it was inevitable that the first human government after the Rathings' passing would have to impose strict controls. As an example, rubbish refuse that the Rathings had allowed to pile up for many years needed removing. A health service had to be set up. Regrettably, despite our granting them every opportunity to streamline our food distribution and dispense with the food rationing system, nothing came of it. We waited for the government to normalize relationships with overseas countries so we can trade with them; they have failed to achieve any material results.

"Furthermore, as you must be well aware of, The Government has declared gambling, smoking and prostitution as activities whose participants are subject to long-term incarceration. Tobacco manufacturing companies closed down. If you can't break your smoking habit, you must buy them from black market dealers at exorbitant prices. Casinos ceased to exist and ladies of the night conduct their business in secret underground cells. Heads of Utilities and public companies and bankers who make losses yet still accepted large bonuses are charged and executed. Prisoners have had their leisure benefits withdrawn and are only allowed billiards and football as sport activities. And all these matters are under the control of and enforcement by the Police's Behavior Force.

"Our civil liberties have been taken away. We now have no freedom. We now lead an existence that is more restrictive than it was when the Rathings ruled over us. We now live in a totalitarian state. Or rather, a dictatorship. There is really only one person who runs this country and it is our glorious Chancellor, Oskar "with a K" Brabanti." Here, he imitated the Chancellor's habit whenever the Chancellor introduced himself. He always said, "I am Oskar – with a K – Brabanti. Chancellor of Great Britain".

"But surely the various Ministers?..." Cello intervened.

"Puppets – pleased with their appointments, ministerial cars, salaries, expenses and perks. They all kowtow to the Chancellor's wishes. No, my friends let us not fool ourselves. We live under a Dictatorship.

"But let me tell you of a 'Government' plan which is being seriously considered and which I heard of the other day. But I must first ask you to not laugh when I tell you of this plan. The Government wishes to cut back on energy waste and excessive use of water. It proposes that henceforth the flushing of lavatories will be restricted within certain laid down hours. One may, of course, use the toilet for the intended purpose but one cannot flush the waste immediately. When the due time permitted for flushing arrives then one may flush."

Cello raised his hand and said, "Excuse me, but such a scheme would never work. How can the Government possibly control when a person decides to flush their toilet?"

Purple Pill smiled. "Very easily. When you flush a valve opens, and allows the toilet tank's water to enter the toilet bowl. Existing toilets will have a gizmo installed that is programmed to not allow the valve to open. You can push and press and yank for as long as you liked but nothing will happen. The valve will only open at the time designated and programmed.

"All newly built toilet bowls will incorporate a timing device programmed in line with Government timing directives.

"All that users must remember is to make a note of permitted flushing times so that they can ensure to flush their toilet during those periods."

"That is control over people's lives gone mad!" a member codenamed Hammer bellowed.

"Precisely," Purple Pill acknowledged. "We are not much better off than we were when the Rathings ruled over us. We are, in fact, worse off in many ways. That is why we must launch a take-over and assume power. Naturally, any insurrection will be countered by the Government calling in the army. You, my newly recruited colleagues, might well ask 'how can we fight the army?' Your Sponsor, October Moon would not have been permitted to divulge this information to you – at least not until now. I am informed that you have both paid your annual subscription of five hundred pounds, so I shall tell you as you are now officially considered as members."

"Excuse me, sir," Cello asked and raised a hand.

"Yes, Cello?"

"Could a resolution of No Confidence in the Government not be raised by the Opposition party and debated in the House?"

Purple Pill smiled and shook his head. "It has been mooted many times but always blocked for a variety of reasons. My friend, Cello, you must grow to realize that the members of the Government rule as a Dictatorship, not a Democracy. Also, that the Opposition is completely ineffectual."

"Well, it *is* a fact that the Government, on assuming power, passed a Bill limiting general elections every fifteen years, so I guess it *is* a dictatorship of sorts." Cello said in agreement.

"Precisely," Purple Pill responded.

"But as I was saying before you raised your perfectly valid question, Cello. We have a secret weapon, one which the army would find difficult to deal with." Here, Purple Pill paused and took a sip of water. With the exception of the two new members, the men gathered round the table grinned, as they were all cognizant of what Purple Pill was about to reveal.

"We have our own army, one more fearsome than any other and one the Government's army would find difficult to defeat." Purple Pill paused again. Some suspected he was rather enjoying his dramatic starring role. "We shall have a Rathing army."

There were soft shouts of 'hear hear' from some of the men. The two new members stared at Purple Pill as if he was mad.

"Forgive me," the new member called Algebra raised his hand. "Did I hear you correctly? A Rathing army?"

"You did indeed, Algebra," Purple Pill replied.

"But I thought all the Rathings had been killed by the Americans? You know, by poison released from their planes."

"Not all. You see, a short while ago some dead Rathings were found in a cave in Scotland. They had collapsed over a handful of new born ones who were still alive."

"So this Rathing rumour is true after all," Cello remarked.

"But not for general public knowledge. This information must be kept strictly within these walls. No word must leak out," Purple Pill stated solemnly.

"One of our members was in a position to have these creatures transported to here. In our basement we have hospital facilities set up under the care of three of our members, two eminent doctors and one who is a well known scientist. Gentlemen. Please stand so you may be recognized." Three middle-aged men stood. "I present Elderflower, Septimus and Bunsen." They all bowed and sat down again.

"These young Rathings are fed well and are growing fast. Soon they will be mating and within a very short time we shall have many more at our disposal. Our good friend, Bunsen has developed a programme whereby the Rathings are being indoctrinated to obey implicitly clear cut instructions. They have had implanted in their brains a microchip program which dictates their immediate obedience to commands issued. As a safeguard, they are programmed with the same chip to not attack their human commanders but only assault those marked as targets by their commanders."

"By Jove!" The new member, Cello remarked. "That will be one fearsome sight – having an army of Rathings advance on you."

"It will, indeed," Purple Pill smiled. "Being advanced upon by a vast horde of giants of massive strength is enough to frighten anyone. And when recognized as Rathings, it would take a brave man to stand his ground.

"But timing will be of prime importance. Our Rathings will not be able to handle modern weapons. Their arms will consist of swords, lances, knives and so on and, of course, their phenomenal physical strength. Therefore, they can be quickly destroyed once faced by phasers, blasters, laser guns and other such weapons. We must ensure a swift victory and by doing so not allow our enemy forces sufficient time to counter our attack with such weaponry."

He took another sip of water and referred to some papers before him on the table. "There's just one other point on the agenda." He turned to the scientist amongst their group. "Bunsen. Would you be kind enough to bring us up to date on the development of the Rathings?"

A tall, thin man of about sixty or thereabouts stood up. "They are doing exceedingly well. As you know, eleven baby Rathings were delivered from Scotland. Unfortunately one of them subsequently died and another one died entertaining Grey Goose. We now have nine of which five are females, all growing, all healthy and all programmed with the microchip. The four males have begun to show sexual interest in the females and coupling has already taken place. The gestation period for a rat is twenty one to twenty three days, but here we are concerned with a hybrid clone and – part rat and part human. Data available from the past, when female Rathings gave birth, indicate a gestation period of about three months. Generally, with their first litter, young female Rathings have given birth to about ten pups. This is the information available from hospital records at the time of the Rathings occupancy of our country. More experienced breeders will give birth to twenty plus in a litter. Therefore, according to my calculations, if all proceeds to plan, in three months time we shall have fifty nine Rathings – that is the five original female mothers and four males plus fifty offspring. Breeding can start again within a very short time and, on the basis of, say, twenty pups in a litter times from the five original females is one hundred plus first litter from the first lot of pups of which, say, half are females, that would be forty females giving birth to first litter number of ten equals four hundred – this can only be a very rough hypothesis as we cannot know the number of females born in a litter, but you can see that within six months we would be talking of many hundreds of new Rathings. Therefore, for a time scale for the launch of our putsch against the Government I would calculate that we should not take any action until we have sufficient Rathings at our disposal." He sat down.

"Thank you. Bunsen," Purple Pill said. "Most enlightening. Naturally, the question of time scale is a matter for consideration and discussion by our Logistics Committee under the chairmanship of our C.O. Your comments, Bunsen will be taken into strong consideration.

"Incidentally, Algebra and Cello. You will note that we are all dressed in normal suiting. This is as it should be for normal meetings. However, when we are on training manoeuvres with the Rathing recruits we wear uniform. Our uniform is a light steel grey tunic and black trousers. We are all officers. We do not have rank designations on uniform; we all know our order of seniority. Our Rathings are rankers but some will be promoted to corporal or sergeant, depending on their capabilities. Their uniform has been designed as a black skirt or kilt and a black tunic. NCOs will have the usual chevrons on their tunic jacket sleeves.

"Your sponsor will take you, in due course, to our appointed tailor who will measure you up and produce your uniform. The current charge he makes is one thousand pounds. You must meet that charge personally.

"Now, does anyone have any questions or other points to raise?"

Bald Eagle waved his hand. "Yes, I do, Mr. Pro-tem chairman. "You will all remember that some expressed concern at the inquisitiveness of the locals at seeing a succession of you come and go from here. Some people began to question what was going on. As agreed, I have arranged for a large sign to be erected at the lodge gate of the East entrance. The builder submitted this for our approval, which I now seek from you gentlemen. He reached down to the side of his chair and raised a printed card for all to see. I thought blue writing might be in order but I leave the decision to your good selves.

The card read:

HEADQUARTERS
SOCIETY OF
INTERNATIONAL SOCIOLOGISTS

It can be in place tomorrow morning."

"Thank you, Bald Eagle," Purple Pill said with a smile. "I think it splendid, as I am sure all here agree. Are all happy with the layout wording and colour?" He looked at his companions, all of whom nodded. "Splendid, your concept is approved by all. Thank you,

Bald Eagle. Now, gentlemen, unless there are any questions, or anyone has anything else to say, I suggest we adjourn to the bar for drinks before an early luncheon."

TWELVE

Patrick O'Connor passed the palm of his hand over his shaven head and smiled at his companion. "This is a really nice club, sir," he said in his strong Irish accent.

"Thank you," Blue Eyes replied. "I take it all went well following Grey Goose's slight mishap?"

"It was more than that, sir. The poor creature was dead."

"Yes, quite, so I believe," Blue Eyes said and nodded. "I take it there were no problems?"

"No, sir."

The two men sat in the lounge bar of the exclusive gentlemen's club in Regent Street, of which O'Connor's drinking companion was a member.

O'Connor had been a sergeant in the same regiment as his companion, before the human army was disbanded by the Rathings when they took over. The other man had been O'Connor's commanding officer, and whilst O'Connor obviously knew the other's surname, he only ever referred to him by his code name of Blue Eyes.

"No problems whatever, sir. I drove to the Lake District with the body in the boot. I used our group's rowing boat at Lake Coniston and dropped her over the side. Nicely bound and padlocked with some weights. She'll be feeding the fishes along with the lad I dropped down there a year or so back. The bodies will never be found."

"Good man," Blue Eyes smiled. "You have again excelled at your allotted task. Well done."

"Thank you very much, sir." O'Connor appreciated Blue Eye's words. His ex-commanding officer had been extraordinarily kind to him since his demob. He had financially supported O'Connor's wife and children when O'Connor had been sent to jail for a short while following a case of aggravated assault on another person in a pub. On O'Connor's release, Blue Eyes had recruited him as a support member of the group Blue Eyes belonged to. O'Connor carried out many tasks of either a secret, sensitive or illegal nature. The Irishman knew, of course, what activities the group members were planning, but he never involved himself in such. In some strange way, he found their antics somewhat questionable. But he needed the job and the very handsome money it paid, so he said nothing and just accepted that, like in the army, officers were of a different breed. And nearly all of the group's members had been an officer in one of the three services.

"And tell me, how is your wife and the two girls?" Blue Eyes asked.

"Very well, thank you. The girls are doing well at their school; they are really enjoying it."

"Oh, I've got a little thing for each of the girls," Blue Eyes said as he got up. "I won't be a second."

He walked to the cloakroom and showed his ticket to the attendant. "I just want to collect something from my briefcase," he mentioned.

He opened his case and took out two small packets. He returned to his table and put the packages on it in front of O'Connor.

"There's one for Alice and one for Sophie, with love from Uncle Blue Eyes."

"Geez, sir. That's very kind of you."

"Pleasure, O'Connor. Just a couple of small toy things I picked up yesterday from Hamlyn's."

O'Connor took a sip of his drink. "As I said, sir, this is really a nice club, sir. Bit different from the other one we've had drinks in."

"Thank you. It is quite pleasant here. Very private."

"D'you belong to many clubs, sir?"

"Three," Blue Eyes replied. "Each one different, yet all the same, if you know what I mean."

O'Connor nodded. "I think I do, sir."

"Care for another?" Blue Eyes asked, pointing at O'Connor's empty glass.

THIRTEEN

Grey Goose was Treasurer of The Group. He was also an ex-Royal Navy Commander before the human population's navy was stood down by the Rathings. He sat in the room he called his office in Gretorex Hal, his long thin legs tucked under his desk chair. Patrick O'Connor sat opposite him.

"I am pleased you could make this meeting as I requested," Grey Goose's thin, reedy voice was accompanied by what he thought was a friendly smile. "I've been studying the group's finances and they are in a somewhat parlous state. Like the country, we too have to make cutbacks. One of these is I regret to say, your emoluments which in any event I have been inclined to believe as being over-generous. We must all make sacrifices for the common good and, therefore, I am obliged to reduce your monthly payment by twenty percent."

"That's a ruddy big cut in income," O'Connor said angrily.

"When needs must," Grey Goose muttered, trying not to show his annoyance at the lack of a 'sir' after the word 'income.'

"This will take effect as from next month. Oh, and whilst at it, I would ask that you no longer continue to drink in the bar. Some of the members have expressed their disquiet at an enlisted man frequenting the officer's bar."

O'Connor rose and leaned over the desk. Grey Goose cringed back in his seat. "We're not in the bloody forces here," O'Connor shouted. "What's this them and us crap? Everyone goes in and helps themselves to what they want. Do they all pay into the honesty box, like I do? Perhaps you should check on that. That's maybe why the finances are in what you call a parlous state. And if you're so bloody keen on savings, are you cutting out the boxes of champagne and fine wines? Or other fancy booze? You're a first class, snooty bastard, Grey Goose. Or perhaps I should say Mr. Jarvis."

"That'll be all, O'Connor," Grey Goose snapped.

"Or what? You'll have me on a charge?"

"You are dismissed," Grey Goose snarled.

"Dismissed my arse," O'Connor replied. "And next time you need to have someone remove a dead creature from your bed, don't call me. OK?"

"I do have others whose services I can call on if necessary," Grey Goose sneered as O'Connor stormed out of the room.

Grey Goose shuffled nervously the papers on his desk. He knew he had been frightened by O'Connor's threatening stance and he was annoyed at that. Also the comment about the dead Rathing upset him.

FOURTEEN

They had just finished drafting out their reports and
Alistair was about to go to the Ministry to see Sir
William when the doorbell rang. Penny answered it
and listened to the visitor for about a minute and a half.
"Alright. Come up," she said and pressed the door
release button. "It's a man who said he's from
something or other investigative journalism."

"Bloody reporters!" Alistair growled. "Don't say
anything about what we're doing. Get rid of him
quickly."

The door opened and a big man of about fifty
stepped into the room. His ginger hair was tousled. He
wore a sports jacket and jeans. Draped over his wide
shoulders was a plastic rain cape.

"Hi," he said. "The name's Kilroy. James Kilroy."

An American accent, definitely Deep South, Alistair
reckoned.

"Thank you, Mr. Kilroy, but we have nothing to say
to the press," Alistair said abruptly.

"Hey! I'm not from the press. Well, I sort of am
but I'm not a reporter. I'm a member of the Editorial
Advisory Board of the Bureau of Investigative
Journalism."

"I see," said Alistair disinterestedly.

"Forgive me for turning up without an appointment
but I was in the area. I've been checking out something
which you guys might be interested in. My sources tell
me you are looking into the rumour of Rathings being
present in the country. Am I right?"

"From where and whom did you get this information?" Alistair demanded.

"I'm afraid I can't tell you that."

"You seem very well informed." Alistair sounded annoyed.

"Naturally," Kilroy replied. "We are an investigative body. We dig around, search for info, we use umpteen sources for information. But I cannot divulge the names of our information contacts. I am currently sourcing out a group of men who I believe are planning some kind of subversive activity against the Government. It's very early days and I don't have very much hard information; I don't reckon even the Government is aware of any danger. I believe I could have a hook up with what you're looking into. I guess this is a bed of information we could share."

"And how d'you see that?" Alistair asked in a rather offhand manner.

"Look here, sir. This group of what I believe is subversives are made up of some very important people. Most are ex-military. All are established figures – barristers, doctors, scientists, theologians, businessmen. I believe there might even be a minor royal involved. Very minor, mind you, but still..." He shrugged. "I'm that near to outing them." He put this thumb and index finger close together but not quite touching. "My problem is that I can't quite pin down what exactly they are planning. I know that they tend to sometimes congregate at a place called Gretorex Hall somewhere in Hertfordshire, but I am having problems moving further with this. I thought that if we can perhaps pool our information and resources we could make good headway. Is what I have just told you of any interest?"

"I appreciate your being so candid, Mr., er..." Alistair paused.

"Kilroy. James Kilroy. And you are?"

"My name's Pellow. I am with the Ministry of Internal Affairs. Mr. Kilroy, I wish you every good hunting in catching these people. However, whilst you are searching this group of men, we are investigating something entirely different."

"Rathings?" Kilroy said.

"We never disclose what we may be investigating."

"But don't you see that the two could be interlinked?" Kilroy said.

"Perhaps. But I don't see any immediate cause for celebration. As you apparently know, we are conducting a government inquiry. All information we gather *ab intra* must remain so and cannot be shared with others. I thank you for your suggestion that we co-operate but I regret to inform you that such will not be possible."

"Don't you want to catch these people?" Kilroy asked in a surprised voice.

"That's *your* brief, Mr. Kilroy," Alistair replied. *Ours* is entirely different. All government inquiries are held *a couvert*. We cannot be seen to be implicated in any other organization's investigations."

"Sure. Not officially, of course. I thought, kinda off the record, you know. In a pub over a drink perhaps?"

"I'm sorry, Mr. Kilroy, but I must refuse on behalf of His Majesty's Government. Thank you for calling to see us but now, if you don't mind. We are rather busy." Alistair took the man gently by the arm and steered him towards the door. But Kilroy wasn't giving up. "Young lady," he called over his shoulder to Penny. "I have it on firm authority that this is your agency. Have you no opinion on the matter?"

Penny was standing by the printer/photocopier. "You heard my colleague, Mr. Kilroy. Thank you for coming to see us and good luck with your investigation. Goodbye."

Kilroy placed a business card on one of the desks. "Call me if you change your mind," he said.

Alistair walked the journalist to the landing. "Tell you what I'll do." He said quietly. "I'll see if the Minister will talk with you. OK?"

"Gee, that'd be great!" the American said with a smile.

When they were alone Penny asked Alistair why he didn't want them to co-operate with the investigations bureau.

"Because as I told our American visitor, government inquiries are not shared with others."

"How d'you know he's American?" Penny said.

"His accent. He spoke deep, Deep South of the Mason-Dixon line."

"I thought he might have been Canadian but, yes, I guess you're right." Penny said. "But I still think we should have agreed to co-operate."

"That's an example of why Sir William assigned me to assist you. It would have created untold embarrassment to the Department and the Government had you agreed to any form of co-operation. I'm sorry, Penny. We must follow the rules."

Penny said nothing.

"I'm on my way to see Sir William," Alistair said. "Will you be alright?"

"Yes, thanks," she replied.

When Alistair had left the office, Penny picked up Kilroy's business card and put it in her handbag.

The telephone rang a few seconds after.

"Hello. Campbell private investigations agency," Penny announced. She listened to the caller speak, her complexion going steadily paler. Her hands were trembling when she put the receiver down.

FIFTEEN

"How are you getting on with Mrs. Campbell?" Sir William asked Alistair.

Alistair sat on the visitor's side of Sir William's imposing mahogany desk and watched the older man move the items on his desk so that they all lined up in orderly fashion.

"Fairly well, sir."

"Fairly?"

"She does not seem very happy working with me."

"What have you done? What have you said?"

"Nothing untoward, sir. Take, for example, the interview with Professor Antonijevic. I thought it went well. She gave me the impression that she thought it was all faked up."

"And was it? I do know you intended to get him to give an opinion to the effect that no Rathings re-existed."

"And that's what he said. No, I think she's been working under her own steam for a long time; certainly since her husband died. Which, incidentally, I knew nothing about."

"Yes, quite. I'm sorry. I should have mentioned that to you."

"I just feel she's a bit touchy. But I'm working on her and she'll come round to our way of thinking in due course."

Sir William leant forward and adjusted the position of some of the objects on his desk. Obsessive Compulsive Disorder, Alistair surmised. He had noted this behaviour of Sir William on many occasions in the past.

Alistair continued, "There are two things to report to you. We had a visit from a journalist of sorts, a James Kilroy, who says he is a member of the Bureau of Investigative Journalism. It appears that he has been looking into a group of men whom he suspects of planning some subversive action – what exactly, he is not clear about. He believes there is a link between this group and the 'possibility' of there being Rathings in the country."

Sir William leaned back. He linked the fingers of both hands and moved them to his chin. "Now that is very interesting."

"He maintains that he is close to revealing who this group is," Alistair said, with a smile. "I am a bit worried that he's getting a bit too close to home."

"Indeed, indeed," Sir William nodded several times.

"He wanted us to co-operate, to work together on this investigation, except that he is checking up on a group of possible subversives whilst we are supposedly trying to establish that no Rathings exist."

"Perhaps I should see this chap, what's his name?"

"Kilroy. James Kilroy."

"Well, we don't want this Mr. Kilroy getting his fingers burned. Perhaps I can help him. Get my secretary to fix up an appointment. Give her this fellow's details."

"Excellent thinking, if I may so, sir. I shall talk to Miss Pilgrim straight away, sir."

"You said you had two things to report."

"Mrs. Campbell apparently intends to phone a contact in Edinburgh whom she thinks may have some knowledge about the Rathings."

"Named and address of this person?"

"I didn't get her name or address but the name of her firm is High and Low Scotland Detective Agency. You know, for Highland and Low..."

"I already gathered that, Pellow, thank you. But no name of the individual in question you said."

"I'm afraid not. But I rather suspect that it's a one-man agency."

"No matter. I shall have that looked into. Is that all?"

"Yes, sir," Pellow said and nodded.

"Good, then you'd better be off handling your other duties. How's the Montrose job going?"

"Making good progress," Alistair said as he rose. "I shall have to go to Edinburgh to finalise things."

"Don't spend longer than necessary in Edinburgh. I don't want Mrs. Campbell to be left for too long on her own."

"Of course. And I shall keep you advised of developments."

"Thank God you didn't use that atrocious Americanism – keep you in the loop. Harrumph!" – Another grunt. "Do you know someone had the infernal audacity to say that to me yesterday?"

"One of those avant-garde new boys, I presume?" Alistair laughed.

"Not here at the Ministry. Thank God we haven't started recruiting from that pool yet. They're not our kind. This was at a cocktail party at one of the charities I am involved in. Fellow had no breeding. Kind of man who tucks his singlet into his underpants I shouldn't imagine." Sir William harrumphed again and picked up his telephone to indicate that the meeting was over.

SIXTEEN

Alistair rang the street level doorbell of Penny's office. He heard Penny answer it. "Yes? Who is that?" It did not register with him at the time that her voice was a bit panicky.

"Oooh, the ghost of Christmas past," Alistair said jokingly in a spooky voice.

"Go away," he heard Penny shout. "I'll call the police."

"Penny. Penny, it's me, Alistair. I was joking."

"Alistair?"

"Yes. Penny? Are you alright?"

"Is that really you?"

"Of course. What's the matter? You sound dreadful. Can you let me in?"

The buzzer sounded and Alistair pushed the door open and rushed up the stairs. Penny stood at her office door. She held a heavy rolling pin in her hand. Alistair walked up to her. "Are you planning on fighting me off?" he said jokingly. "Or baking cakes?"

"It's not funny," Penny said in a quavering voice.

Alistair put his hands on her arms. He drew her towards him. "Tell me what the matter is? You look frightened."

"I'm terrified," Penny replied. "I had a nasty phone call yesterday just after you left. I've been scared all night. I couldn't sleep. I just sat in my flat, listening hard for any strange sounds or creaking floorboards."

"Can you remember what they said?"

"I can play you the recording of the call. I record all calls received and made. It is essential in my line of business."

"Good girl," Alistair smiled. "Let's hear it then."

Penny fiddled around and eventually pressed a button.

The recording was of a man's voice. His accent sounded to Alistair as if he normally spoke with Received English pronunciation but was trying, not very successfully, to sound like a cockney with a reedy voice.

'We know what you're trying to do. Listen sweetheart. Take my advice and drop it. Don't continue with the job. Don't stick your nose in business that has got bugger all to do with you. Drop this assignment. Otherwise you're going to get badly hurt. Even killed. This is your only and final warning. Next time you'll be dead.'

"Friendly chap," Alistair said.

"What do we do, Alistair?" Penny pleaded.

"Let's just hold fire for a bit and see what we can find out about this phone call. In the meantime I shall need to take that recording away."

"Why?"

"For speech analysis. The government has a department that uses behavioural software that decodes the human voice to identify a person's voice over the telephone. Sort of voice driven algorithms."

Penny frowned. "They can do that?" she exclaimed.

"Well, there is no such thing as a voice print as there is, say, with fingerprinting," Alistair explained. "But they can still produce some interesting results." He took his mobile phone from his pocket.

"I wanted to call you last night after I got that phone call but I didn't have your number," Penny said.

"Sorry. That was remiss of me." He took a card from his wallet and scribbled on the back of it. "I've put my home number on the back," he said. Penny put the card in her jacket pocket. Alistair pushed some numbers on his mobile. "Sir William? Alistair Pellow here. I am at Mrs. Campbell's office. It appears that she received a rather nasty threatening call last night warning her to drop the investigation."

"What?" Sir William Henderson shouted so loudly that the word was easily heard half way into Penny's office.

"I have told her to stop the investigation for the time being."

"Put her on to me," Sir William barked.

Alistair handed his phone to Penny.

"Uncle?" Penny said but got no further before Sir William spoke very sternly. "Listen here, young lady and listen well. You are to cease further work on this assignment until we establish what is going on. This is an instruction. Now put me on to Pellow."

Alistair took his phone. He heard Sir William barking down the line. "Pellow. We must discover who is making these threats. As far as I am aware, nobody other than me, you and Mrs. Campbell know about this investigation. What the devil is going on, eh?"

Alistair said "Yes, sir," as he followed a string of instructions he was receiving from Sir William. "Yes, the call was recorded and I shall bring the tape to the office. No, but I shall arrange suitable protection cover for her. I fully understand that you do not want the police involved at this stage. Yes, I will do. Goodbye, sir."

"So what's happening?" Penny asked nervously.

"Firstly, no more looking into the case. Secondly, we've got to get you relocated residence-wise. Is there anywhere you can stay other than at your place for a short while?"

"I don't know," Penny confessed.

"Are your parents around?"

"No. They live in France now."

"Your late husband's parents?"

"They were in the car with Peter and were killed as well."

"I'm sorry, Penny. What about friends? Anyone you know well enough with whom you could stay for a short while?"

"Oh, I know!" Penny exclaimed. "Julie and her husband. Julie's a good friend."

"Good. Call her now if you will."

"Oh," she said suddenly. "I remember now her telling me they were going off for a late winter sun break. To Cyprus, I think."

"Anyone else?"

She shook her head. "I don't have many friends, friends I'd be comfortable staying with, that is. Lots of acquaintances, few friends." She thought for while. "I suppose I could book into a hotel."

Alistair shook his head. "Not that brilliant. Apart from the phenomenal cost of staying in a hotel for, perhaps, several weeks, there's a total lack of security. The person threatening you could soon find out where you are staying. Getting hold of a pass key is comparatively easy and, besides, there are too many people coming and going in a hotel."

"As I'm working for the Government, can't I be put in what you call a Safe House?"

Alistair nodded. "Yes, that is one possibility." Yet Alistair knew that Sir William would be loath to get other Government departments involved. He walked around the office, deep in thought. Eventually he said. "You could always stay at my flat."

"What?" Penny exclaimed.

"I have a couple of spare bedrooms, all en suite. There's a concierge and video entry facilities. It's a gated property and it is very secure. It's almost like Fort Knox; and it's called Knox Court to boot."

"This is most kind of you, but I don't think I could impose on you like that."

"It's no imposition. And I'd feel a lot happier knowing that you were in a secure environment. As I am sure would Sir William. I can clear it with him for his approval."

"Did I hear you correctly when you said you had *a couple* of spare bedrooms?"

"Yep." Alistair nodded.

"So, what's the address? Buck House? Or do you run a hotel in your spare time?"

Alistair thought Penny very plucky, being able to have a sense of humour in the present situation. She went up a further notch in his estimation. He laughed. "It's in Pimlico. Knox Court in Astley Street. It actually belongs to my parents but they don't use it, so they've let me have the use of it. They have their home in Hampshire and if they need to stay in London for any reason, they tend to book into the Royal Overseas Club."

Penny said, "Thank you, Alistair. You are a very kind man and I am very grateful to you. I'd love to stay at your place for a short while."

"OK, let's go then," Alistair said and helped Penny with her coat. "Your flat first to pick up some of your things and then on to my place."

Both of them noticed the middle-aged man in the red Toyota positioned three cars behind Alistair's parked vehicle. Alistair drove off.

"We're being followed," Penny said.

Alistair nodded. "I know. The red Toyota."

The Toyota followed them to Astley Street and parked outside Knox Court.

SEVENTEEN

Alistair approached large double gates leading to an underground car park of a private gated development. He pushed a button on the car's dashboard and the gates swung slowly open. He drove underground and slotted his car in his allotted space. As he parked, Penny noted the large number of expensive cars already parked. They got out of the car and walked to a bank of elevators, which took them up to the main entrance, a large circular hall. Penny thought the flat's location was perfect, being close to the Kings Road and Sloane Square, and only five or so minutes from Pimlico tube station.

The building was beautiful, freshly painted and in pristine condition. At the far end of the hall was a semi-circular counter behind which stood a uniformed concierge, a tall, strong looking man, perhaps in his sixties Penny guessed.

"Evening, Mac," Alistair greeted him pleasantly. "Are the gee gees looking after you yet?"

"Evening sir, madam. Not so far Mr. Pellow, sir. I don't think they know what an accumulator is."

"Oh, Mac. This is a good friend of mine, Mrs. Campbell. She will be staying here with me for a while. Would you be good enough to see about fixing a front door key and an apartment door key for her? I'd be grateful."

"Of course, sir," Macallan replied. "I may have to get the apartment key cut. "Would tomorrow be alright?"

"Fine thanks. And remember to tell me of any costs."

The concierge bowed to Penny as she and Alistair walked to the elevators. "Madam," he said.

"Hello," she replied.

They got into the lift and Alistair pressed the seventh floor button, which Penny noted appeared to be the top floor of the building.

"What a nice man he seems," she said, as the elevator rose smoothly and silently.

"Macallan? Yep. Ex Commandos. Hell of a reliable chap and handy to have around."

"Does he like his name abbreviated to Mac?" Penny asked.

Alistair laughed. "I don't know really. Everyone calls him that and he doesn't seem to mind. He's always just been Mac."

They walked along heavy pile carpet which was so clean it looked like it had been laid only that day. They reached a light grey painted door with the number five in white enamel placed at eye level. Alistair took out his key and opened his apartment door.

They entered straight into a lounge area and Penny could not help but gasp in surprise and wonder at the magnificence of the view from the large floor to ceiling picture windows. Even though the front door was some distance from the bank of windows, the unimpeded view afforded a stupendously uninterrupted vista of the River Thames and the city roofs, wearing caps of snow.

"Wow, Alistair! What a wonderful view!"

"Yep. It is nice."

The apartment and its furnishings were as magnificent as was the view. The drawing room walls were painted a very light French grey combined with brilliant yet subtle white. She immediately recognized the cream coloured sofa as an Ikendi. She knew that it would have cost in excess of twelve thousand pounds. A large Vendome Credenzar sideboard against one wall held a vase of flowers and a few family photographs in silver frames. Some oil paintings and prints were on the wall. She recognized a Rembrandt but whether it was an original or a reproduction, she didn't know. She doubted it was the latter. The sofa and a couple of armchairs stood close to a fireplace with a basket of logs besides it. There was little else in the room, which gave it a rather minimalistic feel.

Alistair took Penny's suitcase from her. "Let me show you your bedroom."

They went up a flight of carpeted stairs to another landing which led to the bedrooms. "There are three bedrooms up here. Mine and two guest rooms. All are en suite. There's also a private riverside terrace, OK for the summer but not recommended at this time of year."

They entered a very large double bedroom with a magnificent king size bed and leather headboard. The room was painted a high gloss white and Penny noted that, like the living room, large picture windows gave unimpeded views of the river and the trees that surrounded it.

"Here's your bathroom." Alistair showed her the en suite bathroom with a deep sunken white bath. A slim line body drying cubicle stood in a corner. Big fluffy white towels hung over a wall rail.

"You're probably wondering why there are towels in here when it is obvious that, like all homes, I have warm air body drying units in all bathrooms."

"Penny smiled. "The thought did cross my mind."

"It's Mrs. Padwaski's idea. Oh, she's a cleaning woman who comes in for about an hour three times a week to Hoover, dust and polish. When she first saw the empty rails she said 'it's not right. Bath rail look naked with no towel to cover. Rail must be dressed'. I could not persuade her otherwise. So each time she comes in to clean, she changes the towels, even though they quite obviously had not been used."

"I see," Penny said. "She is obviously a very determined lady with a set mind-frame."

"You might say that," Alistair gave a laugh. "Oh, there's another bedroom I can show you if you prefer," Alistair said.

"No, no, Alistair. This is just perfect. My heavens, this flat of yours is like being in paradise. It's beautiful."

Alistair smiled. "Thank you. Incidentally, just down from your bedroom is a separate shower room, in case you prefer to shower rather than bathe. You can look around later. Back downstairs is a pretty modern kitchen with all the usual gubbins and there are plenty of toilets scattered around." He gave a laugh of embarrassment. "Oh, and there's also a laundry room.

"I do hope you enjoy your stay here. Let me know if there's anything you need at any time."

"I will do. And thanks. You're very sweet and very kind."

"Rubbish," he said. "Just doing my job."

"Really?" Penny raised an enquiring eyebrow.

Alistair smiled. "Well, not really." He then said. "Look, Penny. I have to go out for a very short while. No longer than half an hour. Now, don't leave this flat, understand?"

"Perfectly," she replied.

When he had left, Penny decided to call her contact in Edinburgh. She keyed in a number on her mobile phone. She heard it answered as High and Low Scotland Detective Agency. Can I help you?

"Hello, Margot. It's Penny."

"Penny? Oh, yes, hi Penny."

"Margot. I want to ask you some questions. Is it convenient to talk now?"

"No, not really. Can you call me back in about half an hour?"

"Of course. Anyway, how are you?"

"I'd be fine if I could sort out the static interference I keep getting on my radio at home. I can never seem to get a clear station."

Penny was immediately alerted to the fact that Margot had a serious problem.

"Try fiddling around with the channel tuner," Penny suggested, playing along with the game of code language they had adopted, particularly when talking to each other in the presence of a client whom they did not wish to know what they were saying.

"Yes. I'll do so. Incidentally, how is Birmingham?"

That was another code cue. Birmingham indicated danger. Penny was becoming concerned but she could not express her worries on the phone. It seemed that someone else was present with Margot. And that person present was a danger. Margot's guarded conversation indicated that the other person might have been listening in to their talk.

"Oh, Birmingham is OK," Penny replied. "But I don't think I'll be going up there soon. Well, listen, Margot. My call wasn't important and if you're busy at the moment I'll call you back another time. Bye then."

"Bye," Margot said, then added, "Be careful, Penny." And she closed the line.

EIGHTEEN

The man who had followed Alistair and Penny from Putney now saw Alistair leave the block of flats and walk towards Sloane Square. The man shuffled as quickly as he could to the front entrance of Knox Court. His feet were hurting him, he was tired and fed up and now had to pretend he was someone he was not. He rang the door bell. Macallan pressed the release button to open the main entrance door. The man straightened his back and assumed a confident air.

Macallan noted the man's strange appearance and dishevelled state. He wore dark sunglasses, which was distinctly odd on a dull grey, snowy winter's day. His mackintosh was dirty and had several grease stains on the front. His shoes were scruffy and his trousers were baggy. Furthermore, his moustache was unkempt, which to Macallan, as an ex-military man, was a mortal sin. The man walked in and up to the reception desk. He whipped off his dark glasses.

"Good day to you," he said, making an effort to be friendly. He also made himself speak in a refined, cut-glass accent, as he assumed someone of the aristocracy would speak. "I am Sir William Henderson; uncle of Mrs. Campbell who I understand is staying here. I should like to see her please. Would you be good enough to tell me her apartment number?"

Are you indeed? Macallan thought. Fallen on hard times, have we? "Certainly, sir." Macallan said. He went to pick up his internal phone.

"I'd rather you didn't tell her I'm here," the man said quickly. "I want to give her a surprise. Just give me her apartment number, like a good chap."

"I understand, sir. But I have my instructions."

The man swore softly under his breath but continued to smile at the concierge.

Penny heard the phone ring. She looked around and saw it on a side table. She hesitated about answering it. Eventually, she picked up the receiver.

"Excuse me, madam. This is Mac here. I have your uncle at reception who wishes to see you."

"My uncle?"

"Yes, madam."

"That's impossible!" she exclaimed. She felt distinctly uneasy. Alistair had suggested she stay at his place only at the last minute and, certainly as far as she was aware, he had not called her uncle to tell him of their decision. She was also mindful of the telephone call threat and Alistair's advice to be on her guard at all times. She made a decision. "May I talk to him on the phone please, Mr. MacAllan?"

"Certainly, madam. Just one second, please."

He passed the phone to the man. "She wishes to speak with you, sir."

The man hesitated before taking the receiver. "Hello," he said in a guarded voice, desperately trying to think what Sir William Henderson would sound like and how he would address his niece. He thought that the less he said the more chance he had of not being caught out.

"Is that you, uncle?" Penny asked.

"It is, my dear."

"How did you know I was here?"

"Oh, I have my ways."

Penny knew that it was not her uncle's voice. She felt dubious about the whole affair. She thought she'd try a subtle test. "Did Peter tell you this afternoon?" she asked.

"Yes, he did." The man was becoming more confident of the outcome. The girl seemed to accept him as being her uncle. He smiled at Macallan.

"Would you put me on to the receptionist," Penny said.

The man handed the phone to Macallan and continued to smile.

"Yes, madam?" Macallan said.

"Mr. Macallan. That man is not my uncle. I believe he could be dangerous. Tell him I have a headache or something but don't let him up. Get rid of him please."

"Certainly, madam," Macallan replied as he reached under the counter for the truncheon he kept there.

"I regret Mrs. Campbell says she cannot see you as she has a bad headache. Perhaps another time, sir?"

The man's smile disappeared. "This is most inconvenient!" he snapped.

"I am sorry, sir."

The man stood at the reception desk, deep in thought. So near and yet so far, he thought. The confounded woman was within reach, on her own, and he was being thwarted.

"If there's nothing else, sir?" Macallan pressed the door release and the front door swung open.

The man remained standing there, debating how he could possibly reach the Campbell woman. The instructions he had been given had been very clear. You are to get rid of that woman. I don't care how you do it. But dispose of her. He knew that failure on his part would not be tolerated by his master.

"If you would be so good as to please leave the building, sir."

The man did not move but stood there rubbing his chin. God, he thought, there must be easier ways to earn a living.

Macallan brought out the truncheon and laid it on the counter top, his hand over it. "Now, sir, if you don't mind."

The man looked at Macallan and recognised that whilst he was elderly he looked quite capable of dealing with any disturbance. He also had the feeling that the receptionist would know how to use the truncheon effectively.

"Damn nuisance," the man said, trying to retain some pride as he turned and walked towards the open entrance.

Sometime later Penny took the lift down to the reception area and spoke to Macallan. She thanked him for his help and just told him that she was being bothered by the man who had called earlier. She went on to tell him that she wished to see no one whilst she was staying there.

Macallan assured her he would ensure she was never bothered.

NINETEEN

Alistair sat at his desk at the Ministry. He had tried to concentrate on some of his other assignments but his thoughts kept drifting back to the enjoyable weekend spent with Penny. She had taken her enforced incarceration well. He knew of other girls who would have complained about not being able to go out and shop or whatever. But Penny, who he knew secretly chaffed at the bit at having to stay indoors, never complained and tried to make light of the serious situation in which she now found herself. To ease matters, Alistair took her out to dinner on Saturday and to lunch on Sunday. He smiled when he thought of how much at ease they were with each other, how they laughed at silly things and discussed deeply more important matters. Penny's suspicious querying of some things, such as her interview with Branko or her seeming annoyance with him for having to report her intended actions seemed to have dissipated.

Alistair realised that he was becoming slightly drawn towards her. He had had numerous girlfriends and many affairs over the years, but none of them had ever excited or stirred him as much as Penny did. He had a growing conviction that he would do all in his power to bed her. Of that he was confident. Once he'd set out to seduce a woman he invariably succeeded, even if, like Penny, they held some reservations about him. They always succumbed in the end.

She had a quality about her that was difficult to define. Of course, she was certainly very pretty, had a wonderful figure and could look most alluring or boyish, depending on her mood, but her beauty went beyond that, it was deep in her soul – a gentle femininity, wonderful sense of humour and a sweet nature at one moment quickly followed by a temper. He had not come across such a combination before. Her fury at her uncle's decision to call her Penelope on her business card, her questioning of Branko's silly slip up in asking him, Alistair, if what he said was what Alistair wanted, all testified to a balanced character with strength and purpose. Discreet enquiries he had made informed him that her father had been a well respected GP, and her mother a classical pianist. Alistair and she were of similar background. Solid middle to upper class backgrounds and he found puzzling her habit of sometimes seeming to talk herself down.

The more Alistair thought about Penny and his intention to entice her into his bed, the more did his mood become elated. He felt light at heart and carefree and extraordinarily happy; a state of mind he had not experienced for very many years.

His reverie was interrupted by his phone ringing. He answered it and heard an American drawl greet him. "Hi, Alistair? Praise the Lord. I've had the devil of a job getting hold of you. This is James. James Kilroy."

"Oh, yes. Good morning, Mr. Kilroy."

"Look, I just wanted to call you and express my sorrow at the sad news about your colleague. I heard the news with some shock, let me tell you. My condolences."

"I'm sorry; I don't understand what you're talking about."

"Penny Campbell. You know, the detective agency gal I saw when I called round recently."

"And?"

"My God! You haven't heard the news, have you? She's dead, my friend."

"What?" Alistair nearly shouted down the line.

"Appears she got into her yellow VW yesterday morning outside her flat and it blew up when she started it."

Alistair felt a sense of uplift. This was all an obvious mistake. Penny didn't own a car and he had seen her this morning. "Thank you for calling," he said. "Why did you think it is Mrs. Campbell?"

"When making some enquiries I learned where she lived. The car blow up was outside the same block of flats. I was given the dead girl's description, which fits. I am sorry."

"Thank you for calling."

"Hey! And thanks for fixing me up with your boss, the Minister. We're meeting up to discuss co-operation. I appreciate your change of mind."

"You're welcome. Goodbye and thanks again for your call."

"Good bye, Alistair, and, again, sorry about your girl colleague."

Alistair put the phone down and picked it up immediately. He dialed his apartment number.

"Penny? Alistair here. "Is everything OK?"

"Yes, Alistair, except that I'm standing here wrapped in a towel I grabbed having jumped out of the shower to answer the phone."

"Good," Alistair said, happy to know she was alright.

"Good because I was having a shower or good because I'm standing here wrapped in a flimsy towel shivering to death?"

"Good because you're alright. I just had a call from that American chap, Kilroy passing on his condolences at the news of your apparent death."

"No, Alistair. I assure you I am standing here very much alive. Cold but alive"

"That is really good to hear. Tell me, why d'you think he thought it might have been you?"

"I don't really know. Because he's besotted with me?"

"Very funny. Is there anyone you know who looks like you?"

"I'm unique."

"I know. Of course you are. I meant someone who could be mistaken for you at a distance."

There was silence for a while. "No. I can't think of anyone." A further silence. "Wait! Hold it! There is a girl who lives in the same block of flats who is a little like me. Well, she is short and slim and her blonde hair is cut in the same style, so I suppose at a distant glance we might be mistaken for each other."

"Did she drive a car?"

"Yes, I often saw her tootle away in it."

"D'you know what car she drove?"

"No. I'm not very good on cars. I know it was yellow."

"That's her. That's the poor girl someone killed thinking it was you."

"Oh my God, Alistair! Poor, poor girl. Why? Why? Who is doing this?"

"We'll find out. Meanwhile it is very important that you stay indoors. Don't go out. OK?"

"Yes. I understand. "

TWENTY

The next day, back at the apartment, Alistair gathered his case and looked at his watch. "Taxi will be here in ten minutes, and then I must go, but I'll be back within two days max, maybe sooner."

He had wanted to make sure that Penny did not have to go out unnecessarily to buy food or to eat out. He'd spoken to the manager of a nearby restaurant and arranged for them to take any orders she may have. He put his case down and moved to one of the side tables, opened the drawer and took out a menu card. "To save you doing any cooking, this is from the restaurant down the road. I've made arrangements with them to provide and deliver here any meals you order. Mac will see that one of the in-house staff deliver the meal to you up here. They'll serve up breakfast, lunch or dinner. You'll see from the menu that they can serve up practically most things except that they may get stuck if you order Lobster Thermidor.

"Oh, I forgot to mention that there's an indoor swimming pool on the lower ground floor. The lift will take you right down there. It's a great pool and you might want to use it. A few lengths in the morning can set you up for the day. I take it you can swim?"

"Sort of, but not very well," Penny smiled. "I get very nervous in the deep end of a pool."

Alistair gave a soft laugh. "In that case, keep to the shallow end and do a few extra breadths there. That's just as good for a work out. Look, Penny. I must say goodbye. I've left the name and phone number of my hotel in Edinburgh on the kitchen table but obviously if you need anything, contact Sir William."

"He phoned me yesterday and suggested he put someone else here with me during your absence. I refused. Apart from the fact that this is your flat and not a hotel, I wouldn't want anyone staying here. And Mr. Macallan is a very good guard dog."

With a smile, Alistair forward to give Penny a goodbye kiss on the cheek. She turned her head at the same time to look at him and they accidentally kissed on the lips. For a few seconds neither moved. Both stood with lips locked together, Penny with her hands on Alistair's arms and Alistair with his gently on her hips. Eventually, seemingly reluctantly, Penny stepped away. "Sorry about that," she mumbled.

A tingling sensation rushed sensuously from her lips through to the tips of her toes. "I'm not," Alistair replied with a naughty grin. "If you must know, I found it rather nice."

TWENTY-ONE

Penny mooched about the flat after Alistair had left. She watched some television. Then she read the daily newspaper delivered that morning. She made herself a cup of coffee, then another. She again moved from room to room. She stood at the picture window and watched the river traffic. She was feeling distinctly edgy. She was itching to go out but knew she shouldn't and wouldn't. She eventually decided to laze in a luxuriously deep bubble bath in an attempt to kill time. It was nearly noon by the time she got out, toweled herself dry and snuggled herself in a fluffy woolen bath robe. The trill of the phone interrupted her listlessness.

"This is Mac, madam. We have just received a delivery of oysters from Sir William Henderson with instructions to pass these to you for your lunch. I am sending the tray up with one of our maids."

"Good Lord, Mr. Macallan! Oysters?"

"That's right, madam."

"Thank you, Mr. Macallan."

"Most people just call me Mac, madam."

"Oh yes, of course. I'm sorry. Mac."

"Thank you, madam."

Penny paced around the room until the apartment doorbell rung. She opened it to see a young girl balancing a large tray on both hands. On it was about a dozen oysters, if not more, a half bottle of champagne and a champagne flute.

"From Zeer Villam," she said in a strong foreign accent. "I take in?"

Penny stepped back and the maid walked in and tottered over to the dining table. She placed the tray down very carefully, turned and curtsied.

"Thank you very much," Penny said, and hurriedly passed to the girl a five pound note as a tip.

The girl smiled, nodded, said thank you and walked out of the room.

Penny moved to the table and looked down at the large platter full of shelled oysters lying on ice with cut lemon pieces lying amongst them. She bent down and sniffed but, of course, could smell nothing. She smiled. How considerate of Uncle William, she thought. Except that I don't like oysters. The slippery, slithery pulp makes me feel sick as it slips down my throat. She was sure that Alistair would have enjoyed them if he had not already left.

She tried to eat one, but gave up the attempt. She knew she simply could not stomach them. But how to get rid of the oysters? She thought about it for a short while, and then an idea struck her. She picked up the platter and took it into the toilet. She sat on the rim of the bidet, scraped an oyster from its half shell and dropped it down the lavatory pan, flushing the toilet afterwards. She continued this until all the oysters had been flushed away to join the other multitude of effluent matter in the waste pipes.

Her task completed, she opened the champagne, poured some in the flute glass and sat down in front of the television. She was watching some inane afternoon programme when she suddenly smacked her forehead with the palm of her hand and said out loudly, "What am I doing wasting time here? I should go to Edinburgh and check on Margot."

She rose and went to her bedroom and got dressed quickly, grabbed her coat and dashed out of the apartment. As she walked through the reception hall,

Macallan called out, "I've been asked to ensure your safety at all times, madam."

Penny smiled. "Yes, but not to make me a prisoner. I have an important task to fulfill and should be back soon Please don't worry and thank you, Mr. Macallan."

Macallan could only stand there and watch her go out of the front door.

TWENTY-TWO

Penny grabbed a taxi and told the driver to go to Heathrow airport. At the airport she booked herself on a BA flight. She settled in her seat, ready for the near two hours flight to Scotland.

At Edinburgh airport, she walked over to the flying taxis rank and got into the first vehicle. "Would you please take me to Melville Street?" she said.

The driver turned and smiled at her. He was very brown – she reckoned that he was most likely an Iraqi or Afghan – certainly Middle Eastern. His mouth was full of gold teeth. "Aye, right ye are, lassie," he said in a broad Scottish accent. He activated some buttons on the dashboard of his jet pod and typed in 'Melville Street'. A recorded female voice relayed instructions. "For Melville Street – M E L V I L L E street take the D50 designated pathway corridor. Travel at exactly five hundred feet. You will be alerted when you are close to destination. You will then traverse onto the E12 exit pathway corridor and descend to three hundred feet. You will see on your port side an indication arrow directing you to the landing strip. Your journey time will be fourteen minutes. Walking time from landing strip to Melville Street is between five and ten minutes, depending on walking speed. The fare cost is ten pounds. Thank you for calling Activia, sponsored by Jet Pods Incorporated." There then followed a jingle in which the word Activia was repeated several times.

Penny was impressed with the whole performance. "This is the first air taxi I've ever taken," she admitted. "The whole thing is amazing."

"Aye. Many people think we fly wherever we like but can you imagine the chaos if there's no control? Flying taxis crashing into each other, plummeting to the ground, deaths galore."

"So how does it work then?" Penny asked.

"There's designated routes at designated flight levels; north to south fly at seven hundred feet; south to north at six hundred and fifty feet. East to west fly/drive at five hundred feet – the route we're on. Returning west to east is flown at four hundred and fifty feet. The journeys is quick because there's no cross traffic, no side roads as such. The only drawback is that we can't drop you off right outside your destination address because we need a strip of about forty foot long on which to land. But there are so many landing strips that you are always within a short walking distance of your destination. As the lady said, in your case between five and ten minutes but it could be shorter if you decided to run." He turned to look at her and laughed, displaying even more gold fillings in his mouth.

"Where are you from?" Penny asked.

"Edinburgh."

"I mean, where were you born?"

"Edinburgh."

"But you're not Scottish."

"Why, lassie? Because I'm brown? I'm Scottish, believe me. I've got the right passport an' I've even got to like haggis and the bag pipes."

They landed, taxied to drop off point and Penny paid him and included a generous tip.

She walked to the building in which Margot had her office. There was no reception desk. A board on the wall advertised each tenant's name, location – floor and room number. Margot's office was closed, the door locked. Penny knew that like her, Margot worked alone, so Penny assumed that Margot may be at a client's office. She thought she'd double check, so she knocked on the door of the office opposite Margot's. It had a name plate on the door proclaiming it as being the Milk Marketing Board Data Centre. She walked in and saw an oldish woman sitting at a computer inputting data.

"Hello?" Penny called.

The woman stopped and turned round. "Yes? Can I help?" she said.

"I'm sorry to trouble you, but I wonder if you know when Margot might be back."

"Oh, I'm sorry, dear. Are you a friend of hers?"

"Sort of. We've worked together on some cases."

"Well, I'm sorry to have to tell you that she won't be back. The poor girl is dead. Tragic."

Penny was really startled. "Dead? How?"

"Well, her neighbour in the next door flat heard a tremendous noise of something tumbling down the stairs. She knocked on Margot's door to ask if all was alright and she got no reply. She tried a few times again after that – still no reply, so she called the landlord. He rang the door bell several times then he used his pass key to gain access. They found poor Margot in the hallway at the foot of the stairs. Dead, she was. Broken neck. Seems she stumbled over her cat which must have been weaving around her feet on the stairs as she was walking down. And she, such a lovely young lady. I know the police are trying to trace her brother."

"Her brother?" Penny knew that Margot, like her, was an only child.

"Aye. He visited her here at her office some days before her death. Came with a friend. Ever such nice young men, but there's no record in Margot's papers of his address."

Penny felt sick. The walls of the office in which she stood began to sway. She clutched hard at a desk to stop herself from fainting. Margot had warned her of danger but it had never occurred to Penny that the danger would be directed at Margot. "Thank you," she said hurriedly to the old lady, and left the room quickly. She had to get out into the fresh air.

She rapidly walked across to Margot's office. From her handbag, she took a set of pro-line pick keys. She quickly unpicked the lock and stepped in to Margot's office. Penny was thankful for having taken the Locksmiths course in Wakefield two years before. Learning how to unpick a door lock had proved useful on more than one occasion in her line of business. She walked over to Margot's desk. Penny was convinced that Margot's death had not been an accident. She had been killed and obviously because she had some information her killers did not want her to divulge. Penny hoped that Margot might have left some notes or sign of what she knew. Penny did not expect to find any file with this information lying in a desk drawer. That would be an obvious place for her killers to check. Both Penny and Margot had discussed the best place to hide incriminating evidence and they agreed that should be between the pages of a book; not foolproof but better than a desk drawer. Penny moved swiftly to the bookshelf in Margot's study. She worked methodically, taking the first book on the left hand side, turning it upside down and shaking it. Nothing fell out of the book. She did the same to the next one and worked her way along the shelf. When she shook the twelfth book, several handwritten pages fell to the floor. Penny replaced the book on the shelf and picked up the fallen papers. It was handwritten notes, headed 'Draft'. Before she could read any of it she heard the front door being opened. She quickly hid the papers in her bag. She stood stock still. It was too late for her to find a hiding place; besides which, if she were discovered hiding in a cupboard it would be obvious that she was there clandestinely. She decided that the best thing to do with brave it out with whoever was entering the office. She stood at the study door. The front door opened and she saw two men enter the hallway. They were both wearing suits and dark overcoats.

"What the he…!" one of the men began to exclaim.

The other quickly said, "Might I ask who you are and what you are doing here?"

Penny replied, "My name is Jean Metcalf and I am a friend of Margot Turner. I've just come in. She said I could use her office whenever I'm in town. The door was not locked so I assume she must have dashed out to get some milk or whatever and didn't make sure to bang the door closed after her. In fact, I thought it was Margot returning when you came in. And you are?" she raised an enquiring eyebrow.

"We're business associates of Miss Turner. She asked us to check over some things. We're going to be a while and are sorry to disturb you, but you might find it more convenient if you left us to get on with it and come back in, say, a couple of hours?"

"Right," Penny said with a smile. "I wouldn't want to get in your way. If Miss Turner returns before I'm back would you please tell her that Jean Metcalf popped in?"

"Sure, will do," one of the men said.

Penny's journey back to Edinburgh airport was by conventional road taxi. On the flight to Heathrow she took from her handbag the file of papers she had found in Margot's office. She began to read what was a draft report with the subject headed Helen McClory.

It appeared that this McClory woman had asked Margot to trace her cousin who lived in Achiltibutie in the district of Assynt, West Sutherland. Letters were returned marked 'no longer at this address' and the cousin's telephone number was unobtainable.

Initial enquiries made indicated that the army moved all crofters from the North Assynt Estate and relocated them in some of the 18 communities in the area. Margot's Correspondent spoke to a Mr. McLaren in Inverkirkaig who said that some time ago (before the villagers were moved by the army) some climbers went to the cave at Uamh an Claonaite and shortly afterwards called the local police station. Then several helicopters arrived with teams of search and rescue persons. Mr. McLaren said that he had seen the men lower down to the helicopters nets containing "big, heavy things"; he did not know what they were.

A young man who was visiting the area took some pictures with a long range photo lens camera, some of which he gave to Mr. McLaren. Mr. McLaren gave the Correspondent a few spare photographs.

Penny studied the accompanying photographs. They were not very clear, but the things being lowered in nets look like large bears. Apparently, some locals disputed this and they said they were Rathings. This created disagreement within the communities.

Penny looked carefully again at the photographs that had been pinned to the draft report. The shots had been taken at some considerable distance and it was difficult to see clearly what the things were that were being netted down to the helicopters. But whatever they were, they were large. Penny reckoned that if she looked at the photos under a magnifying glass she would get a better idea as to what those nets actually held.

She returned to Alistair's apartment, went into her bedroom and flopped on the bed. Margot had not stumbled on any cat. Margot had been murdered, of that Penny was sure. And she was sure that she had held in her hand the material that had brought about Margot's demise.

She lay there for a while. She felt that events were assuming very strange shapes ever since she was asked by her uncle to accept this assignment. And she was floundering in deep waters; paddling madly trying to keep afloat. Things were not quite right. Penny believed she owed it to Margot to find out what was going on.

She searched the flat in an attempt to see if Alistair had a magnifying glass. She eventually found one by some books on the bookshelf.

She studied the photographs. Despite looking at the picture from every possible angle, it was still not easy to recognize what was being transported in the sling.

TWENTY-THREE

Penny then suddenly remembered the visit of James Kilroy. Perhaps he could throw some light onto the shadowy corners of uncertainty that troubled her. She recalled having taken his card from her desk drawer and putting it in her handbag. She went to her handbag, found the American's card and called him from her mobile.

When she said who she was, she heard him expel a deep breath.

"Thank the Lord you're OK. I called you colleague, Alistair when I heard you'd been killed, but it seems like I was wrong. Are you OK?"

"Yes, I am, thank you Mr. Kilroy. I wondered if we could meet. Just you and me. I'm sorry but Alistair doesn't seem to be too keen to co-operate with anyone outside the Government machinery."

"Oh, I don't know about that. He kindly fixed me up to his boss, the Minister, so I guess he might be softening his stance. But, hey! Sure I'd very much like us to meet up and see what common ground we might have here. When can you make a meeting?"

"Ideally now," Penny replied. "I want to see you without Alistair's knowledge and he is out today. I'm sorry if it all sound clandestine, but I need help, which I think you might be in a position to give, and I need to do this without anyone else's knowledge."

"I see," Kilroy said. "Tell you what. You seem to be in a fix and I'll do what I can to assist you. What d'you say about our meeting in an hour? Say, at the

Natural History Museum. You know? The one in Cromwell Road.

"That would be wonderful, Mr. Kilroy," Penny said.

"Call me James Please. Otherwise you make it sound like I am a geriatric."

"James. Thank you. Shall we meet at the front desk, Cromwell Road entrance?"

"Yep. That sounds fine. We can savour a coffee in the café there and have a chat. See you in one hour. Cheers."

Penny put her mobile in her handbag. She quickly went to the bathroom to wash her hands and splash some water on her face. She tidied up her makeup and she then took the elevator to the ground floor. "I'm off again, Mr. Macallan," she called out, as he stood at his desk with a bemused expression. "Yes, madam," he replied with a slight frown.

"Off to the Natural History museum and shan't be long. Bye." She waved to him as she went out of the door. She hailed a cab and arrived at Cromwell Road before Kilroy.

She was standing by the reception desk when a thatch of ginger hair caught her attention. She saw him hurrying in. She waved at him. "Hello, James. I'm here."

He saw her and smiled. They shook hands and he led her to the new downstairs café. Once seated with their respective coffees, Penny got down to the matter without delay.

"When you came to my office you said you were looking into the activities of a group of men whom you thought may have had some connection with my brief from the Government to establish the true facts pertaining to the rumour about Rathings. May I ask how you connected the two?"

"Through my source," Kilroy replied.

130

"I need more than that, James."

"I can't divulge my contact's name."

"I don't want their name. What I need to know from you is how you connect your group of men with my group of Rathings – if Rathings do in fact exist."

"Oh, they exist all right. I have that on good authority."

"Still not good enough. What good authority? I know you don't want to give any names, which is fair enough. But what about your contact's background? Their job? Their involvement in all this?"

Kilroy leaned back and smiled. "Boy. You're one tough cookie. But I admire that. Look, what I am prepared to tell you is that my contact is a male cleaner at Gretorex Hall."

"And why should you trust what he is telling you?"

"His employers – the men at Gretorex Hall – cut his wages very substantially with no notice of their intention to do so. The man is married with five kids. This cut in wage is hurting him. He explained to his boss the problem he faced with such a big cut, but was more or less told 'hard cheese'."

"He is obviously an employee with a grudge," Penny said. "So he could be making it up to get his own back."

Kilroy shook his head. "I don't think so. I'm going to show you something in a moment which will convince you that my contact is telling me the truth.

"Gretorex Hall is a massive place. The teams of cleaners cleanse the whole house. The exception is the basement area where they are not allowed. That location is strictly verboten. One morning, my contact was taking a break from sweeping and was standing in a kind of recessed bay area having a breather when he heard some movement along the corridor. He looked out and saw one of the security guards leading a chained Rathing from one of the rooms to the door leading down to the cellars. Naturally, my contact was astonished at the sight, but he had the foresight to pull out his cell phone and snap a picture. The security guy was too anxious looking at the Rathing to notice the photo being taken. And my contact had the sense to not use any flash."

He pulled out of the inside pocket of his sports jacket a photograph. He passed it to Penny. It was dark and grainy but showed clearly a man leading a Rathing by a nose-ring chain. There was no doubt, even given the poor quality that the creature with the nose-ring was a Rathing. This was no human, dressed up in a fake costume. This creature *was* a Rathing.

"It is a bit fuzzy and obviously my contact is no Yousuf Karsh, Robert Capa or Sergei Vaznikov, but I'd say that that is pretty conclusive evidence," Kilroy remarked.

Penny was staggered at the evidence she held in her hand. "May I keep this to include in my report?" she asked.

"I'm sorry, I'm afraid not," Kilroy said, reaching out to retrieve the picture. "I propose to show this to the Minister when we meet. Sorry. But why don't you mention it in your report? That'll be just as good. Sorry, I just don't have the time to have a copy for you"

Penny handed the photograph back. "Do you think that this might in any way be a fake?"

Kilroy shook his head. "No. But we could get an expert in fancy dress costumes or a specialist of sorts to check it. The stance is clearly that of an animal and not a human and my contact saw it walking and has sworn to me that it was an animal. But, hey, listen, Miss Penny. You'll always have those who dispute any evidence. I guess if the good Lord was so inclined as to send down Noah's Ark, complete with animal pairs, and drop it in the middle of Trafalgar Square, you'll find a fair sprinkling of folk say it's bogus, a fake."

He stood up and put out his hand to Penny. "Sorry, I've got a great many things to do and I dropped them all so as to make this meeting. I guess I've got to skedaddle. Let's keep in touch."

"That would be nice," Penny said with a smile.

"Perhaps we could make dinner next time?" he asked.

"Perhaps," Penny replied non-committedly.

TWENTY-FOUR

Penny stood on the pavement outside the museum. She was pleased that it had stopped snowing and that a weak sun was hovering in the sky. She decided to forgo a taxi journey back to Pimlico and instead go by tube.

As she made her way along the pavement she saw a crowd of people standing and staring up at a manned elevated monorail train that stood stationery between stations. Electricians or mechanics were being sent up to it by hydraulic platforms. Penny knew that electric motor fed by dual third rails and contact wires/electrified channels enclosed in their guidance beam often broke down. It was because of the frequent monorail breakdowns that she rarely elected to travel by that means.

She stood for a few minutes watching the men unscrew the underside of the monorail and fiddle about with the mechanics within. Most of the rail passengers were crammed against the windows trying to see what was going on but they could not, of course, observe the men working beneath them.

With a sigh, Penny turned away and continued to the underground station. The platform was surprisingly quite crowded. As more and more people arrived, so the crowd pressed forward and Penny soon found herself standing close to the platform edge. She heard a driverless tube train approaching and at the same time felt a hand on her back push her hard. She tottered and knew without a doubt that she was about to fall onto the rail right in front of the arriving tube train. Then two things happened. An elderly man standing next to her grabbed her arm and pulled her back. And at the same time Penny was conscious of a scuffle behind her and people shouting "He pushed her."

"Never stand too close to the edge, my dear," her saviour said. "It can be dangerous. Here, let me help you to a bench. You look quite pale." He and Penny pushed their way through the crowd. Most had got on to the train but some were still there, holding on to a middle-aged man with a straggly moustache. Penny was vaguely conscious of all this confusion but had not realized that the man accused of pushing her was the same as followed her and Alistair to Alistair's apartment.

"Have you called the police?" someone asked. "This bugger pushed the girl to go under the train."

"The Transport cops are on their way down," someone else replied.

"I know. I saw him. Gave her a hard push, the bastard!" another announced.

Penny collapsed on a platform bench. Her legs were shaking and she was feeling quite frightened.

She saw two policemen arrive. They listened to the various people. Someone pointed her out to the policemen. One of them came over to her. The other stayed with the detained man.

"Are you alright, Miss?" he asked.

"Yes, thank you. A bit shaken but not hurt," Penny replied.

"Can you tell us what happened?"

"I don't really know. There were so many people on the platform that I found myself standing on the very edge of the platform and then I felt this had land on my back push me hard."

"Are you sure about that, Miss? Could it perhaps have been natural pushing by the crowd as they moved forward to get on the train?"

Penny shook her head. "I'm really not too sure. It could have been as you've just said."

The policeman gave her a kindly smile. "If you don't mind, I would like you to accompany us to the station where we can investigate this matter more thoroughly. We'll check the film in the CCTV camera and that should explain how it happened. Are you alright to come along now or do you wish to sit here for a while longer?"

Penny thought the young policeman very kind and considerate. She said she could accompany him and his colleague straight way. The detained man and a handful members of the public who were witnesses to the event, accompanied the police to the Police Station.

The time spent at the Police station took far longer than Penny would have liked. A police sergeant interviewed her at some length. She made sure to make no mention of the Ministry of Internal Affairs or Sir William. She played her role as a young innocent, completely unaware as to why someone tried to push her under a train.

She was told that it was unusual for an attacker to be spotted and detained. The Sergeant stated that the detained man was adamant that he did not deliberately push Penny but that he, in fact, had been pushed against her by the swelling crowd anxious to be first on the arriving tube train. The Sergeant went on to explain that there was no evidence to dispute the man's claim; the CCTV film had been handed in but it appeared that it had not been functioning and was awaiting repair. It was his word against hers and the handful of public spirited attention-seekers who had been present.

She learned that the man who she believed had pushed her was called Philip Green and worked at a merchant banking firm in the City. This fact troubled her. She had no connections with any merchant banks. Her enquiries had not involved any merchant banks or bankers. Why should a man who worked in such an organization want to harm her? She was beginning to suspect that the whole episode was possibly a genuine unintended push due to the surge of the crowd.

Eventually, Penny left the Station but was told that she might need to be interviewed again, if the situation warranted such.

TWENTY-FIVE

It was nearly 5.00 p.m. before she returned to Knox Court. She went up to Alistair's apartment and made herself a strong cup of coffee. She had been offered coffee at the Police Station but it had tasted like warm dish water with milk sprinkled in. Now, seated in the flat with a decent cup of coffee in her hands, she began to gradually calm down.

She telephoned Sir William.

"Uncle, it's Penny."

"Yes, Penelope?"

"Firstly, I want to thank you for the oysters. It was a very sweet thought of yours."

"Did you enjoy them?"

"Yes, I did, thank you," she lied.

"Good. I was a little concerned after I'd ordered them and they were on their way to you. I suddenly remembered you once saying that you did not enjoy oysters."

"Ah, that was when my palate was still unsophisticated," she continued to fabricate. "Yet I am a little puzzled as to why you decided to send me lunch."

"I know that Pellow is out of town and I wasn't sure how you might cope with having something nourishing. It was just a thought."

"A very kind one. Thank you again, uncle."

"A pleasure. Is everything going well? I trust there have been no more untoward incidents?" Sir William was increasingly concerned at the threats made to

Penny. He was furthermore concerned as to who was behind those intimidating actions. He had racked his brains to find the answer, so far with no success. "How is your report progressing?" he then asked Penny.

"Extremely well, uncle. I should be in a position to submit it to you in a day or so."

"Splendid, splendid. Oh, do make sure that Pellow has sight of it before you send it in."

"Yes. I will. 'Bye then."

"Good bye, Penelope."

Penny closed the line. She shuddered. "Don't call me Penelope!" she inwardly shouted at her uncle.

Penny decided to try out the swimming pool. She hoped it might help her relax. She realized that she didn't have her swimming costume so she took a pair of plain panties and bra which, at a very quick glance, could be just about mistaken as a not very glamorous costume. She put on a white flannel dressing gown and she took the lift down to the lower ground floor.

She was relieved to note that nobody else was in the pool. It was painted a light blue. The pool room was dimly lit. Soft light danced off the walls and shimmered below the waterline. Penny felt a bit more comfortable about her make-shift bathing costume. She changed in a cubicle, quickly showered and then walked carefully to the shallow end of the pool. The water was at just the right temperature and Penny very carefully paddled from side to side. At one stage she looked down and noted the myriad little reflected lights – triangles, asterisks and circles shimmering in the water. It was very quiet and cool and peaceful in the pool. She floated on her back for a while and was gradually becoming relaxed when she heard a door open and someone come into the pool area. Her body immediately tightened from fright. She turned on her stomach and tried to see who had come in. She saw no one and assumed that they had gone into a cubicle. She immediately realized that she had possibly placed herself in a dangerous position by being down here on her own, although part of her urged caution and less panic.

She got out of the water, changed and took the lift back up to the apartment.

She phoned down to Macallan. "Mr. Macallan, sorry, Mac. This is Penny Campbell. Do you know any way that I can get hold of a computer with Microsoft Office Word or similar, for me to type out a report? You don't happen to have a spare one lying around somewhere?"

"Leave it with me, madam. I shall see what I can do," Macallan said. There was a knock on the door half an hour later. A very tall young man stood outside holding a supermarket carrier bag. "I have a computer in here for you, miss," he said.

"Please come in," Penny said. "Thank you very much. Where did you get this from?"

"It's a spare one we have in the office."

She looked puzzled. "I'm sorry? Who are you?"

"I'm one of the staff here. Mr. Macallan instructed me to bring this to you."

"It's wonderful. Thanks ever so much."

The young man smiled. He took the computer from the carrier bag. He also extracted a disk. "I've brought an empty disk, which you can use when you come to print out what you've entered in the computer."

Penny smiled. "Thank you. You've been most helpful. And will you please thank Mr. Macallan for me?"

"Yes, miss."

"Thank you. I can set up the computer from here. Thanks again. I'll let Mr. Macallan know when I have finished."

After the young man had left, Penny set up the computer, poured herself a coffee, and sat down and began typing her notes recording the day's events. When she finished, she sat back and read what she had written. It was obvious to her that, as confirmed by James Kilroy's photograph, there were Rathings still alive. She had an inkling that that was not what her uncle wanted to hear. But her job was to report on her findings and not create a work of fiction. She had completed what she had been assigned to do. She put the disk in an envelope and the envelope in her bag. She was in no hurry at the moment to print out her report and hand it in to her uncle. She would do so when she felt the time was appropriate, and when she could get hold of a printer.

TWENTY-SIX

Macallan called her in the apartment. "I apologise for not informing you sooner, madam but I have, in fact, only just received this message from one of our staff members. "It appears that Mr. Pellow called you a short while ago when you were out and he asked that you phone him please. He left his number."

"Where've you been?" Alistair demanded when she had called him.

"Did you try my mobile?" she asked.

"There was no reply," he answered shortly.

"Oops! I think I left it on my dressing table. I was in the swimming pool downstairs."

"I was told you were out. The swimming pool is not out. Where did you go?"

"Is it that important to you, Alistair?"

"I asked you a question, Penny." He sounded angry.

"I met James Kilroy, you know, the American newspaper man."

"What on earth for? And you were told not to go out."

"Nobody tells me what to do – or not to do. People ask me," Penny snapped back at him.

"Don't stand on ceremony. You know damn well what I mean."

"Alistair. Please stop treating me like a child."

"Do you realise how dangerous it could be for you?"

"I went there by cab. It was perfectly safe, Alistair."

"This time maybe. Please, please don't do that again."

"OK."

"Promise?"

"I can't say definitely that I might not have to go out again."

"Even at the risk of possible injury to yourself?"

"Come on. Unlikely." She thought it best not to tell him about the incident at the tube station.

"You're quite impossible, you know. Either that or you have a very short memory span and forget things easily. Have you forgotten the girl who was killed at your block of flats when her car blew up? And why did you not tell me about the man pretending to be Sir William who tried to gain access to the flat? I suppose that slipped your mind as well."

"Where did you learn that from?"

"Mac."

"Does he report everything I do to you?"

"Only when I ask him to keep an eye on you."

"Alistair, I appreciate your concern. I really do. But I am being very careful. You see how clever I was in dealing with my supposed uncle? I only take a cab – usually from right outside your block of flats, and I am on my guard all the time.

She laughed, hoping to lighten his mood. And then, at a further effort to ease the tension, she changed the subject. "How is Edinburgh?" she asked. She thought how far from funny it would be if he said he'd spotted her in Edinburgh.

"Very pleasant, as always."

"Is it snowing up there or have you temperatures in the high thirties?"

"Snowing?" Alistair laughed. "They don't have a thing like that up here. I am at the moment sitting in

143

my bathing trunks by the open air swimming pool, sipping a Pina Colada and sunbathing."

"So it *is* snowing," Penny said.

"Of course it's snowing. Can you imagine Scotland without snow when the stuff is falling all over the south of England?"

"And the hotel?" Penny asked.

"Very good. Everything's fine and it was an uneventful flight. Sorry, I can't discuss this with you at the moment as I'm due to go into a meeting and everyone is waiting for me. Let's talk about it later."

"Look after yourself, Alistair." Penny smiled to herself. "And remember to ration those Pina Coladas, OK?"

"Will do," Alistair laughed back.

They continued their conversation without touching further on the investigation and Penny was happy to sense that Alistair's initial annoyance had abated somewhat and he had began to sound his light hearted usual self.

His final words to her were "Stay indoors."

Penny was not to know that Alistair was not calling her from Edinburgh but from Melrose, a town south of Edinburgh. He had hired a car after his meeting in Edinburgh ended and drove down to Melrose. There he held a meeting with six men in an ordinary suburban semi-detached house in an ordinary suburban street. Had Penny called on her mystical third eye to view the proceedings she would have assumed, quite rightly, that these men were concerned about the existence of Rathings. They were all older than Alistair and obviously his superiors as he always addressed each one as 'sir'. Sir William's name was mentioned several times as, indeed, was Penny's on more than one occasion. The meeting lasted no longer than thirty minutes. Each of the six men used his mobile phone to make a call. Alistair and the men then left the house. Alistair drove off in his hire car. The others departed in separate chauffeur-driven limousines that had been parked elsewhere and summoned to the house.

TWENTY-SEVEN

Penny decided to continue with her enquiries. She went out again and took a cab to West End Central Police Station in Savile Road where she asked to see an old friend who had occasionally helped her and Peter out with their enquiries, such assistance being very much off the record.

"Sergeant Border will see you now, madam," the front desk constable said and pointed her in the direction of the sergeant's office.

Jimmy Border was not a tall man but he was solidly built and had the physique of a heavyweight boxer. "Hi, little Penny!" he said, extending his arms in a warm welcome. "Well, it is nice to see you again. It's been a long time, Penny. What? Three, four years?"

"Five since Peter died."

"Aye. And time does fly by. I'm fast approaching retirement age. But tell me. How are you getting on since Peter's unfortunate accident?"

"Oh, I'm managing, Jimmy. Thanks."

"So, to what have I done to deserve this honour of a visit?" the sergeant asked.

"You've always been so helpful in the past and I need to pick your brains."

"Not so many brains left at the moment, but I'll do me best."

"I've been asked to make some enquiries regarding the rumour doing the rounds about Rathings having been seen."

Jimmy Border let out a big guffaw. "Rumour's the right word. A load of stuff and nonsense."

"So you don't believe it's true?"

"Aye. That's right."

"Is that the official police stance?"

Another resounding laugh emanated from the sergeant's mouth. "Hey, Penny. I'm just a sergeant based in one of the police stations. I'm not likely to be involved in official police viewpoints. But if you want the honest truth, I believe it is so. The police force hasn't got the time to go chasing after dreamed up stories, conjured out of the air by looney-brained individuals. Believe me, it's all cods wallop."

"So you have no juicy lead to give me?" Penny persisted.

"Nothing to give you – other than a great big kiss, except the missus would kill me if she learned I was smooching beautiful women."

Penny smiled at the sergeant. "You'll never change, will you, Jimmy." She went up to him and kissed his cheek. "Now, don't tell your missus what we've just done," she teased.

Jimmy Border looked at her in a serious manner. "Penny. I have no information on this rumour other than it is just that – a rumour. But if I hear of anything to the contrary I'll let you know straight away. OK?"

"That would be wonderful, Jimmy. Thanks, and thanks for seeing me."

"Always a pleasure – especially if I can get a kiss on the cheek."

Penny smiled and waved goodbye to him as she made her way out of the police station.

TWENTY-EIGHT

Penny passed a library. She had a sudden thought, so she went in and found the Holographic section.

"I should like to book a holographic session straight away please," she told the young girl at the Reception Desk.

"Certainly madam. For how long a duration?"

"Oh, thirty minutes."

"If you could give me the contact details I shall set it up for you."

Penny gave the girl her parents' names and address, telephone number and their personal holographic address. Penny sat on a sofa and waited whilst the girl went about fixing the arrangements.

Eventually, the girl came up to Penny and said, "I've connected to Mister and Misses Henderson and they are in their holographic capsule. Your session time will start in five minutes. The cost of this service is twenty five pounds. "

Penny paid her and she guided Penny to a small cubicle that housed a plain table and two chairs around it. Penny sat down and waited. After a short while, a faint shimmer made its presence known on the table and her mother's and father's holographic images gradually took shape. They were only some twenty four inches tall but the 3D digital projection was so clear that she could see every line and furrow on their faces.

It had been well over a year since Penny had seen her parents. They both looked tanned and fit.

"Hi Mummy and Daddy," Penny cried out in excitement. "I thought I'd surprise you."

"Darling!" he mother called out and blew her a kiss. "How are you, my love?"

"Oh, I'm fine. And what about you two?"

"Well, father seems to spend all his time either playing boules on the village square with the locals or wandering around a golf course," Penny's mother laughed.

"Don't believe a word of it!" Penny's father exclaimed and gave a hearty guffaw. "I spend a great deal of time smoking my trusty old pipe and doing French crossword puzzles. Not to mention my slave labour tasks in the garden."

"Very clever, Daddy," Penny laughed. "And what about you, Mummy?"

"I played the piano at an evening do in the village and the next day the head teacher of the local enseignement primaire – that's primary school – asked me if I could help out with some music lessons for the little ones. I've been doing it for some six months now and –"

"Keeps her out of mischief!" Penny's father joked.

"That sounds great, Mummy."

"But tell us about yourself. What are you doing? Is everything all right with you?"

"Yes, I'm fine," Penny replied. "Everything is good."

"Have you never thought of coming to live over here?"

"No, Mummy. I am very happy here in England."

"It's gorgeous here," Penny's father said. "The people are very friendly."

"The food is out of this world," her mother explained. "Fresh fruit and vegetables, delicious fish and scrumptious cheeses. And property is cheap. You could buy a small apartment or cottage and if you live close to us you can always use our swimming pool."

"Sound tempting," Penny said so as not to upset her parents' enthusiasm for her to go out to France."

"You still running your detective agency?" her father asked.

"Yes, Daddy."

"And how's it going?"

"So, so, but not too bad, thanks."

They chatted on about family matters when Penny heard a small bell ring softly.

"Oops!" she exclaimed. "My time is up. 'Bye you two lovely ones. We'll talk again soon."

"Bye, darling," her mother cried out and waved and blew kisses at her.

"Cheerio, sweetheart," her father shouted and waved at her.

The images of Penny's parents gradually dissolved and disappeared. Penny sat still, looking down at the now empty table. She had been so happy seeing and talking to her parents but also felt a slight tinge of sadness – missing them and thinking of her own comparatively lonely existence. After a few minutes she rose and left the holographic chamber.

As she was already in the library, she thought she'd do some quick research on the Rathings. The Rathings had been supposedly annihilated by the American's poison spray when she was only a few years old, so her knowledge of how they had behaved towards the human population was based on hearsay or stories told to her by her parents and other family members and friends. She had blithely accepted the Rathings' presence as a thing of the past, something that did not affect her. That is until now with her involvement in the new assignment from her uncle.

She went to the relevant section – Local History. There were umpteen books on Rathing history. She eventually found one which gave her details of their creation. She took the book, found a seat in a quiet corner, and began to read.

The book explained that their creator, Professor Jens Andersen had been transferring the nucleus of a single human cell containing its entire DNA into a cow's egg, from which all the genetic information had been removed. The combining of human and animal cells to create a hybrid embryo prompted him to consider the implications if these embryos were not destroyed at the prescribed time limit of fourteen days. Furthermore, he wondered how successful he might be if he created chimeras, clones that possessed two types of cell – one from each progenitor – as opposed to mixed genetic material that would form a clone. What would be the result if he transferred the nucleus of a human cell to an egg harvested from a rat and another one from a magpie? What if he did not destroy it within the prescribed fortnight, but let it develop and mature?

Professor Andersen decided to call on the assistance of Doctor Mordecai Stern, a cytologist and both scientists worked secretly on their experiment which they called The Kytos Project.

She took a break from her reading and sat back and looked around. There were not many people in the library. Two old men were deeply involved in a game of chess. A small group of schoolchildren sat quietly studying and a young mother, with a baby in a pram next to her, was going through a load of microfiche. A middle aged man was deeply engrossed in a book and equally fixated in picking his nose. Penny threw him a nasty look, but he was completely unaware of her presence or, indeed, that of any others. He just kept exploring his nostrils with his index finger and flicking on the floor what he'd extracted.

"Gross!" she said loudly but even so, the man did not react.

Penny returned to reading the book before her.

The author went on to explain that the two scientists successfully isolated embryonic stem cells from rats and from magpies. Then, being familiar with the genome sequence for humans, rats and birds, Andersen and Stern had started by knocking out some of the specific human genes and replacing them with rodent or avian genes, of which they knew the function. The difficult part was the decision to bypass the conventional process of transferring the cloned embryos from a petri dish to the uterus of a female host. They could not risk that, so instead they took the big step of placing their work on plates for early development in the growth tanks and then seeking the permission of the owner of Rumrunner Cove in Cornwall to locate the embryos there.

Penny reckoned she had read enough about the Rathings. She also found the book rather heavy going, so she closed it and returned it to its shelf. She already knew that the clones developed into Magars (the part human, part magpie concoction), Droons (a malformed and ugly clone which resulted from an accident in the early experimental stages, and the Rathings who matured and became the dominant species on Rumrunner Cove, and eventually over-run and governed the country. Thank God none of them are still around, she thought. Or are they? She wondered.

Penny decided to leave the library. She walked to the exit and as she passed the nose picker she stopped and leant towards him. "You may care to use these," she said, throwing a small packet of tissues into his lap, "for the discoveries you are making in your nostrils.

It's much more polite to place your dirty treasures in there than throwing them on the floor, you gross little man." With that, she stalked out of the library, leaving her wrath as a vibrating aura around him.

TWENTY-NINE

Philip Green was allowed his one phone call and he contacted the man who gave him his orders to kill Penny. The man was not in his office but at his home. Green explained what had happened and that he was being held at a Police station. "Leave it with me," Green's boss said. "And after you are released I want you to see me at the bank on Monday and give me a full report on this debacle."

Some minutes later, the Station Commander received a phone call. He listened most carefully, asked a few questions, and then said, "Right. I'll deal with it from here on."

The Commander went down to the Duty Sergeant. "I believe you have a man called Philip Green in detention. On what charge is he being held, Sergeant?"

"No charge as yet, sir, except he is suspected of attempting to push a woman on to the tube line, sir."

"I wish to see him. I'll see him in his cell, so no need to bring him out."

One of the Desk Sergeant's colleagues accompanied the Commander to the holding cell and opened it. "Thank you, Constable. I'll ring the panic bell when I am ready to leave."

The Commander went over to Green who was sitting on the cell bench. Green looked absolutely miserable.

"I've had a call," the Commander said. "Looks like you've been a silly boy."

Green said nothing and looked down at the floor.

"I've been asked to get you released, which I shall do. You are then to go straight to the office of your boss and explain yourself. Understood?"

The Commander rung the panic button and a Constable opened the cell door.

The Commander walked to the Duty Sergeant's Desk. "Who is handling the Green arrest?" he asked.

"CID sir. Sergeant Sullivan, sir. But he's gone out for a while."

"Has the woman who claims to have been pushed made a formal charge?"

The Sergeant shook his head. "No, sir. Said she was pushed but didn't know by whom."

"CCTV evidence?"

"Afraid not, sir. I wasn't working."

"Right," the Commander said. "So we have no evidence. I've spoken to Green who assures me he was being pushed by the crowd and had his hands up when he was pushed into the woman. I take it he has been questioned?"

"Yes, sir. Denies the charge."

"With no evidence there can be no charge, Sergeant. Release him," the Commander ordered. "It would seem that this is a complete misunderstanding. I'll authorize and sign the release form. And tell Sergeant Sullivan to see me when he returns to the Station."

"Yes, sir," the Duty Sergeant nodded.

THIRTY

Alistair was due home just after lunchtime. Penny was looking forward to seeing him.

The cab from Heathrow to Pimlico seemed to take an age. Alistair realized that it would have been far quicker had he taken the Piccadilly tube line instead or a flying taxi.

His mobile rang. It was Sir William ordering him to collect Penny and for both of them to meet him at his office. Alistair cursed silently at this last minute instruction. He wanted to relax at his flat after his hectic meetings in Scotland and not have to listen to his boss pontificating about God knows what.

Penny heard the key in the front door. She saw Alistair enter. "Hello, Alistair. Welcome back home."

"Hello, Penny," Alistair gave her a big smile. "It's really great to see you."

"D'you want a drink or prefer something else?" she asked.

"Something else sounds nice," Alistair remarked with a lecherous grin.

She waved a finger at him. "Don't be naughty," she mock-scolded. "You know what I mean."

"Can't, I'm afraid. Orders from your uncle. We are to go and see him straight away."

"Oh, no," Penny groaned.

Alistair shrugged. "Never mind. We can look forward to hearing what exciting things Sir William needs to see us about."

"That really is a nuisance," Penny pouted. "I was planning on doing some laundry as I desperately need some clean clothes."

"Didn't you have time to do it before now?" Alistair asked.

"I've spoken to the confounded washing machine but it keeps saying 'Recognition unknown'. I pleaded, shouted, whispered sexily to it – but no response. Dead as a Dodo!"

"Oops!" Alistair exclaimed. "Of course. The machine control is voice-activated and hasn't been programmed to recognize your voice. I am sorry. I should have thought of that."

"No, I'm sorry, Alistair. But it doesn't matter really. If you don't mind me walking around with clothes smelling of last week's assorted odours, then I guess I too could live with that – provided I can borrow a clothes peg from someone."

Alistair laughed. "Come on," he said. "It won't take a moment to sort out and then we can go and see your uncle."

They walked to the Utility section of the apartment and into the laundry room. Alistair fiddled about with the mechanics of the washing machine and the spin dryer. "Say something," he said. "Anything – just so it can recognize your voice."

"Alistair is a genius."

"Thanks, Penny. Very apt. You realize you will have to say that each time you want to do any laundry?"

"You are joking!"

"Yes. I am – regrettably."

As they walked out of the laundry room, Penny noticed a partly opened door and in the room behind were a small table and some chairs.

"Have you got an office down here?" she asked.

"Not really. It's a Holographic office."

"Gosh!" Penny exclaimed. "I talked to my parents the other day by holographic connection. It was so good to see them in front of me."

"Where did you do that?" Alistair asked.

"At the local library."

"Use this one any time you want. It's easy to operate," Alistair said.

"That would be lovely. Are you sure you don't mind?"

"Not at all. It doesn't cost anything and is far better than using a public facility."

"Thank you so much, Alistair. You are most kind."

"Think nothing of it. If you don't mind doing your laundry when we get back, I suggest we make tracks to your uncle's office."

*****

"Glad you made it before I had to leave," Sir William greeted them. "I can't be long; have a meeting to attend."

"You wanted to see us," Alistair said.

"That's right. Has Penelope brought you up to date?"

"I've only just got back and came immediately here. Haven't had time for any de-briefing, I'm afraid, sir."

"I understand from Penelope that her report is about ready, but I want you to look it over before it is submitted."

"Uncle?" Penny said quietly.

"Yes, my dear," Sir William said.

"Would you mind very much calling me Penny and not Penelope? You know I don't like that name."

"But it *is* your name."

"I do prefer Penny."

Sir William nodded but did not smile. "Very well. I shall try, but old habits are hard to break."

"I will really appreciate it, uncle."

Sir William said nothing for a minute or so; it looked like he was gathering his thoughts. Finally, he said, "Pellow. Whilst I appreciate your offer to have Penel... my niece stay at your place, I do not like to know that there is someone, or more than one, conniving in conducting a campaign of intimidation. Despite my several enquiries, I am unable to pinpoint who the culprit or culprits may be."

"Uncle. I think you should know that I have the name of someone who tried to push me under a tube train. I feel sure he is connected to the other incidents."

Both Sir William and Alistair exclaimed "What!?" at the same time.

"Explain yourself," Sir William said with a scowl.

"I have already mentioned on the phone to Alistair, er, Mr. Pellow that I arranged to see a Mr. Kilroy to see what I could learn from him."

"That's the man I spoke to you about, the newspaper chap," Pellow cut in.

"Yes, yes, I know," Sir William said in an irritable voice. "Go on, er, Penny."

"You were specifically told not to leave the apartment," Alistair said angrily.

"We will not dwell on that at the moment, Pellow." Looking at Penny, Sir William snapped. "Go on."

"We ended up in the police station and..."

Alistair smacked his forehead. "Oh God!" he exclaimed. "This gets worse."

Sir William turned to Alistair and said in a very stern voice. "Pellow. If you cannot contain yourself, you shall be asked to leave my office. Is that clear? I will not, I repeat, will not have these constant interruptions from you."

159

Alistair looked sheepishly at the floor. "I am sorry, Sir William."

Penny continued. "His name it seems is Philip Green and he works as a security man in a merchant bank."

"The bank name?" Sir William asked brusquely.

"I wasn't told."

"No matter. We can resolve that quite easily. Now will you kindly tell me why you saw this newspaper man, what's his name?"

"James Kilroy," Penny said.

"You went out despite my explicit instructions for you to stay indoors?" Sir William barked.

"I'm sorry, uncle. I had to do it."

"You will please address me as Sir William in my office."

"I'm sorry unc ..., I mean Sir William."I'm afraid there's more," Penny said. "Mr. Kilroy has information from someone who works as a cleaner at a place called Gretorex Hall. That someone took a picture with his phone which clearly shows a man leading a creature that is without doubt a Rathing."

"Are you very sure of this?" Alistair said tonelessly.

"From what I saw, yes." Penny noticed a quick, worried look exchanged between the two men.

"And you are quite sure that someone tried to push you on the rail line?" Sir William asked.

"Yes. Someone tried to push me under a train onto the tube line station. The man was arrested and I had to go to the Police station to make a Statement." Penny continued.

"Penny. Please tell us what happened. In detail," Alistair requested.

And so she did. She told them everything that had happened from her arrival at the Natural History museum to her eventual return to Knox Court.

Sir William spoke: "You had no call to see this man, Kilroy. You put yourself in danger as a result and you have also endangered this whole investigation."

"How can you say that, uncle?"

"Sir William," Alistair whispered a reminder how she should address her uncle.

"... You asked me to undertake an investigation in the course of which I have to contact anyone who may have information pertaining to the investigation." She was beginning to become annoyed at her uncle's attitude. "Forgive me for saying this, but I think it grossly unfair for you to say that I may have endangered the investigation. My enquiries have established to some degree the existence of Rathings. Is that not what you wanted?"

Sir William said nothing. Instead, he began to move the items on his desk into an orderly line. There was a heavy silence in the room until Alistair said to Penny. "I don't think Sir William actually meant that."

Sir William still said nothing but looked at Alistair beneath his beetle brows. After several seconds of silence he said, "Thank you, Pellow, but I am quite able to clarify any of my statements, should thus be necessary. I do not need a spokesman to justify or otherwise my comments." He turned to Penny. "You may not have been aware that I am due to see this newspaper man later this afternoon. Obviously, he would have imparted to me the information he passed on to you – without the risk of anyone falling under a tube train."

"I did not know of your impending meeting with Mr. Kilroy," Penny said.

"You would have, had you informed Mr. Pellow of your intention to see Kilroy." He turned to Alistair. "I understand that you informed Mrs. Campbell of the necessity of her clearing with you first any action or meeting she proposed to make."

Alistair nodded. "Yes, sir. I did."

To Penny Sir William said, "Well, there you are."

"I discovered that my contact in Edinburgh who runs her own investigations agency is dead. I suspect she's been murdered."

After another protracted silence, Sir William said to Penny. "Your friend's sad demise has nothing to do with this case and with what we are talking about at the present moment. That incident is, quite frankly, of little interest to us." He looked at Alistair, "This meeting is concluded. You may both leave now, but I shall want to see you both tomorrow.

"Pellow, establish if the man who attempted to push Mrs. Campbell on to the rail line is still being held. I want you to take no further action other than to establish that fact. Then be good enough to inform Miss Pilgrim of the status. I repeat. Take no further action. I shall say goodnight to you both."

With that Sir William walked out of his office on his way to his meeting.

Alistair took hold of Penny's arm and gently steered her towards the door. "Come on, Penny," he said quietly. "Let's go home."

"Are you angry with me, Alistair?" she asked as they walked down a corridor.

"No, Penny, I'm not angry. Just exasperated with you. Do you realize what a dangerous position you put yourself in?"

"I'm sorry, Alistair. I was just doing my job and I was on the tube because I decided to not waste money on a taxi fare."

Alistair patted her arm. "All right. It's not the end of the world. But you are a bit of a loose cannon at the moment and your uncle is worried for you. From now on you go nowhere without me, understood?"

She nodded. "Yes, Alistair," she said.

THIRTY-ONE

It was late afternoon by the time they got to Alistair's flat. Alistair said he had to make some phone calls to establish whether or not the arrested man was still held in detention. Penny said she'd rustle up something for them to eat.

Whilst Alistair was on the phone, Penny went into the kitchen and began her dinner preparation. She first put a few potatoes on the stove. She then found some chicken breasts in the fridge. She placed them between two pieces of greaseproof paper and beat them flat with a rolling pin. She seasoned the chicken fillets, dipped them in the flour, beaten egg and breadcrumb. The potatoes were now ready. She drained them and mashed them with some cream, butter and a smidgen of grated nutmeg. She dug out a small packet of mixed vegetables which she put in a steamer and placed in the microwave. They were ready in two minutes. The creamed potato mash was being kept warm and the chicken breasts took a couple of minutes on each side to cook.

"Dinner's ready," she called.

Alistair walked in. "That was quick," he said.

"Unlike most bachelors you do have a well stocked food larder," she said with a smile.

"I like my food and I enjoy cooking," Alistair said. "Mmm, smells good. So tell me, Penny, what delicacy have you created?"

"No delicacy, Alistair. Just plain and simple Wiener schnitzel with creamed potatoes and veg.

Unfortunately you don't seem to have any lemons so there's none to squeeze over the chicken."

"Ah, I've slipped up there. No lemons. How about lemon juice?"

"You got some?"

"Yep. In the cupboard over there. Top shelf."

They ate their meal in comfortable silence. Penny was conscious of the fact that Alistair seemed pre-occupied. His replies to any questions she asked were monosyllabic.

THIRTY-TWO

In the morning Alistair knocked on Penny's bedroom door and brought her a cup of coffee and a fresh orange juice on a small tray. He insisted on making breakfast whilst she showered.

When she came down she saw he'd laid the table, had the coffee percolator on the go and had cooked scrambled egg with slivers of smoked salmon on hot buttered toast. On a side plate were some croissants.

As he'd made breakfast, Penny volunteered to do the washing up.

Alistair was reading the morning paper which had been delivered when he suddenly called out to Penny.

"Hey Penny, listen to this." He began to read aloud an article on one of the inside pages. 'A Mr. James Kilroy, 52 was killed yesterday afternoon in a hit and run incident in Cromwell Road, London. He was on the Editorial Advisory Board of the Bureau of Investigative Journalism and was unmarried. It is believed that he was heavily engaged in attempting to expose a ring of subversive individuals but at this stage it is not known what activity they may have been involved in. The police have appealed for any witnesses to come forward. Several eyewitnesses said that they had at first thought a movie was being made as the car was driving fast and aimed directly at the victim. They had expected him to either jump aside or for the car to swerve away from him. When the car hit Mr. Kilroy, they knew it was a deliberate killing. The incident took place at about 3.30 yesterday afternoon.

166

The weather was clear and traffic was light. The police suspect foul play may be involved.'" Alistair put the paper down. "Poor chap."

"I bet he was targeted by the people he was investigating. How dreadful," Penny said, coming into the lounge area. "Poor, poor man."

"He was due to see Sir William yesterday," Alistair remarked.

"Should we call my uncle's office about this meeting he wants with us?"

Alistair shook his head. "No. We'll wait to hear from Pilgrim's progress."

"Who?"

"Miss Pilgrim, his secretary."

The phone call from Miss Pilgrim came through at 10.00 am. Alistair was informed that he and Mrs. Campbell were required to be at Whitehall at 11.30.

At 11.20, Alistair and Penny took the lift up to the fifth floor where Sir William's office was located. Alistair had driven them to Whitehall and had slotted his car in the Department's garage, inaccessible to any other than Government officials with passes.

Sir William offered them coffee, which they accepted, and then he got down to business.

"Pellow. What is the situation with the man arrested when trying to harm Penny at the tube station?"

"He was released by the Station Commander who stated that there was no case to answer. I did, however, establish his place of work. It is with a firm of merchant bankers called Bormoni and Challoner."

"Who?" Sir William demanded.

Alistair looked at the piece of paper in his hands. "Bormoni and Challoner, sir. He's a security guard there."

"Really? How interesting. Most interesting."

"I thought I might go down there and make some enquiries."

"No. Don't do that Pellow. Leave that with me. I'll assign somebody else to that task. You have enough on your plate plus keeping an eye on my niece. Did you confirm this man's name?"

"Yes, sir. Philip Green, as Mrs. Campbell said. I couldn't establish if Philip was with one 'l' or with two."

"No matter. Green, eh? Now, we come to the matter of what we do with you Penelope. We still have a problem as to your safety."

"Well, sir," Alistair interjected. "Short of putting an advert in The Times or The Globe reading: 'To whom it may concern. Please note Mrs. Penny Campbell is no longer searching for anything so will you please stop hounding her,' she won't be safe until we discover who is behind these attacks on her."

"Quite so, Pellow."

"We could put her into Holloway prison. She'd be safe there," Alistair said with a grin, which Penny didn't see.

Penny looked frightened. "You wouldn't, you couldn't do that!" she exclaimed.

"I think you will find that Mr. Pellow was trying to be funny," Sir William said in a tone which was far from amused.

Sir William studied Alistair before speaking. "Tell me, Pellow," he said, "how would you feel if my niece were to continue to stay at your place until this matter is resolved?"

Alistair grinned. "It would be my pleasure, sir, to help out the Department."

"Harrumph!" Sir William grunted. "I trust it is not too great an intrusion in your personal life?"

"None whatsoever, Sir William," Alistair assured him. "Having Mrs. Campbell stay at my place is no problem at all, sir."

Sir William settled back in his chair. "Good. That's settled then. It looks like you still have an additional resident in your flat until we can resolve this matter. And chain this confounded girl up against a radiator or something to ensure she doesn't go walkabouts again. Now, Penny, do you require any further monies towards your fee?"

She shook her head. "No, uncle. I mean Sir William. The cheque amount was more than adequate."

"All right. Remember to put in for your expenses, tube fares and so on. Thank you both. This meeting is now concluded."

Alistair waited until Penny had gone out of the office door when he whispered to Sir William, "I read about Kilroy's death, Sir William. May I ask if you had your meeting with him?"

Sir William nodded. "I did indeed. He had a photo taken of a Rathing at Gretorex Hall."

"My God!" Alistair exclaimed quietly.

"Don't worry. I insisted that he leave it with me – supposedly to have it checked on."

"And the hit and run?" Alistair asked.

"Most unfortunate, but sometimes it is necessary to contend with the death of one in order to save the lives of many," Sir William said. He then added, "You'd better go to see Penelope who is waiting for you in the corridor."

THIRTY-THREE

Two heavily built, well-muscled men, smartly dressed – one wearing blazer and flannels, the other a suit – walked through the main entrance of Bormoni and Challoner and went to the reception desk.

"Good morning, miss," one of the men said politely to the young lady at the desk. He produced from his inside jacket pocket an identity badge. "Special Branch," he said with a smile. "I believe you have a Philip Green working here."

The girl said, "One moment, please," and began to type the name into her computer. "Ah, yes. He's one of our security officers."

"We should like a word with him please. He's in no trouble, but might be able to help us with our enquiries."

"I'll page him for you, sir," the girl said. She picked up a microphone and pressed a switch. "Will Mr. Philip Green, Security, please report to reception on the ground floor," she announced.

Some minutes later the two men standing at reception saw a middle-aged man with a straggly moustache and dressed in a uniform approach the desk. His longish straggly hair reached his collar. He shuffled forward as if his feet hurt him when he walked.

"There he is," the receptionist whispered to the men.

They stepped up to him. "Mr. Green?" one of the men, the one wearing the suit asked.

Green looked nervously at them. "Yes, yes. That's right."

"Thank you for seeing us. We're from Special Branch."

"Special Branch?" Green gasped. "I haven't done nothing. What's this about?"

"We just need your help, sir in respect of some enquiries we are making. You are in no trouble, I assure you. We believe you are in a position to give us some information. Is there somewhere quiet we can go to for a chat?"

Green pointed towards a corridor. "There's an empty room down there," he said.

"Good," the man who'd spoken earlier said. "Would you lead the way?"

They all entered a small room. It looked as if it might be a storage area. There were rows and rows of typist chairs against one of the walls.

Nobody sat down. The man wearing the suit said, "Would you be kind enough to give us the name of the man in this bank who issues instructions to you?"

Green gulped. "Well, there are a number of people who …"

The suited man interrupted. "The person who instructed you to push a young lady on to a tube line rail line."

"That's a lie. I never did," Green objected.

"Mr. Green," the Special Branch officer said. "I have assured you that you are in no trouble. We need your co-operation. We are asking politely. If you do not co-operate, we may need to arrest you and question you at headquarters. Now, all that could be avoided if you give us a name. After that, we shall leave and you can go back to your duties and you won't hear from us again."

Green looked nervously at the two men. "Do I have your assurance on that?" he asked.

"Without doubt, sir. The name please."

"I've received instructions for some time now from a Mr. Jarvis. He's a senior executive in the bank."

"His first name is?"

"I believe it's Clarence. Yes, that's right, Clarence Jarvis."

"Thank you for your help, Mr. Green. Now, that wasn't too hard was it?"

"I have your guarantee that there won't be any comeback on me for telling you this?"

"I did not say that, sir. What I said is that you won't hear from us again. I can assure you of that, as best as I am able to."

"My God! You lot are all slimy bastards," Green swore.

"We did not hear that comment, Mr. Green," the well-suited man said.

Both Special Branch men walked out of the small office, said goodbye to the girl on the reception desk, and walked out of the building.

THIRTY-FOUR

When they left her uncle's office, Alistair suggested they go and have a coffee. Once seated, a waitress floated over towards their table. She was wearing glider boots. She took their order. Once they were served, Alistair said, "As you are likely to be at my place for a while may I suggest that we pop over to your flat now and that you collect any things that you feel you may need to have?"

Penny stirred her coffee. "I'm sorry about all this palaver, Alistair. I know you probably hate having your routine and independence thrown out of gear by having me stay with you."

"Don't talk rubbish. It's great fun having you about my place. And anyway, having tasted your dinner effort last night, I think I'll rather enjoy having my meals prepared for me."

"Are you really serious about not minding?" Penny asked.

"Positive." He gave a laugh. "Now about collecting some of your things from your flat. Will they all fit into this car or do I need to fix a trailer on the back?"

Penny smiled at him. "Oh, I rather think you'll need to drive a lorry to my place. A great big lorry."

Alistair nodded. "Good. So all will fit in the car."

Penny looked around her flat. She thought how small and nondescript it was compared to Alistair's place. Whilst Alistair sat in the lounge she begun putting various things in a large suitcase she'd taken from the top of a cupboard. It did not take her long to collect the things she thought she'd need, and soon she plumped down in an armchair opposite Alistair.

"That's it," she announced. "All done and dusted. I'm ready to go when you are."

He got up. "OK then, Penny. Let's mosey along."

"Very funny," she laughed. "You're a real whizz for getting out of tight corners. Come on then, let's leave this dump and whizz over to where the other half live."

Alistair joined her in laughter and drove off towards Pimlico.

*****

They had dinner that night at a little restaurant in South Kensington where it appeared to Penny that Alistair must have frequented frequently as he was greeted by all the staff like a long lost brother.

After dinner, Alistair suggested that they have coffee and a brandy back at his flat, which Penny was happy to go along with.

Back at Knox Court Alistair put on a CD of smooth blues and searched the drinks cabinet for some cognac. Penny meanwhile got the coffee percolator started.

Alistair came in carrying an exotic looking bottle and two brandy balloon glasses. "I think we should celebrate," he said.

As Penny poured out the coffee she looked at the bottle of cognac Alistair placed on the table. "That is a most interesting looking bottle," she said.

"And a most interesting cognac," Alistair continued. "This, my dear Penny is a Martell Creation Grand Cognac in a handcraft Baccarat decanter."

"It looks expensive," Penny said.

"It is, but I didn't buy it. It was a present from an erstwhile girl friend."

"A special recent one?"

He shook his head. "No. Long time ago. We broke up shortly after but she refused to take back her present, which I offered."

"Baccarat isn't cheap," Penny commented.

"Neither is the cognac," Alistair added, as he poured out two generous measures. "She could afford it. Her father is President of an American airline." He raised his glass to Penny. "To you, Penny. My best wishes to your future P.I hunting."

Penny smelled the aroma of marmalade and jam that permeated from the brandy glass. She took a sip and was overcome by the silky smoothness and powerful finish of the drink. "Mmm," she murmured. "This is heavenly. I've never ever tasted brandy as smooth and delicious as this."

Alistair smiled as he sat down. "I'm glad you like it."

They both sat in companionable silence, savouring the smooth cognac, sipping their coffee and listening to the melodious music.

After a while Penny said, "Alistair, there's something I need to ask you. Why d'you think my uncle gave me this assignment?"

"I presume because he wanted it solved."

"But why me? There are many better experienced and qualified private investigators."

Alistair shrugged. "Because he believed that you could establish the facts?"

"But he said this morning that he wasn't entirely sure that I would succeed."

"I doubt he really meant that."

"He didn't give me the job as a favour to me because I am his niece?"

"I would doubt that. Altruism does not figure high in your uncle's portfolio of personal traits. He assigns jobs to people whom he believes can come up with the goods. That's why you got the job. However, I think you should know that your uncle is working on a project that requires him to present a report from an independent source – such as yourself – confirming that your investigation indicate that there are no Rathings existing. To him, that is of paramount importance."

"What is this project?"

"I'm afraid I can't tell you that."

"Well, can you tell me if you agree with it?"

"In principle, yes. But I think your uncle's plan is lacking direction in many respects. It is somewhat amateurish, and overburdened with unnecessary individuals and the complete set up is a bit of a waste of time."

"Golly, Alistair. You don't mince your words, do you?"

"I'm telling you the truth. And the truth sometimes hurts."

"Have you told my uncle how you feel about this project – whatever it is?"

Alistair shook his head. "No."

"Why not?"

"Because I have other plans in mind."

"You're being very dark about all this. What's so special about this project that you and my uncle have in mind that you cannot tell me?"

"You will know what it is when the time is right. It would be unfair to you to make you privy to this information at this stage of proceedings."

Penny shrugged. "Well, it all sounds very mysterious to me. Very cloak and daggerish."

Alistair laughed, got up and refilled their glasses. "Don't worry, Penny. Just relax and enjoy the moment.

Life's too short for one to worry about things they can do nothing about."

Penny smiled at Alistair. "You are quite right. And this brandy will soon send me to sleep when I go to bed."

That night neither Penny nor Alistair slept well.

Alistair lay in his bed and thought of Penny sleeping in her room, a room a mere stone's throw away. His desire for Penny had grown in intensity during the short time he had known her. Every moment he spent with her he discovered a new aspect of her character, a new beautiful colour added to her rainbow of brilliant beauty. He had to admit to himself that his desire to possess her physically had grown. He'd often experienced sexual attraction, the intense desire to have sex with a girl, and he very much wanted to have sex with Penny. He also was aware that his feelings for her run a bit deeper than just sexual attraction.

As he tossed about in his bed he wished he was sharing it with the beautiful, sensuous girl next door. And the more he imagined her naked body lying next to his, so did his erection grow. He gave a sigh, turned over on his side and squeezed his eyes tight in a desperate attempt to sleep.

In Penny's bedroom, she too tossed and turned in her bed. Her five years of celibacy were like five hills, each growing higher as they progressed, each becoming harder and more difficult to scale. She had so often longed to be held, to be loved but she had always stood back, afraid to commit. Was it the memory of Peter that was holding her back? Was it his ever presence that had made her reject any form of physical contact with a man? But now, for the first time in five years, she felt her resistance wavering. Alistair was the only man she had met who had stirred within her her love of sex. And now her body yearned for him to have her in

177

any way he liked. Yet her mind flitted with uncertainty. Her only previous sexual experience had been with Peter. And unlike many women whom she knew who could enjoy sex without any emotional entanglement, Penny needed tender, sensitive trust at the same time as physical fulfillment. Sex alone was not enough for her. And at the moment, she was not yet sure how much conviction she had as to how upright and honorable was Alistair. She still had a niggling feeling that he was playing a double game of sorts.

Her hand moved down to her groin and her fingers began to caress her vagina. But, like that morning when her uncle had first called her, she stopped at exciting herself with full masturbation. Her hand moved away, she gave a sigh, turned over on her side and squeezed her eyes tight in a desperate attempt to sleep.

THIRTY-FIVE

The apartment was very quiet when Penny woke up in the morning. She went into her bathroom and quickly splashed some water on her face, then walked onto the small landing and down the steps to the lounge area. Alistair wasn't there. She went into the kitchen to make some coffee and saw a note by the percolator. It read **'Penny. Have gone for a swim. A.'**

She quickly dashed up to her room and put on her bikini, which she had brought back with her on her and Alistair's visit to her flat. She threw on a bathrobe and took the lift down to the swimming pool.

Alistair was the only person in the pool. He was doing the crawl fast and vigorously, up and down the length of the pool. At each end, he dived under the water and made his turn, pushing hard against the pool tiles.

She quietly disrobed and slipped into the water at the shallow end. She bobbed up and down watching Alistair's strong swimming style. He had swum at least twenty lengths before he became aware of her presence. He stopped and swum leisurely towards her. "Good morning," he greeted. "How are you this morning?"

"Fine thanks, Alistair."

"D'you want to use this as a swimming pool as opposed to a bobbing up and down pool?" he asked with a laugh.

"There's no need for you to be cocky, just because you're a good swimmer," Penny replied. "Besides, a

179

find bobbing up and down, as you put it, very therapeutic."

Still laughing, he held out his hand towards her. "Here, let me help you conquer your fear of the deep end. Trust me."

She took his hand. "I do trust you, Alistair. Very much," she said.

"Now lie on your back," he instructed, "and relax. That's it. Good girl."

He placed the palm of his hand on the small of her back and supported her as he walked her towards the deep end of the pool. When they had reached the deep end, Alistair said, "Now move your legs as you do when you swim, and use your arms to propel yourself backwards towards the shallow end. Don't worry. I'll be here to support your back if necessary."

They soon reached the shallow end. "Remember," Alistair counselled. "Your body will always float back to the surface if you relax it entirely. And if you find yourself in the deep end, just turn and float on your back and make your way towards shallower ground. This is what you've just done." He smiled at her. "I wasn't really holding you up. I had my hand just below the surface to steady you if you began to sink, but you didn't. And d'you know why?"

She shook her head.

"Because you were confident and not afraid. You knew I was there for you and so you relaxed. A most important tactic when in water is to relax the body, not tighten it up. If you can do that, we'll soon have you swimming lengths."

They swum around for a little while until an elderly couple came in, and so they decided to get out of the water.

They stood on the pool side, drying themselves with their towels. "We can have a shower upstairs," Alistair said.

As they dried themselves, they each looked surreptitiously at the other's body. Penny found Alistair's well muscled, sculptured body and hairy chest extremely attractive. She also could not help observe the bulge in his swimming trunks which signified that he was either very well endowed or had stuffed a couple of socks down the front of his pants.

Alistair sneaked glances at Penny's very skimpy bikini and was struck by the protuberance of her nipples which pushed hungrily and were clearly evident against the wet fabric of her bikini top, as if pleading for release. He had seen before prominent nipples but none as attention seeking as Penny's. He found them sensuous and very sexually exciting. Her breasts were not large but were proportionate to her build. He noted that her feet were delicately well shaped and small and without any corns or bunions, with slim toes ending in nicely rounded unpainted toenails. But what held his fascination were her nipples. He had an intense wild desire to whip off her bikini top and clamp his mouth over her breasts and nipples.

"Ready for coffee?" he asked.

"Yes please," Penny replied very sweetly.

THIRTY-SIX

It was 6.34 p.m. Clarence Jarvis sat at his desk in his large office at Bormoni & Challoner, Bankers in Throgmorton Street, London. As a director of the bank, his office was situated on the Executive tenth floor, which afforded a panoramic view of the City's roofs. Opposite him sat two of his operatives, both employed as security guards by the bank. Like O'Connor, they handled peripheral duties specifically for Jarvis.

Both were middle-aged, rather non-descript in appearance, but held in fairly good regard by Jarvis. The slightly fatter one was called Phil Green; the other, slightly younger man was Alan Thompson.

Jarvis had chosen this hour for the meeting as he knew no executive staff would be around on the tenth floor and that the bank's offices would be virtually empty.

"Your status report, gentlemen, if you please." His reedy voice sounded tired.

Green was the first to speak. "The girl's got some man hanging around with her. I thought at first he might have been police, but changed my mind when I saw where he lived."

"Which is?"

"Pimlico. A rather exclusive collection of apartments called Knox Court."

"Go on," Jarvis instructed.

"I hung around for a while to see if she'd go out again but she didn't. But the man did. That gave me a chance to get her on her own. I went to the receptionist man and pretended to be her uncle wanting to see her. She refused to see me. I think she's on her guard after your call warning her to drop the case."

"Thompson?" Jarvis looked at the other man.

"Well, sir, Phil and I keep interchanging so she doesn't click on to the fact that she's being followed. They went to a pub. I got caught short, dying for a piss, and had to go into the pub's Gents but they didn't clock me. Oh, I also turned her office over to give her a bit of a fright."

"It is incumbent on both of you to get rid of this girl. She could cause us a great deal of trouble," Jarvis remarked. "Which of you is responsible for the car bomb?"

"Me, sir," Thompson said.

"Not a very good job, was it? You managed to kill the wrong woman," Jarvis frowned. "That will undoubtedly put our target more on guard."

"It was an error," Thompson admitted. "I thought our target had gone back to her flat as I saw her drive up in her car. I fixed the charge on it, thinking it was her car. I tell you, the one killed looked the spitting image of our target."

"It's an easy mistake to make, sir," Green interposed.

"We do not make mistakes. Easy or otherwise," Jarvis snapped. "I've already had a report from my police contact about the fiasco you created at the tube station, so we won't dwell on that, Green, except to say that I am extremely disappointed at your inadequacy and failure."

"Sorry, sir," both men chanted simultaneously.

"I want this assignment concluded without further delay. That's all. Take the Executive lift straight down to the garage basement where I assume you left your car.   That way you won't come across anyone. Goodnight."

After the two men had gone, Jarvis sat and contemplated the events of the last few days. These extraordinary delays in getting rid of a potential problem-maker in the guise of a female detective were beginning to irritate him. He wished in some ways that he and O'Connor hadn't fallen out with each other. He knew that had O'Connor been given the task it would have been satisfactorily completed long before now. He wondered if Thompson and Green were actually up to the job.

He was also far from happy at the way things had gone within The Group. Because of his experience in banking, he had volunteered to be the Group's financial officer. Blue Eyes was appointed Commanding Officer but Blue Eyes had soon assumed that his position within The Group gave him carte blanche to dictate on various matters, as if The Group was a business. The Group was merely a body of men with a shared interest. To ensure a smooth running, they had formed a Committee, with designated positions within that Committee but such were honorary and held no power. Blue Eyes had surreptitiously assumed a mantle of executive power, and this annoyed Jarvis.

Grey Goose was also disturbed at current rumours that Bald Eagle had demanded that he, Grey Goose, be asked to leave The Group. Bald Eagle had appeared to be furious at the incident with Grey Goose and the young Rathing. Confound it! He had not deliberately embarked on a killing spree, Grey Goose cursed. Grey Goose was determined that Bald Eagle would come to regret his stance on the matter.

Grey Goose gave an inner shrug. If they want me to leave, so be it. It'll be their loss more than mine. I can always find ways to continue my pleasurable pursuits, but they don't have anyone near capable of handling efficiently The Group's finances. They'll soon run out of money and will be obliged to increase contributions from members. On the other hand, I could manoeuvre matters by judicious steps so as to ensure that I could come out of this in a more powerful position. He smiled to himself as a plan began to slowly evolve in his mind.

He sighed and moved to his drinks cabinet. The sun is well beyond the yard arm, he muttered as he poured himself a generous gin and tonic over pebbles of ice he'd taken from a small freezer. A couple of drinks and then his driver would be summoned to drive him home.

THIRTY-SEVEN

This evening, a figure tiptoed into the bedroom. It was of a tall, thin man. He moved to the bed and picked up a spare pillow that lay besides Bald Eagle. He very carefully placed it over the old man's face and pressed down hard. Bald Eagle struggled for breath but was far too old and weak to fight off his assassin. He soon succumbed into the arms of the ever eager Mistress Death.

Grey Goose slipped out of the bedroom with a sly grin across his face. Now go put your proposal to kick me out to the Committee, he said softly to himself.

*****

They found Lord Gretorex dead in his bed the next morning. A local GP and member of The Group codenamed Septimus Forceps was called. He made a vey perfunctory examination of the dead man and he had no hesitation in completing the death certificate confirming cause of death as a pulmonary artery embolism.

Later that day, an Extraordinary General Meeting of all members was called. Blue Eyes took the floor.

"Gentlemen. It is my sad duty as C.O to inform you that our honorary President, Bald Eagle, was found dead in his bed this morning. I believe that cause of death is a heart attack suffered during the night.

"We will at a later date discuss and make arrangements for a fitting farewell tribute to be paid to

186

our good friend and colleague. Today's meeting is to vote for a new President."

He saw Grey Goose raise his arm. "Yes, Grey Goose?"

Having been aware that this meeting would inevitably be called, Grey Goose had briefed his supporters on his plan, and he now caught their eyes as he stood to address the members.

"Sir. Thank you for giving me the floor. Like you and all present, I too am bereft at our loss. You, Blue Eyes have played an invaluable part as Commanding Officer in steering our group safely through the vicissitudes of today's existence and I would propose to the assembled body that our C.O be accorded the position of President of The Group. It is a step up and a role which I know he would hold in an honourable and most professional manner."

Before any counter-proposal could be made, if, indeed, one were to be made, one of Grey Goose's supporters, a vicar code named Victor Pious, shouted out. "Splendid, splendid. I second the motion." There seemed to be general approval with the proposal. It was put to the vote and passed.

Then the next step in Grey Goose's plan was played out. From the front of the hall another of his inner group stood up. "Gentlemen. We are all aware that Grey Goose and Blue Eyes have not always been in accord with each other. But now we can be nothing but impressed with Grey Goose's most unselfish, most gracious gesture of burying the hatchet by proposing Blue Eyes as The Group's President. Such generosity should be acknowledged by our appointing Grey Goose as The Group C.O."

A voice from the back of the hall: "I second the motion."

This was put to the vote but was not immediately approved. Unseen by the majority of members, Grey Goose leaned over and whispered to one of his supporters, code named Pink Panther. Pink Panther nodded and then addressed the assembly. "The Committee is aware, although the full membership may not be, that Grey Goose as Treasurer has just saved The Group some considerable money. He has achieved this through judicious use of purchasing arrangements and this means that we shall not be called on to increase our already substantial subscription. To show our heartfelt appreciation, I believe we should adopt the appointment just proposed, which I now repeat. I propose Grey Goose be appointed C.O." Another member called out, "I second the motion." This time it was approved by the full membership.

"In view of the elevation of Grey Goose, there is an opening for a new Treasurer. Is there anyone who wishes to assume that position?" Blue Eyes asked.

"I propose Purple Pill," a voice called out.

"I second that," another shouted.

"Purple Pill," Blue Eyes said. "Are you prepared to accept the nomination?"

Purple Pill stood. "Yes, Mr. President. I am."

"We shall put it to the vote," Blue Eyes stated. It was passed.

"I must ask for your attention on one matter which we must now consider," Blue Eyes announced. "We must establish what Lord Gretorex has stated in his Will regarding this house. We all know that he had no family but that, of course, need not have precluded him from bequeathing this place to a charity or anyone else."

Several members, worried at the implication, began to whisper amongst themselves.

"In such event," Blue Eyes continued, "we would no longer be able to use Gretorex Hall for our activities. To this end, I propose that I contact Lord Gretorex's solicitors and establish from them the position or when they propose to read out the contents of his Will.

"I would also like to ask our new Treasurer, Purple Pill, to check our finances in case we have to consider purchasing another suitable establishment," Blue Eyes concluded.

Grey Goose was ecstatic but disguised his delight well. He had achieved his objective; as C.O, he now held power, which he would exercise in the same way that Blue Eyes had done, except that it would be under Grey Goose's agenda.

And Blue Eyes, as President, held an ineffectual position as a figurehead. Blue Eyes had been effectively sidelined into a backwater. That had been Grey Goose' intention.

However, Grey Goose's ecstatic feeling became somewhat muted when he heard Blue Eyes speak. From Blue Eye's performance so far, Grey Goose wasn't too sure that his plan was travelling on the intended path. He felt that, as C.O, he should make his presence felt and voice heard, so he called out, "Surely, Mr. President, that is a role for me, as C.O."

"No," Blue Eyes replied tersely. "That is for the Treasurer."

The gauntlet had been thrown down by both parties.

THIRTY-EIGHT

Alistair and Penny once again decided to have dinner out. This time they took a taxi to the West End and ate at the new La Petite Maison restaurant in Bond Street. Penny felt more comfortable with the menu, as it was in French and English. As it was, she spoke French well and recognized many of the dishes offered. They lingered over their dinner and did not take a taxi back to Pimlico until it was gone midnight.

They agreed to spoil themselves with another snifter of the Martell Creation cognac they had the night before. A glass of that and a small coffee was a fitting finale to the evening.

They sat opposite each other, savouring the silence. Eventually Penny said, "Ally, do you work out in a gym somewhere?"

He gave her a questioning look. "How d'you mean?"

"I noticed that you have a good physique."

"Thanks, it's kind of you to say that. No, I don't really workout in a gym. I find it somewhat pathetic to be stuck indoors walking on a treadmill machine, when one can enjoy the weather outdoors and walk for miles, enjoying changing scenery. Until recently I played rugby but I'm getting a bit too old for it now. So I do plenty of swimming and I find that is excellent healthy exercise."

"Yes, you are a good swimmer," she said.

"Thank you. If you want, I'd be happy to help you with your swimming."

Penny shrugged. "Well, it does depend to a large extent on how long you're prepared to have me stay here."

Alistair smiled and nodded. "I know. I only hope your uncle gets the right person to follow up on the man who tried to push you under the tube. Incidentally, did you hear from the police about the break-in at your office?"

She shook her head. "I haven't been in the office for some days, of course. I did check with them and they said they hadn't. I'm not too hopeful."

"Penny," Alistair said in a serious voice. "It's funny that we were just speaking about my playing rugby because I had a call at the office from the captain of the rugger team I used to play for. Apparently, their regular hooker has injured himself and is unable to play in the match on Saturday. The team captain asked if I can help them out and stand in for their regular team player. I used to play hooker before I felt I was getting a bit ancient, so I said yes, because they're all pals and I can't let them down."

"I thought a hooker is a slang expression for a prostitute. Are there men prostitutes in rugby as well?" Penny said, pretending to be posing a serious question.

"In rugby a hooker is the player who uses his feet to get the ball in a scrum."

"Is that what you are, Alistair? A hooker?"

Alistair nodded. "Yep. And no funny comments from you if you please."

"Can I come and watch you hook?" Penny asked.

"Very funny. I'd love you to, if you'd really like to come and not be bored."

She shook her head. "Bored watching male prossies in a field? No way."

"That's it," Alistair pretended to be upset. "We can't have your sort tainting our hallowed rugby club pitch. You're banned."

"You do that Alistair Pellow and I won't cook you a dinner ever again."

Alistair raised his hands in mock surrender. "Ok, OK, I surrender. You can come to the match."

They both fell about laughing at their childish antics.

Alistair drove them both to The Stoop rugby ground in Twickenham. The stadium was home to Harlequins rugby football club but Harlequins had decided to open it to other clubs as a playing venue at a high rental charge. Today's game was between Alistair's team called the Old Oxonians and a visiting Cornish team called Truro Nomads RFC.

Alistair was determined that Penny should not be alone at any time in the stadium. He had arranged for a friend of his to be with her throughout the game and afterwards, until Alistair had showered and emerged from the changing rooms.

His friend's name was Andy Kendal and he was a very pleasant young man probably in his mid-twenties Penny guessed. Penny knew absolutely nothing about rugby and Andy sat alongside her and explained the rules of the game. He also bought Penny a diet coca cola at half time and asked her if she'd like a hamburger or something to eat. She thanked him but declined his kind offer. He had a pint of beer and he and Penny were joined by several of Andy's friends.

When the final whistle went at the end of the game, the score was 24- 18, the Cornish team being hailed as the winners. Penny and Andy walked along with the departing throng and waited for Alistair by the entrance to the ground.

"He shouldn't be too long," Andy assured Penny. "I know he'll have the quickest shower imaginable and will be out here pretty pronto."

As they stood around, some friends of Andy were standing a little way away and they called him over to join in a joke someone was just relating. "I won't be a sec, unless you'd like to come also?" Andy said. Penny shook her head and turned it upwards and nodded in the direction of Andy's friends. "That's alright, Andy. I'll hold on here. Go on and join your friends. I'll be fine."

Phil Green, the man who had been stalking Penny, had followed Penny and Alistair from Pimlico and had entered the stadium and sat in a seat just behind Penny. He had stood watching Penny and Andy. The moment Andy moved away from Penny, the man stepped up behind Penny. He stuck his finger into the small of her back and whispered, "This is a knife. One false move or sound from you and I'll push it upwards into your lung. You'll die a slow, painful death. Understand?"

Penny just stood there, terrified out of her wits. She nodded vigorously. She looked over to where Andy stood with his friends but he was unaware of her situation, so engrossed was he in listening to a girl chatting away to her group of friends.

The man behind Penny grabbed her tightly by her arm and walked her swiftly towards the car park and his red Toyota. They had just reached his car when Alistair came out of the stadium player's entrance. He looked around to find Andy and Penny when the loud laughter from Andy's friends drew his attention. He walked quickly over. "Where's Penny?" he demanded. Andy turned with a smile and said "She's just over ..." He looked around hurriedly. "She was standing there just a moment ago." He and Andy scanned the thinning crowd when Alistair saw Penny being hustled into a

Red Toyota. Alistair ran like mad to where his own car was parked. Andy chased after him but Alistair shouted "Go home, Andy. I can handle this."

Alistair gunned his car, narrowly missing a woman who was reversing slowly out of her parking space. He saw the red Toyota exit and turn left along the main road. He drove as quickly as he could to catch up.

He followed the Toyota as best he could. The Toyota weaved its way through town traffic and Alistair was becoming quite worried that he might lose sight of it. Their journey took them through Ealing, Uxbridge and Harrow and Alistair was trying to figure out where the devil the Toyota was heading to. They eventually reached Pinner. Alistair lost his target. The Toyota seemed to have vanished. Alistair drove slowly through a housing estate, where he had last seen the Toyota. He kept glancing to his left and then to his right, but with no success of sighting the other car.

Unbeknown to Alistair, the Toyota had pulled up in a drive of a terrace house. The man bundled Penny out of the car, unlocked the house front door and pushed her into the house. He led her into the front room. He made her sit on a kitchen chair and he wrapped gaffer tape around her ankles and to her wrists which were pinned to the seat back.

Phil Green was exhilarated. He had at last successfully accomplished his allotted task. He went to a cupboard, took out a bottle of whisky and two glasses.

"Want a little snifter, dahlin?" he showed the bottle to Penny. Penny shook her head,

"Well, I think we'll 'ave a little fun first before I do the necessary," he smirked. "If you don't want a drink, 'ow about a lollypop?" He moved closer to Penny and unzipped the fly of his trousers. "Go on, 'ave a suck on this."

"You stick that anywhere near or in my mouth and I'll bite the damned thing in half and spit it out at you," Penny snarled, unbridled fury stressed in every word. Although she was shaking with fear, she believed that when threatened the best form of defence was attack. Her tactic worked because the man quickly zipped up his flies.

"OK, then, dahlin'. We'll get down to the serious business. I'm gonna pull down your knickers so no funny business or you'll really regret it. I'm going to screw you first solo, then might call some friends to join in the fun." He undid the tape around her wrists which bound her to the chair and was just bending down to put his hands up her skirt and pull down her panties when the door bell rung.

THIRTY-NINE

Alistair drove up and down the streets of the housing estate. He was sweating heavily from anxiety and pent up frustration. He was about to reverse out of the street in which he was when he gave a glance to his left and saw it. The red Toyota was parked in a drive. Alistair drove quietly and parked outside the property. He quickly got out of the car and walked up the drive. He thought he'd ring the door bell in the first instance.

*****

The man stood perfectly still, half bent over Penny. Then he rushed to the window and looked out. He was hoping to see who was at the door but the angle did not allow this. He could not see who the caller was. But he did see, and recognize the caller's car. There it stood, parked outside the house, the grey snazzy sports car of that rugby playing thug boyfriend of the girl tied to the chair by her feet.

"Fuckin' hell!" Phil Green silently swore as he turned and dashed into the kitchen, unlocked and opened the back door and scooted into the back garden. He hurriedly pushed open the back gate and beetled as fast as his fat little legs would carry him along the back alley cinder path. He was just yards into his run when he heard the house front door being kicked in. His speed rate immediately increased a hundred-fold.

When there was no answer to the door bell ring, Alistair did not hesitate to take a few steps back and then kick in the cheap panelled front door. He dashed into the hallway, looked around and went into the first room to his right. He saw Penny on the chair, staring at him her eyes wide open in terror.

"Penny! You OK?"

"Oh God, Alistair! I thought it was his friends come for a ..."

For a gangbang, Alistair thought but said nothing and bent down to undo the gaffer tape from her ankles.

Alistair helped Penny out of the house. "Come on," he said. "I'll take you home. Did that bastard try anything? Did he hurt you?"

Penny shook her head and laughed when she thought of the threat she had made to bite the fellow's penis in half. She didn't say anything to Alistair about that.

When they'd reached the gate they noticed a young woman pushing a pram and going into the drive of the house next door.

"Excuse me," Alistair said. "Could you help us please? Do you know who lives in this house next door to you?"

The young woman looked at Alistair and then Penny. She apparently thought they looked respectable enough to divulge that information to. "Alfonso something or other. But he's in the Med right now."

"The Med?" Alistair queried.

"Mediterranean. He's a steward on a cruise liner. Will be away for at least another week."

"But there was a man here," Alistair said.

"Oh, that'll be Alfonso's friend. Alfonso said his friend would be staying here for a few days. Haven't seen or spoken to his friend, though." She leant over the pram and gave cooing sounds to her little bundle of joy that lay there, warmly wrapped against the cold and with dribble running down his chubby chin.

As the woman entered her house Alistair said "Thanks for your help." He then said to Penny, "I'm just going to make a note of this car's reg number. We can see if we can trace the owner."

FORTY

Alistair drove fast to Pimlico. They didn't speak much during the journey. When they arrived at Knox Court they greeted Mac briefly and took the elevator to Alistair's apartment.

Once indoors, Alistair asked Penny if she'd like something to drink, alcohol, coffee, tea? She shook her head. She was still shaky following her close shave and she was making a determined effort not to cry.

"How about a nice, relaxing bath with lots of bubbles?" Alistair suggested. "I can run one for you."

That sounded perfect to Penny. "That would be lovely," she said.

"And if you like, I'll bring you up a nice cup of tea,"

"Mmm. That sounds lovelier still. Thank you, Alistair. I really don't know what I'd do without you."

Alistair smiled at her. "Right," he said. "I'll go run your bath. I'll give you a shout when it's ready."

Penny lazed in the bath, enjoying her cup of tea. She was still ensconced in the water which she had refreshed with more hot water and she was beginning to feel tired. She closed her eyes for an intended minute or so and awoke with a start when she saw Alistair standing by the bath with a big grin. "Sorry to intrude when you're naked in the bath but I kept calling you and got no reply. I hoped you hadn't drowned."

"Ooh, sorry. Have I been in here too long?"

"There's no such thing as too long when enjoying a bath."

"Brrr. The water's gone cold," Penny shivered slightly.

"I'll run some more hot water in. Then I'll leave you in privacy as I've established that you are still in the land of the living," Alistair said. "I'll see you downstairs when you've finished."

About one hour later Penny went down to the lounge. She had on a fluffy bath robe. "I hope you don't mind my state of dress, Alistair. But I just couldn't face getting dressed again. Anyway, I think I'll be going to bed shortly."

"Of course. I understand," Alistair replied. "You've just gone through a pretty traumatic episode D'you want something to eat?"

Penny shook her head. "No thanks. Oh, unless you'd like me to cook something for you?"

"Good heavens, no. I'm quite capable of cooking something if needed. Anyway, it's getting quite late so I might call it a night as well."

They said goodnight to each other and went up to their separate bedrooms.

FORTY-ONE

The tension between O'Connor and his wife, Sinead was near breaking point. Her first reaction when O'Connor told her of his pay cut was anger, unmitigated and uncontrolled fury. She cursed and uttered maledictions against Grey Goose. Then she threw a teacup against the wall and burst into tears, blubbering in an uncontrollable manner. Her third performance was to discuss with O'Connor the resultant problems they would have to face. Whilst O'Connor had no way of coping with her first two reactions, he felt more comfortable discussing the situation without accompanied histrionics.

Sinead pointed out that their two children, Alice and Sophie would have to be taken out of their fee paying school and moved to a comprehensive. Aside from not being able to meet school fees, they would also have a problem with meeting their mortgage payments. A move to a small house in another area was inevitable. As they discussed the matter, more and more difficulties presented themselves. There was definitely no easy way to resolve their dilemma.

Sinead was implacable in her attitude and O'Connor could in no way appease her. She asked him if he had done something wrong, had slipped up badly on an assignment, to cause him to be demoted and his salary so drastically reduced. She did not appear to believe his explanation.

O'Connor stormed out of the house after Sinead had thrown a saucepan at him – fortunately empty – and told him that he was completely useless. He got into his car and drove off.

He drove for hours and for miles and eventually found himself on the outskirts of Bristol. He pulled into a pub car park and sat in his car smoking. Five cigarettes later, he got out and entered the pub. He ordered a pint of Guinness, found a quiet corner table and lit yet another cigarette. Thoughts of his predicament and its effects on his family tumbled around in his mind. He felt totally bereft of ideas. He ordered another beer, and another and another and after four pints of Guinness he was no nearer finding any answers to resolving his difficulties. One thing he was determined to do was to ensure that his wife and children were spared a change in their way of life. And suddenly he knew what the answer was.

He asked the barman if he could have some paper and an envelope. The man gave him a sheaf of old menus printed on one side. "You'll have to use the other side which is blank. Sorry I've nothing else, mate."

O'Connor thought of all the questionable assignments he'd undertaken for The Group, including the water burial of the young female Rathing. As a good Catholic, he knew he had sinned and he wondered if God was now punishing him for the unforgiveable acts he'd taken. And if he was being punished then his now intended action, a grievous and serious sin he was about to commit, might as well be added to his punishment list.

O'Connor knew that he had quite a few sizeable death and life insurance policies [essential in his line of work] and he reasoned that on his death the payout would see the family comfortably off for a long, long time. He had made the decision to commit suicide. But because insurance companies do not usually pay

202

out on policies where the holder has committed suicide, it was important that there was no suspicion of suicide. A car crash may be an answer, or a hit and run accident; essentially nothing of a suspicious nature. At the same time, O'Connor was furious at the way he'd been treated by The Group and Grey Goose in particular. If the good Lord was to send O'Connor to damnation because of what he'd done, he reasoned that it was only fair for those sinners to also receive their just desserts. The only one he felt sorry to hurt was Blue Eyes, whose name he did not intend to include in the listing.

He wrote his note in such a way that it would not read like the last words of a man intent on suicide. He gave the names of all the members of The Group. He wrote of the accidental death of Grey Goose's Rathing partner at Gretorex Hall. And he gave exact details of where the body lay in Lake Coniston. He put the letter in the envelope and addressed it to 'The Editor, Daily Star, London'.

He was about to seal it when he stopped and opened it. He took the paper out of the envelope. He had changed his mind and decided at the last moment to include Blue Eyes' name on the list. Whilst Blue Eyes had indeed helped him in the past, Blue Eyes was also the driving force behind the group's intended putsch against the Government. O'Connor considered it only right that Blue Eyes pay his just deserts for his treasonous plans.

The letter read :

The Editor, The Daily Star, London.
Sir

I work for a group of men who are planning a revolt against the Government. They use Gretorex Hall in Hertfordshire as their headquarters.

203

These men are all important people. They give the impression that they consider themselves above the law. I am writing to you about them because I realise that what is happening is against the law.

These men are training Rathings into an army. The Rathings were not all killed by the Americans. No sensible person wants those creatures roaming about. But this group of men do!

The people are:

Bryan Addison (Estate Agent)   Peter Althrop (Barrister)   Rev.   William Blake (Vicar) Carlton Padstone (Police)   Bill Harris (Surgeon)   Septimus Gregson (GP)   James Bosworth (Police – CID)   John Normanston-Brown (Judge)   Christopher Biggins   (Businessman) Branston Ogilvie (Doctor)   Samuel Isaacs (Banker) Lord Gretorex (of private means)   Albert Franck (Surgeon)   Alistair Featherstonehaugh (Government) The Rev. Victor Smith   (Vicar)   Jayston Saunderson (RC Priest)   Sir Oliver Vaux (of private means)   Alan Cuthbertson   (Banker)   Patrick Donald   (Barrister)   Marquis of Chlomley   (of private means)   Ptolemy   De Bruine   (Actor) Peter Kingston   (Quantity Surveyor)   Isiah Levison (Finance   Trader)   Clarence   Jarvis   (Merchant Banker)   Sir   John   Carlson-Smythe   (Judge) Edward Leeks (Senior Engineer)   Oscar Wainrose (Scientist)   John Lewiston   (Police)

There are a few others who have recently joined and whose names I do not know. All people in the Group are given code names.

The letter went on to describe Clarence Jarvis's involvement in the death of the young female Rathing, how the young Rathings were nursed at Gretorex Hall and how O'Connor accepted that he was responsible for breaking the law by acting on behalf of the Group members. He ended his letter by making it obvious that he would contact the paper in approximately a week, thus giving no clue as to his intention to commit suicide. He wrote :

I realise that I too will be arrested and sent to prison for my crimes. I deserve such punishment and will take it like a man.

I have not written this to the police as there are a few police chiefs in The Group. If one of them received this letter they would suppress it. I know I can rely on you to see that justice is done. I shall contact you in about one week to find out who you think I should see in the police.

Meanwhile, thank you for your kind co-operation.

Yours respectfully,   Patrick O'Connor

He finished his beer and walked out. He planned to find a postbox. He hadn't put a stamp on the envelope because he didn't have one but he was fairly confident that it would be delivered to the newspaper.

The driver of the heavy goods vehicle swore that he hadn't seen the man stepping out suddenly onto the road. Nor could he have heard the man cry out just before he was smashed to the ground by the lorry. O'Connor's intention to commit suicide was never realized as in his drunken state he quite innocently and inadvertently stepped off the pavement in front of the lorry before he was momentarily aware of the vehicle's presence. There was the screech of brakes, a woman screaming as she saw the man mowed down by the HGV. The medics said afterwards that the man was obviously drunk and that death would have been instantaneous.

Crumpled beneath the broken body was a heavily bloodstained envelope containing a letter that would never be delivered.

FORTY-TWO

Blue Eyes called O'Connor's mobile but got no reply. He needed O'Connor's services. After numerous unsuccessful attempts, he telephoned O'Connor's home. Sinead O'Connor answered.

"I thought you would have been told, Mr. Blue Eyes," she said when Blue Eyes asked to speak to her husband. "I foolishly believed when I heard your voice that you had called to express your condolences."

"Condolences? I'm sorry, I don't understand. For what Mrs. O'Connor?"

"Holy Mary mother of God! But you're all a strange lot, and there's no denying that," she shouted. "For being responsible for my Pat's death, you swine."

Blue Eyes frowned and gripped his phone tightly. "Do please calm down, Mrs. O'Connor. I know nothing about your Pat's death. Please explain because this is the first I know about it and it disturbs me greatly."

"Pat and I had a row. He drove to Bristol and got tanked up, according to the police. He was run over and killed by a lorry."

"Dear Lord!" Blue Eyes exclaimed. "I am so, so sorry to hear this."

"You weren't that sorry when you cut his wages. That was what the row was about."

"Cut his wages? Pat had his salary reduced?"

"As if you didn't know."

"I assure you, Mrs. O'Connor. I did not know. This is the first I've heard about it. I certainly did not authorize any such thing."

"You've got a strange company going there, Mr. Blue Eyes. You're like kids playing a game. Grown men calling themselves Blue Eyes and Grey Goose. And God knows what else."

"It's essential security."

"Oh aye, I know that. My Pat never spoke about what he did or about the firm but he said your company is involved in secret national security matters that's why you all have those funny names. Like your company Treasurer, Grey Goose, may his soul rot in hell, 'twas him who cut my Pat's wages."

"Grey Goose cut your husband's salary?"

"He did that, the bastard."

"Mrs. O'Connor. Please believe me. I had absolutely nothing to do with such action. Is there anything, anything at all I can do? Will you please allow me to help? Can I look after the funeral arrangements? Do you need any financial help for the immediate time?"

"Mr. Blue Eyes. I thank you for your past financial help and I shall always be grateful for that. But at the moment I want nothing from you or your friends. I don't want to see or hear from any of you. And when you see your friend, Grey Goose, tell him my curses will forever hang around his head, may the devil die horribly like my Pat did." Mrs. O'Connor began crying and she then banged her phone down.

FORTY-THREE

On Saturday morning Alistair mentioned over breakfast that he would be away for most of the day as he had a number of other duties to attend to.

He drove to Acton, found the street and the dwelling he had to visit and he parked outside the rather shabby terrace house. He rang the doorbell and the door was opened to admit him. He went into the house. Seated in the kitchen around a small table were the same men with whom he had had a conversation with in Melrose. Their conversation was a long and serious one. At one stage, one of the men said to Alistair "Are you quite sure about this?" Alistair replied, "Definitely, sir."

After two hours discussion, without a break for coffee or a drink of any kind, everyone rose from the kitchen table and made their way out. Alistair was the last to leave. He picked up the house keys from the table in the narrow hall. Once outside, he double locked the front door and got into his car. There was no sign of any of his companions.

Alistair drove southwards from Acton.

*****

On that same Saturday morning, after Alistair had left, Penny decided that she really should visit Gretorex Hall and find out for herself if Rathings were present there. She checked trains and buses and felt that travelling by public transport would take a long time. She considered cycling, but gave that up as a bad idea. She considered engaging a minicab then had another thought.

"Hello, Bill," she said when he answered the phone. "It's me, Penny. Yes, I'm fine, thanks. And all of you? Oh, good. Bill, I'm calling you because I badly need your help" She explained her having seen a photograph of a Rathing at Gretorex Hall and her intended visit to Hertfordshire and the purpose of such visit.

"You mean you need a chauffeur," Bill said with a chortle.

"No, no!" Penny contradicted. "Of course, it would be nice to be driven down there but I thought that as a newspaperman you would be keen to establish for yourself the existence of Rathings at Gretorex Hall. And for my part, once I can see the evidence for myself, I can complete and submit my report to the Government."

"Where are you now?" Bill asked.

"In Pimlico, Knox Court in Astley Street. It's close to ..."

"Don't worry. I'll find it. Shall we say in an hour? I've got some things I must finish first before I go traipsing to the countryside."

"Bill," Penny interjected. "If you do not feel this visit would be of news interest, then please don't worry about driving down there. I can make my way by other means."

"Come on, Pumpkin," Bill countered. "It is of interest but I must finish some things first before I make tracks to you. I'll see you in about an hour."

True to his word, Bill walked up to Mac fifty five minutes later and asked to see Penny. Penny came down, kissed Bill on the cheek and walked with him to his car. They drove off towards the Alice motorway.

"So what exactly are we going to do once we get to this place of yours?" Bill asked.

"I had a meeting with an American from the Bureau of Investigative Journalism. He said that a subversive group is based at Gretorex Hall and that they are breeding Rathings there. He showed me a photograph which seemed to indicate this."

"Seemed to?" Bill queried.

"The picture wasn't all that good. It was taken indoors with a mobile phone and without a flash, so it's a bit grainy but my American contact said that his informer swore it was a Rathing, and I am inclined to believe that.

"Shortly after he told me of his suspicions, he was run down and killed. It appears to have been a deliberate killing."

"Wait a minute!" Bill exclaimed. "Are we talking here about James Kilroy?"

"Yes."

"Nasty business that. I knew the chap slightly; seemed a regular sort of bloke. I can now see your interest in all this."

They drove on without speaking. After a while Bill said, "That place in Pimlico where your boyfriend lives in quite something."

"He is *not* my boyfriend, Bill," Penny snapped. He works for the Ministry of Internal Affairs and is putting me up for a short while.

"Well, they must certainly pay big salaries to Government employees for him to afford a swish place like that."

"It's not exactly his," Penny corrected. "It belongs to his parents who are undoubtedly loaded."

Bill just said "Hmm".

As soon as he hit the Alice motorway (in the year 2060 all motorway designations were changed; names replaced numbers, so the M4 motorway became the

Alice motorway) Bill gunned the car to 70 mph, then Penny noticed the speedometer creep up to the nineties.

"Exhilarating what? Enjoying it?"

"Not really. Shouldn't we keep to the speed limit?" Penny said quietly.

"If I wanted a speed control inspector I would have asked my mother to accompany us." Bill grinned at Penny. "You sound just like her. In any case, this is the top limit allowed by the Central Computer."

"I'm sorry. I've been terrified of car speeds since Peter's accident."

Her hands were tightly clasped together and Bill glanced down and noted that there was whiteness about the knuckles.

Bill immediately decelerated to a steadier speed. "I'm sorry," he said. "I should have been a bit more sensible."

Penny felt more at ease, having noticed the speedometer hover around the 60 mph mark. Her clenched hands began to relax.

"No. It's I who should apologise. I'm sorry for being so wet," she said.

"You're not being wet. Anyway, there's no deadline arrival time, so we'll trundle along at a leisurely rate."

They turned off the Alice motorway and connected with the Linda motorway (previously the M25). The traffic was much heavier on Linda. Signals indicated the fast lane as closed. After some miles, they realised why. There had been an RTA of several vehicles. Police cars, fire engines and an ambulance were in attendance. It looked like quite a nasty accident and Penny felt a reflux from her stomach as it burned the back of her throat.

Bill glanced at her and noted her pale complexion. "Are you OK?" he asked.

Penny nodded.

"I'll take the next exit and we'll find somewhere to have a cup of tea."

"It's not necessary to break our journey," Penny said quietly.

"Well, I could certainly do with some tea, and I'm sure you wouldn't turn your nose up at it. There's an exit we're coming up to."

They drove around until they found a cafe. It was a quaint little place. A waitress walked up to their table. She had a broad beam and a broad bosom, accompanied by a broad smile. She had stuck a pencil in her curly brown locks. "What can I get you?" she asked in a well modulated voice.

"I see you do Devon teas," Bill smiled at her. "Two please and would you make the tea Earl Grey?"

"Certainly sir," she said, removing the pencil from her hair and writing down the order on a small pad.

"Oh, and some lemon pieces for the tea. No milk."

The waitress nodded and moved towards the kitchen.

"I'm sorry, I should have asked you what you wanted before ordering," Bill apologised.

Penny shook her head. "No, what you ordered was perfect. Except that I would have preferred Yak milk instead of lemon." She laughed.

They ate their scones with cream and jam in companionable silence until Penny said, "What d'you plan to say to them when we reach the Hall?"

Bill shrugged. "Oh, I'll think of something."

"D'you think we'll learn anything there?"

"I don't know, Penny. But I hope so. If the people at Gretorex Hall are in any way connected with this Rathing business, we might get closer to finding out what's happening."

When they had finished and Bill had paid the waitress, they walked to Bill's car. On the way they passed some people wearing glider boots. These are shoes with a rocket booster, similar to a jet pack used in space exploration. The glider boot wearers hovered a few inches above the pavement.

"Hideous abominations!" Bill growled.

"I've got two pairs of those," Penny said. "A light blue pair and a pink pair. They are so comfortable. With a press of a tiny button you rise above the floor and skim just above the surface. It's a wonderful sensation to slip on your glider boots and float on air. No more trudging up stairs! Just glide up them."

"D'you know something?" Bill remarked in an angry voice. "There are people who got so used to using glider boots that they virtually stopped exercising their legs. By not using their leg muscles, they gradually wasted away and atrophied. Their legs are two thin poles with no muscle and little flesh. We carried an article in the paper some months ago on the dangers of glider boots. Glider boots are an utter abomination!"

"Wow!" Penny exclaimed. "Thank God I don't use mine often."

"Good! You really shouldn't use them at all," Bill responded and opened the car doors.

They rejoined the Linda motorway, and then turned off at South Mimms onto the A1. After a short while, Bill left the A road and drove along a series of B roads until they turned a corner and saw a magnificent Elizabethan manor house standing proudly in the distance behind high perimeter walls.

FORTY-FOUR

Bill stopped by the gate. He pointed at the sign which read 'Gretorex Hall. Headquarters International Society of Sociologists.'

"So, they're passing themselves off as sociologists," he remarked.

"Perhaps they are," Penny stated. "We have no evidence at this stage that this place houses subversives. It could have been no more than a suspicious comment made by the American newspaper man."

"True, so let's find out for ourselves," Bill replied as he drove through the gate and along the long winding drive.

After a short distance they came across a man who waved them down. A large Alsatian dog strained at the leash which the man held tightly. Bill pulled up beside the pair. "I'm sorry," the man said. "This is private property. I must ask you to turn back."

"I take it that this is the headquarters of sociologists, as it proclaims on the board at the gate?"

"That's right. That's why it is private property. No members of the public are allowed access."

"Well, my girl friend here is a sociologist so she is entitled to visit."

The man scowled. He wished today had been a weekday when no more than two or three members might be present. Being a Saturday, many more had turned up to meet in the bar and to have lunch at the Hall.

"Just a minute," he said. He walked some short distance away and pulled a mobile phone out of his pocket.

"I've got two people here who say they are sociologists, so I can't stop them from driving in. You'd better warn the others. I'll send them to the main house entrance but direct them the long way round to give you time." He listened for a minute then said. "OK." He walked back to Bill's car. "I'm sorry to have kept you, sir. I just wanted to check that there was no conference in session or anything like that. If you drive on to the main entrance someone will meet you there. I suggest you take that route," he pointed to a narrow path that lead off to the right. "That's the scenic route that goes past the fishing lake and is a much more pleasant way to take."

"If the public aren't allowed in here would it not make sense to have a gate at the entrance?" Bill asked.

The man shrugged. "I suppose so, but I'm not going to suggest it."

"Why not?"

"I'll be out of a job then, won't I? There'll be no need to have someone patrol the place."

Bill smiled. "Yes. I see your point. Anyway, thanks."

The man saluted Bill and said "heel!" to the dog as he turned and walked away.

"Wasn't it kind of him to suggest this way? It's very pretty," Penny said. "Why did you say I am a sociologist?"

"We wouldn't have been let through otherwise."

"But I know absolutely nothing about sociology. What happens if someone asks me anything about it?"

"Say nothing. Leave the talking to me."

"OK, boyfriend," Penny said with a smile.

"That man was extraordinarily polite after his phone call," Bill remarked. "I also suspect that his suggested route to the house could well be a delaying tactic. He obviously warned whoever he spoke to of our arrival. I bet they're getting organised before we make an appearance."

Penny gave a little giggle. "My goodness, but you are a suspicious fellow, Bill."

"You might well say so."

Bill suddenly turned off the path he was driving along and continued along another path that brought them to the back of the Hall. As they drove along, Penny suddenly saw Alistair's car parked alongside one of the building's walls.

"That's Alistair's car!" she exclaimed.

"What? That metallic grey McLaren F12? Boy! Your boyfriend sure is loaded." Penny raised her eyes to heaven at the boyfriend inference. "Those cars cost an absolute fortune," Bill continued. "I don't care what you say, Pumpkin but the Government certainly seem to pay their personnel healthy salaries."

"Yes, but what *is* he doing here?" Penny said.

"Perhaps he dabbles in Sociology in his spare time," Bill replied.

"Bill! Bill! Look!" Penny practically screamed whilst pointing towards some marmalade coloured outhouses. "What?" Bill said in a startled voice, then having seen what Penny was drawing his attention to he swore "Bloody hell's shit!"

There before their very eyes they saw a man leading two Rathings, each creature having a chain ring fixed to its nose. The Rathings looked young; each was no taller than six foot and nowhere near a Rathing's maximum attainable height. They shambled along and entered one of the outhouses.

Bill moved off slowly, shaking his head in wonderment and what he had just seen. He had to stop suddenly when a man stepped in their path and waved them down.

"What the hell are you doing here?" he demanded.

Bill got out of the car. He towered over the other man. "Look, old man," Bill said in a very quiet voice. "I don't like being sworn at, especially when I have a lady in the car. Comprende?"

"I'm sorry for sounding terse," the man apologized, weighing up Bill's considerably greater size. "But no one is allowed in this part of the grounds."

"We are sociologists and were directed here, although I do admit I might have taken a wrong turning."

"The entrance is in the main building on the other side," he pointed in that direction. "Please proceed there, sir."

Bill returned to his car and drove off along the circular road and duly arrived at the front of the house. There was no one waiting to greet them.

"They obviously don't expect us to arrive yet," Bill remarked with a smile. "Let's give them a surprise."

"Not as big a surprise as we've both just had, seeing those Rathings."

"You're damned right, Pumpkin," Bill said with a grin.

He helped Penny out of the car and they both walked up the stone steps to the front oak door. Bill turned the Alhambra style round ring lever handle that opened the latch and he pushed the heavy door open. They walked into a large hall and stood quietly, admiring the high ceiling and mullioned windows. They heard a gentle cough behind them. They turned to see a tall, fit-looking man watching them. "Good day to you," he said in a very cultivated accent.

"Hello," Bill replied. "What a magnificent place you have here."

"It is indeed," the man smiled. He looked to be in his late forties/early fifties and was impeccably dressed. He was also far bigger than Bill. "We are most fortunate." He then addressed Bill. "I understand that you are a sociologist?"

Bill shook his head. "No. Not me. It's my girl friend here, Penny Cowdrey. And you, sir, are...?"

"My name is Padstone. I am the manager here."

He had volunteered to pretend to be the Society's manager.

"It's good of you to permit us to look around. We were just tootling past when we noticed this place. Penny and I were quite surprised to see the sign indicating this as being the headquarters of the International Society of Sociologists."

"If you'd like to follow me, I'll show you around."

Penny said "Thank you" and sidled up to Bill. "Who the hell is Penny Cowdrey?" she whispered. "An old girl friend?"

"You don't want your real name bandied about here," he whispered back. "And no, it's not an old girl friend's name. One I just made up. And, incidentally, that man we've just met is no manager here. I know him to be Carlton Padstone, an assistant chief constable crime and counter terrorism of the Thames Valley police."

"How d'you know?"

"Come on, Pumpkin. I'm a newspaper man. I've seen him at receptions and briefings his given to the press."

Padstone waited for them to catch up. "This is the breakfast room," he said, opening the door to a room.

He showed them various other rooms. As they walked along a corridor Bill noted that Padstone had passed a door and not stopped to show them the room. "What's in there?" Bill asked and pushed open the door. "Oh, nothing," Padstone quickly replied but was too late to stop Bill and Penny looking in. A phalanx of tiny children's beds was lined up against both sides of the long room.

"Is this the bedroom for dwarf sociologists?" Bill said jokingly.

Padstone gave a forced laugh. "These are beds ordered by a local private children's school who unfortunately cannot accept them yet as they are currently refurbishing the place. We offered to hold them here for them, which we feel is a charitable thing to do. They should be collecting them within a week or so."

They walked on and passed a door behind which could be heard a loud, sonorous basso profundo voice. They stopped at the door. "May we?" Bill asked Padstone, who nodded.

They opened the door and saw a very tall, distinguished looking man, probably in his fifties, addressing a gathering of about a dozen other men. In true life, the speaker was an actor named Ptolemy De Bruine, who had volunteered to pretend he was a lecturer on different aspects of sociology. What neither Bill nor Penny realised was that allowing them entry into the room was a deliberate ploy to test out their genuineness of being sociologists. The members of The Group had long prepared themselves for such an eventuality. They realised that there was every likelihood of inquisitive visitors poking around, so they had rehearsed a little charade to satisfy meddlesome callers.

The men sitting before Ptolemy turned round to see who had entered. Penny stared at the sea of faces; they were a complete blur. Then she blanched. Staring at her with a very surprised look was Alistair.

"Forgive me, Professor," Padstone remarked. "This young lady is a sociologist..." he motioned to Penny. "And she expressed a wish to look around the place."

"Welcome, my dear. I am Professor Bruin and my colleagues here are, like me, all sociologists. We are just discussing Research Methodology which sociological research, as you will know, is divided into two categories. May I ask which camp do you feel inclined to support? – Quantitative design or Qualitative design?"

Penny turned and looked at Bill, her eyes like two large orbs staring at him in desperate, abject terror.

"My girl friend has only just started her course in sociology through the Open University. She is currently working on comparing PCL-R, that is Psychopathy Checklist, Revised with the related four factors and PPI or Personality Inventory and working with the Triarchic model. She is also undertaking a longitudinal study of Maori culture. You will forgive her reticence, Professor Bruin but as a comparative beginner in this field she feels overwhelmingly embarrassed by being in the presence of such obviously highly experienced sociologists." He turned to Penny. "Isn't that so, darling?"

"Yes, darling," Penny replied. Then turning to the men in the room, she said, "I am highly honoured to be in such august company. I thought we'd be looking around an empty house and never for one moment thought there would be such a gathering of eminent practitioners. I have only just started my course so would not dream of discussing any aspects of sociology with such brilliant gentlemen as yourselves."

"And you, sir, seem to be well versed on the subject. And you say you are not a sociologist?" De Bruin said.

"A smattering I've picked up whilst helping Pam with her studies."

"And your name, sir is?" De Bruin persisted.

"Walker. Bill Walker."

De Bruin smiled. "Well, Pamela and Bill, it has been a pleasure to see you. I'm afraid that we must now continue our lecture."

Both Penny, and to a lesser degree Bill, were surprised when the men loudly applauded Penny.

When they left the room, Padstone asked them if he could offer them some tea or coffee or a drink in the bar. Bill thanked him but turned down his invitation, explaining that they had a long journey home.

On the way back to London Bill laughed out loud and turned to Penny, giving her a wink. "That was a brilliant bit of crawling you did. 'I am highly honoured to be in such august company.' You were absolutely perfect."

"Thank you. Can you tell me when I became your girl friend?"

"I could hardly introduce you as a private detective on a case. And anyway, I rather liked describing you as my girl friend. It added a nice touch to our masquerade."

"Masquerade," Penny mumbled. "I see. Was all that goobly gook of PPi and PC something and tri whatever all goobly gook as well? Darling?" She emphasized the last word heavily.

Bill did not reply immediately. Instead, he pulled up on the hard shoulder and leant across to look at Penny seriously.

"Listen, Penny. It was obvious that they were testing us out. They weren't sure if either of us were sociologists, so they set up a little charade and fired a question to you about Quantitative or Qualitative design, which was nothing but verbal garbage." Bill smiled. "Oh it related to sociology alright, but was so obviously a hook to see if you would be caught out. I had my suspicions about their authenticity, so I countered by referring to a psychopathy checklist which has absolutely nothing to do with sociology. Any genuine sociologist would have picked up on that immediately and recognized that as a supposed sociologist you most certainly would not have been involved with a psychopathy Checklist or Psychopathic Personality Inventory, let alone a Triarchic model, and they would have pointed that out. They didn't. Which goes some immeasurable way to confirming to me that they are as likely to be sociologists as I am to be the Dalai Lama.

"Where did you learn all that about Psychopathy?" Penny asked.

"I read a lot. Fortunately, that bit jumped to the forefront of my mind just when needed. Penny. I think those people are dangerous. They appear to be very well organized and they're quick with answers to counter any investigative question. They are obviously highly intelligent, educated men but men with, I suspect, a dangerous streak.

"Think about those children's beds we saw. Our friend, Mr. Padstone was quick with an explanation but I don't believe they belong to any school. I am inclined to agree with our American friend, Mr. Kilroy. I am sure that those beds are for small Rathings. I frankly think Sir William should retire you from this assignment. But what really intrigues me is witnessing for myself those Rathings. It goes to prove that the rumours were not false but based on fact. This whole situation throws open an entirely new aspect on things."

"Bill," Penny whispered. "You remember we saw Alistair's car there?"

Bill nodded.

"I saw Alistair sitting in the crowd of men in the hall. And he saw me."

"Hell's teeth!" Bill exclaimed.

"I'm frightened, Bill. I'm not sure how he is going to react now he knows that I am aware of what he is involved in."

"I totally agree."

"Bill, d'you think you could drop me off at my flat in Teddington rather than Alistair's place?"

"Well, I don't think you should go back to Pimlico. Tell me, does this chap Alistair know of your flat in Teddington?"

Penny nodded.

"Then Teddington is not a good idea."

"Well, I can't afford a hotel booking."

"You must come and stay with Ellie and me until we can sort something out."

"Thanks, Bill but that really would be an imposition."

"Rubbish. We're heading for Barnes. Your friend doesn't know my address, so you'll be safe there.

"What about my stuff at Alistair's place?"

"I don't suggest we stop there to pick it up. Knowing the speed performance of that McLaren, your friend will probably be there already whilst we're still trundling along this motorway we're coming up to."

FORTY-FIVE

They had just reached the motorway junction when they both saw Alistair's car parked on the slip road. On the roof of his car was a blue flashing emergency light which he obviously placed there and plugged in the wire through the window and onto his dashboard. The strobe lighting cut through the evening sky announcing its presence as a vehicle entitled to be there.

"He's a wily bugger!" Bill swore. "He must have realized when you saw him that it would be unlikely that we'd head for his place. He must have shot up here like the speed of sound to watch out for us. I must confess I didn't see him coming up on us. He is now going to follow me. And he's placed an emergency flasher strobe on his roof to stop any police patrol asking him what he's doing parked there."

"How does he know it's your car?"

"Apart from perhaps recognizing you in the front seat, he'd probably checked with their security guard for a car description when we arrived."

"What are we going to do, Bill?" Penny asked anxiously.

"Do? Nothing. Whilst this Van den Plas can do great things she's no match for that flying spitfire of your friend. Don't worry, I'll deal with him."

Bill drove to Teddington and after some difficulty, found a parking space.

"Saturday's always a bad day," Penny said as they walked up to her flat.

"Every day's a bad parking day in London," Bill complained.

Some twenty minutes after they'd arrived, her front door bell rang.

"That'll be him," Penny whispered.

Bill walked to the front door. He opened it. One of his ham-like fists reached out and grabbed Alistair's jacket. He pulled him into the hallway. Although Alistair was strong and fit, he *was* shorter than Bill and Bill had the advantage of extra height and weight. Alistair wisely did not try and fight back but stood in the hall, brushing down his crumpled jacket.

"Right, sunshine," Bill snarled. "What's your game?"

Alistair did not reply but looked over at Penny. He smiled. "Is this gorilla your new bodyguard?" he asked.

Bill stepped towards Alistair. Penny quickly moved towards them. "What were you doing at that meeting at Gretorex Hall?" she demanded.

Alistair said, "Look, I'd better explain," He stretched out his hand to Bill. "My name's Alistair Pellow."

Bill did not shake his outstretched hand. "So explain," Bill said menacingly.

"I'm an officer with MI5, seconded by Government HR to the Ministry of Internal Affairs. My job has been to monitor the activities of a group of dissidents. I have played an undercover role in order to gain access to these men. You must believe me."

"Show me your ID card," Bill demanded.

"Come on," Alistair replied. "I am hardly likely to walk into the lion's den carrying an incriminating identification of that kind."

"So why should we believe you?" Bill said.

"Call this number," Alistair produced his IED and scrolled down until he found the number he wanted. "It's the MI5 duty officer's line. You must first say the word 'Alabaster' before anything else. Otherwise, they won't connect you."

Bill pulled out his mobile and dialed the number on the screen before him, held up by Alistair. "Alabaster", Bill said. He was connected. "This is Bill Murray, Editor of The Globe newspaper group. I have an Alistair Pellow here who claims to be an MI5 operative. Before I pass on to him any information he seeks, I need to verify his credentials. No, he doesn't have any ID – says he left it in another jacket. A brief description will do. Thank you." The person Bill had spoken to wanted to verify who Bill was. He answered, "Yes, Globe Newspaper Group. Editor." He then gave the newspaper's telephone number and address. He was also asked for his email. He eventually said, "You'll need my mobile number as I'm not in the office just now. OK, thanks. I'll wait for your call."

"They're checking up on me and will call back shortly."

"I'll put the kettle on," Penny said. "I'm sure we could all do with a cup of tea or coffee."

Ten minutes later, Bill's mobile phone rang. "Bill Murray," he answered. "Yes, that's right. Thanks Yes, he's here. Just one moment." Bill passed his phone to Alistair. "They want to talk to you."

Alistair listened then said, "Alabaster grows on trees. Yes please, it's all OK and above board. Just go ahead please." He passed the phone back to Bill.

Bill studied Alistair as it was obvious that he was being told what the MI5 agent looked like. Finally he said, "A knife wound on his left shoulder. OK, that should do it. Thanks for your help." He closed the connection. "Take your jacket and shirt off, if you will. I need to see your knife wound."

Alistair took off his jacket and shirt and turned his shoulder to Bill.

"OK. Seems you're the genuine article," Bill said. "Sorry if I was rough with you when you arrived."

"Please don't worry about it," Alistair replied. "You were fully justified."

"So, what's happening with this mob of reprobates?" Bill asked.

"These men are all important persons in their respective professions."

"I know. I recognized Assistant Police Chief Constable Padstone pretending to be the manager of the building."

"So you know him?" Alistair said with a smile.

"Of course. I'm a newspaperman. I've attended briefings he's given. Luckily, he didn't recognize me. In fact, I doubt if he knows who I am. Anyway, go on."

"These men have been agitating for some years, wanting to bring down the Government and take over the running of the country. They realized that their chances of success were remote. Any move on their part would have been countered by the Government calling in the army. But then, some months ago, lady luck threw a winning dice in their corner.

"Some rock climbers discovered dead Rathings in a cave in Scotland. These Rathings had obviously been killed when the Americans saturated the area with the DTX toxin. However, hidden away under the dead bodies, and seemingly protected from breathing in the toxin, were a handful of baby Rathings. Wheels were set in motion and these babies were shipped down to Gretorex Hall. There, these men set up a hospital laboratory and nurtured them and began to breed from them. The gestation period is short and so before long the men started building up a Rathing army. They intended to force the Government down by using this Rathing army to counter any offensive adopted by the human army.

"My job was to monitor their progress and report to my superiors." He turned to Penny who had brought in on a tray three cups of tea. "You will recall that I left Knox Court on a number of occasions – supposedly to visit Edinburgh. But I also met with my boss the head of MI5, an army general, the Commissioner of the Metropolitan Police and a senior Government minister and I brought them up to date on the Group's plans.

"Because their proposed launch against the Government is imminent, all of those men are being arrested at this very moment." He turned to Bill. "So you have an exclusive breaking news story, Bill. It is Bill isn't it? I heard you say that on the phone when you were talking to the MI5 D.O."

"That's right." Bill extended his hand. "Bill Murray. Nice to meet you, Alistair."

Alistair finished his tea quickly and got up. "Look, I must make tracks and see how things are getting on." He turned to Penny. "Are you staying here or would you like to return to Knox Court?"

Penny looked enquiringly at Bill. Bill said, "Now you know Alistair's one of the good guys there's no reason for you to be afraid of returning to Pimlico."

"Good," Alistair said. "Will you come with me or go with Bill?"

Penny looked over at Bill, who smiled at her. "Go on, go with Alistair. I'll wend my way home."

"Thank you so much, Bill," Penny said, walking up to him and giving him a kiss on the cheek. "You've been such a great help today."

"Always a pleasure, Pumpkin," he replied with a grin. "Now you take care and keep in touch." He turned to Alistair. "Look after her, will you," He stated, almost as if an order.

"I will do, Bill," Alistair assured him.

They all left the flat and went to their respective cars.

FORTY-SIX

Six men sat round the large table in one of the smaller rooms in Gretorex Hall. They were the members of the Executive Committee.

In the absence of Blue Eyes, it would have been normal for Grey Goose, as Commanding Officer to chair the meeting. However, on instructions received from Blue Eyes, Purple Pill was appointed chairman of this meeting. Also present were Grey Goose, the scientist code named Bunsen, Hammer, Elderflower and Septimus Forceps.

"Gentlemen," Purple Pill addressed the assembled committee members. "As you will no doubt know, Blue Eyes is on an official visit to Europe and is unable to attend today's meeting. I have been asked by him to chair this meeting as opposed to it being led by Grey Goose as C.O as there are some issues we must discuss, some of which concern your recent actions, Grey Goose."

"Oh?" Grey Goose exclaimed. "And what may they be?"

"Your unilateral decision to cut the wages of staff..."

Grey Goose fumbled about with the papers that lay before him on the table and interrupted. "Our finances are not as healthy as they once were. As Treasurer, I had felt it necessary to effect certain savings...."

"You shall have plenty of time to answer once all the charges have been read out," Purple Pill interrupted him and said sternly.

"Charges?" Grey Goose looked at all around the table. "For heaven's sake! Is this some kind of Court Martial?"

"If you wish to consider it as such. I shall continue. The other charge is that you have – again solely as a unilateral decision – mounted a campaign of harassment and attempted murder against the female detective appointed by the Government to investigate the veracity or otherwise of the rumour concerning Rathings."

"Oh, yes?" Grey Goose sneered.

"Attempted murder?" some of those present murmured.

"But, what is of great concern is that you arbitrarily took certain actions which will materially affect our plans."

Grey Goose spoke in a slow measured way but as his argument continued he became strident. "Do any of you realize what a danger to our cause that detective girl could be? We have struggled for years to find a way of achieving our objectives and we now have the perfect solution. A Rathing military force. But no one outside of our group must learn of the existence of Rathings. If this reaches the ears of the Government or of the public our plan will be shattered." Here he thumped the table with a closed fist. "No one amongst our group seems to be doing anything to stop her in her enquiries. I therefore took the decision to act for the common good. I have been doing this for US," he shouted the last word. Is that an offence?"

Purple Pill said nothing for a while but sat looking down at the table. He spoke eventually, in a cool, measured way. "Grey Goose. Your attempt to make savings is understandable and, is, I am sure, appreciated by all. But may I ask why you did not refer your proposals to the Committee?"

232

Grey Goose had now calmed down. He spoke in a slow, measured way. "I did not think it necessary. Controlling The Group's finances was my responsibility as Treasurer at the time, and I took it."

"I appreciate what you say, but I think you will agree on reflection that you should have sought the Committee's endorsement or otherwise."

"Of course. I shall bear that in mind for future decisions."

"I am not sure whether you shall be making future decisions on behalf of the group."

"Oh, really?" Grey Goose said. "What is that supposed to mean?"

"Unlike you, I don't make unilateral decisions. That verdict will be reached by all Committee members who are present here," Purple Pill replied.

Purple Pill now addressed all the members. "In the meantime, I regard it as incumbent on me to draw to your attention, Grey Goose, the extreme inappropriateness of your actions.

Purple Pill then detailed the attempts made by Grey Goose to deter Penny's investigations.

He then touched on the problems created by Grey Goose in reducing the wages of the cleaning staff, resulting on one extremely displeased member taking a camera picture of a Rathing being led to its quarters and showing it to a newspaper man. "In the first place, the Rathing should not have been moved about in the main building. That is a statutory ruling which somebody will have to answer for.

"We employ gardeners, cooks, housemaids, cleaners, drivers, guards and odd-job men, to name but some. Most, if not all, are aware of our objective to replace the present Government. Most, if not all, share our view point. Like us, all who work here, realize that our objective is best reached with the additional force

233

of the Rathings. No word of the Rathings present, or of our intended goal has been broadcast abroad. None of these people have mentioned our activities to anyone in the village or elsewhere.

"Do none of you not sometimes wonder why that is so? Well, let me tell you. Money. It all boils down to money. All staff are paid well in excess of their acceptable market rate. They also receive handsome bonuses twice a year - at Christmas and in the summer. I daresay that some are becoming quite wealthy due to the wage they receive. You see, gentlemen, money talks and, in turn, it buys silence. Of course, a factor in our favour is that none of them are particularly ethical, principled, so that is distinctly to our advantage. If any one member of staff speaks to outsiders of our activities, they know that we face arrest. In turn, this would cut off their sizeable income. So they keep silent.

"What you have done, Grey Goose by reducing the pay of the cleaners is to give them reason to be perfidious. With loss of income, there will be no loyalty.

"You did not tell us that you had reduced Patrick O'Connor's pay."

"I am sure I did."

"No, you did not," Purple Pill said.

"Oh, didn't I?" Grey Goose exclaimed. "I am sorry. It must have slipped my mind."

"Alzheimer seems to be creeping up on you pretty quickly, Grey Goose." Purple Pill noted sarcastically.

"Well, as I said. I am sorry it slipped my mind. There was so much happening at the time."

"O'Connor is dead."

Grey Goose removed his spectacles and put them on the table. "Dead? How?"

"He stopped breathing," Septimus Forceps said in an angry voice. "That's how one dies."

"I meant how did he die?"

"Run over. Following a row he had with his wife about the substantial cut you made in his pay."

Grey Goose shrugged. "I am, of course, sorry to hear this but I can hardly be blamed for whatever disasters fall on those who have a pay cut. At least he wasn't made redundant."

Purple Pill looked hard at Grey Goose. "We do not propose to sit here discussing all the trivia with you. Suffice it to say that our President expects to have your immediate resignation from The Group. This request from our President was discussed earlier on by all those present here, and agreed on."

"Look here," Grey Goose expostulated. "You cannot arbitrarily put such conditions to me. This is totally unacceptable."

"We just have done," Hammer growled.

Purple Pill continued. "It has always been our policy that staff be paid handsomely. That premise has been our standard from the outset. What you, Grey Goose, have done in one full sweep is to knock down the very fabric of our success. Be aware, very much aware, that should any one member of staff feel that they have been unfairly treated they will have no compunction but to betray us. You can be quite sure about that.

"If our finances are low, then all we need to do is increase our yearly subscription. Even if this means our paying an extra one thousand pounds a year, we can all afford to do so. We must look after, nurture, our employees if they are not to betray us.

"I now call on the Committee to rescind Grey Goose's action and to bring back the payment to the cleaners to at least its original amount. But I would go

235

further and strongly suggest in view of the insult these cleaners were given, that we increase their wages by a nominal ten percent."

There were several calls of 'hear, hear,' and 'agreed'.

"But what about the cleaner who spoke to the newspaper chap?" Bunsen asked.

"We shall have to engage ourselves in finding out who that individual is and deal with him accordingly," Purple Pill said.

Purple Pill continued: "I now propose the motion that the cleaners and any other staff whose wages have been reduced are immediately advised by myself, as Treasurer, that this was an administrative error and that their wage level will be not only maintained, but increased by ten percent. All those in favour?"

Grey Goose looked furious. "This was not an administrative error," he shouted.

No, perhaps it wasn't," Purple Pill countered. "It was a childlike error. But I thought you might prefer us to term it as administrative.

"I know my colleagues agree with me when I say that we wish to have your immediate resignation from our group. Verbal will suffice."

"How dare you put such an ultimatum to me?" Grey Goose shouted.

"We will accept your resignation whether said now or not. You will then be accompanied to the room you use as your office and will be permitted to remove personal items only. You will then hand in all keys you hold to your escorts." Purple Pill looked around the table. "May I have two volunteers to see that Grey Goose complies with these instructions?"

All six foot four inches of Hammer rose from his chair. "It will be my pleasure to escort this man," he looked with disdain at Grey Goose, "and see that he does as ordered."

"I'm more than happy to do so also," Forceps said with a grin.

"You, you can't do this," Grey Goose expostulated, spittle flying from his lips.

"We just have," Hammer grunted; his tone menacing.

"You will leave now, Mr. Jarvis," Purple Pill said, using Grey Goose's proper name and thus clearly indicating that Jarvis was clearly no longer considered a member of the group.

"Allow me to see you out," Hammer said menacingly, grasping Jarvis's arm in a vice-like hold and steering him forcefully towards the door.

Purple Pill then referred to some notes he had made earlier in the day. "I had a phone call from Blue Eyes just before his departure. He asked that we discuss the possibility of transferring to Scotland the Rathings from here. In view of events, I believe it would be prudent for us to do so with some haste. Have the females produced yet?" Purple Pill looked over at Bunsen. "Any day now," the scientist replied.

"As soon as they have, it is imperative that arrangements are put in hand without delay to have them transported to Assynt. The caves will be the most conducive location for them and the safest, away from prying eyes. In any event, that is the location we had earmarked for their intensive training and it will not be too soon for them.

"That does mean, of course, that you, Bunsen and Forceps and Elderflower will have to relocate to Scotland for a while. I trust this will not be inconvenient to you?" Both Bunsen and Elderflower assured Purple Pill that it would not present any problems. "I shall have to check with Forceps when he returns from looking after Jarvis," Purple Pill said as he rose from the table. "Thank you, gentlemen, this meeting is now concluded."

FORTY-SEVEN

After Penny's abduction at the rugby match, and being very much aware of her tendency to shoot off on her own in the pursuit of her enquiries, Alistair decided he would invest in a tracking/location finder device.

When he saw Penny, he gave her a small yellow plastic button.

"I think it very important to ensure that should anyone else attempt to kidnap you that we – that is you and I – can keep in some form of contact so I can trace your hereabouts. You do have a tendency to not always carry your mobile phone with you. Therefore, I have bought a tracking device and that little yellow button is your part of the package."

"Thank you for your concern, Alistair," said Penny. "Do I rub this so it makes me disappear?"

"You rub it, yes. On the side like here," he took the button and showed her where to rub it. "But it doesn't make you disappear. It helps me to appear. In other words, I can trace exactly where you are. OK? Now, I suggest you put that button in your handbag or coat; at least somewhere where you are sure to keep it with you at all times."

"How is it going to work?" Penny asked.

"The equipment at my end, which I will have in my car, will have VHF tracking technology to receive signals from your little yellow button. Your button can transmit from underground car parks or even steel containers. Your signals will enable me to pinpoint accurate location. It's a perfect answer if you continue to make these secret journeys around town without telling me. Of course, if you did that I could have saved myself £700 paying for this gear."

Penny put her hand to her mouth. "Oh sorry, Alistair. I'll try and pay you back."

Alistair laughed. "Don't be a chump. It'll go on expenses. The Government will pay it."

"Well, thank you for your concern, Alistair. It really is appreciated."

"No problem," Alistair replied with a grin.

FORTY-EIGHT

Green and Thompson had finished work as security officers at the bank for the day and they left together and went to their favourite East End pub for a beer. There, they bumped into an old acquaintance of Green. This man's name was Alan Jordan. He was a well known crook in the area and had been jailed on several occasions for a range of misdemeanors.

Green had an idea which he shared with Thompson. Both of them had been promised each a payment of £500 by Mr. Jarvis and they were becoming increasingly concerned that their lack of success in accomplishing the job given to them would result in their receiving no payment.

Green's idea was for them to recruit Alan Jordan and offer him £200. "Look, mate," said Green. "We're having buggered all luck in carrying out Mr. Jarvis's instructions to stop that girl. Each of us working separately is not a good idea. We need to combine forces. Agreed?"

Thompson nodded. "Yes, Phil. Seems right."

"Well, I was thinking we could do even better with an extra pair of hands, if you get my drift?"

"What d'you mean, Phil?"

"Alan over there," he nodded to where Jordan stood nursing his beer, "is good at this sort of thing. He did the Montgomery kidnap, if you remember."

"Oh, yes! That's right."

"Well, we'd 'ave to pay 'im, like. I reckon two hundred would do it."

"But we're only getting five hundred."

"Each. So one hundred each towards paying Jordan still leaves us with four hundred quid each. Better than nothing – which is what it looks like being at the present moment."

Thompson nodded slowly. "Yes. Yes, I see what you're getting' at. I think it's a good idea."

"Shall I put it to him then?" Green asked, and Thompson nodded.

Green walked up to Jordan and after exchanging pleasantries about the state of the country, and the lack of seemingly available females, Green put his suggestion to Jordan.

Jordan was a small man, thin-faced, with slicked back, gelled black hair. He never stood still but always moved around, either tapping his feet or continually shrugging his shoulders or stretching his neck upwards. He listened to Green's proposal and shrugged several times. "Nah, mate. I *might* consider it for a monkey," Jordan replied to Green's suggestion.

"Five hundred? I'll have to talk to my mate," Green replied.

Green and Thompson discussed it at some length. Their original suggestion would have left them each with £400. Now Jordan was asking for £500. This would leave each one with only £250. They turned down Jordan's suggestion.

Four days later, in the same pub and at more or less the same time of evening, Jordan joined Green and Thompson and bought them each a pint. He realized that he had tried it on with suggesting £500. It was obvious that those two were not high rollers, especially as the job they wanted doing could be done by a twelve year old orangutan. He surmised that they were probably being paid £300 between the two of them and they were desperate for the job to be done.

242

He said, as he shuffled his feet, "I've been givin' it a bit o' thought, like. Two hundred would come in handy right now, so OK, I'll do it for two."

The three men shook hands on the deal.

Jordan told them what he wanted them to do. "Find an empty garage somewhere – not miles out of town. Make sure there is a tin bath or a large container that can hold plenty of water. And there has to be an internal tap and water supply. When you've done that, let's meet again here."

"What you got in mind, Alan?" Thompson asked.

"Gettin' the job done and me two hundred quid."

Early one morning two days later Alan Jordan drove the three men in his white van to Astley Street in Pimlico and parked opposite Knox Court.

"I'll give it one week waiting here to see if she comes out. After that, I'm out of it."

*****

Alistair and Penny were in his apartment. He suddenly jumped up. "I forgot all about the little gifts from Scotland." He went up the stairs to his bedroom and a few minutes later he came down holding two packages.

"This one's for Mac," he said. "It's a Scottish delicacy which I don't particularly like but Mac adores."

"Oh, what is it?" Penny asked.

"A haggis, no less."

They both laughed.

"I'll give it to him tomorrow. And this is a little thing for you." He handed her a small box.

"Wow, Alistair! You shouldn't. What is it?"

"Well go on. Open it."

She began to unpick the parcel tape.

"Just tear the paper, Penny," Alistair pleaded.

243

She did and opened a small box. She lifted out of it a small gold broach fashioned like a thistle.

"Oh, Alistair! It's beautiful. Really beautiful. Thank you so much."

"I can pin it to your blouse." Alistair offered.

He did so and stood back to look at it. "It really looks good on you," he said.

Penny walked over to the wall mirror. "Golly! It's beautiful, so tastefully elegant and sophisticated looking." She went to stand beside him, stood on tip toe and said "Thank you, Alistair. Thank you so much." She tried to give him a kiss on the cheek but he took her chin gently and bent forward and kissed her on the lips.

Penny didn't resist. His kiss was gentle. She opened her lips in response, her tongue eagerly seeking his. Their kiss grew in intensity.

Alistair's blood was coursing in a state of deep arousal. His desire to possess Penny grew strongly.

There was a seemingly desperate urgency in their bodies melding into each other. It was as if the realization that their time together was now limited that was driving them to seek the physical satisfaction both had craved for some time.

Alistair held Penny tightly as they kissed. She could feel his erection pressing against her thigh. Her kisses became more passionate.

Alistair lifted her and carried her up to the bedroom landing, into his room, and laid her gently on his bed.

He undid her trouser belt and began to ease her trousers off. She raised her hips to help him take off her trousers. As he unbuttoned her blouse, she tore at his shirt buttons. They both began to frantically undress.

Alistair gazed longingly at her body, from her upright breasts right down to her tight, slightly tanned stomach and light blonde pubic hair.

"Alistair," Penny whispered throatily. "I'm afraid. I haven't for a long time."

He silenced her with a soft kiss on her lips. "You don't have to do anything," he said.

Their initial physical congress was at first slow, even hesitant from Penny's female perspective on sex and love. Her five years of self-imposed celibacy weighed heavily on her conscience; she was worried that she was being unfaithful to Peter. She knew that it was foolish for her to feel so, but she nevertheless could not dispel her concern. Yet Alistair was gentle with her and he refrained from imposing his own masculine agenda. They both explored each other's body for the first time, gently caressing each other. Penny remained extremely nervous. To help relax her, Alistair just caressed her shoulders and arms and sometimes her hips. When Alistair moved his hips to press against Penny's stomach, he felt her stiffen. She turned and pressed her back against him. Alistair realized that Penny was not ready to conjoin in the full sexual act and he was sensible enough to not force the issue.

They eventually fell into a light sleep.

In the morning, Alistair was awake first. He looked down at the still sleeping Penny. His eyes now explored her face, without fear of her watching him. He carefully studied her soft lips, partly open and showing the edges of her perfect white teeth. He noted her long eye lashes and ear lobes that invited nibbling at. His look travelled down her body, noting her litheness and light summer tan.

He was suddenly aware that she was looking at him. He smiled at her. "Good morning, Alistair" she whispered and smiled warmly at him.

Penny moved on her back to be closer to Alistair. She was deeply appreciative at his kindly understanding of her nervousness the night before and the fact that he had not forced himself on her. She was now mentally ready to accept him. She spreads open her legs in clear invitation.

They kissed and they made love. Easy and gentle to begin with, then their movements became more frenetic as any initial hesitancy was dispelled and they each became familiar with the other's motions and responses.

Penny climaxed several times, screaming out on each occasion that she was about to do so.

Afterwards, Alistair made to move and get out of bed. He gave Penny a gentle smack on the bottom and said, "Come on, Mrs. Campbell. Shower, then breakfast."

She felt a twinge of guilt when she heard him call her Mrs. Campbell. For a few minutes she felt that she had been perhaps unfaithful to Peter. She had held back from any emotional entanglements for so very long and had clung on to her memory of Peter during that time. Now she felt certain Peter would not want her to end her life a dried up old prune. She was sure he would be pleased at her happiness. Yet the guilt persisted because, whilst Peter had been an adequate lover, he had been young and inexperienced and in no way did his lovemaking match up to the finesse of the older, more experienced Alistair. Penny had never had such wonderful orgasms with Peter as she had just had with Alistair. She resolved in her mind that Peter was of the past; a good, happy past but the past nonetheless.

Alistair was of the now. And she was so happy to have met him and shared moments with him.

As she showered, myriad thoughts went through Penny's mind. She was trying to reconcile her views on Alistair and to reach a balanced perspective. On one side of the coin, she found him to be kind and considerate, attentive, gentle and exciting. He was undoubtedly intelligent and held a good job. He was loyal to his country and his superiors. He was strong and brave. He was fun to be with. And he was a most wonderful lover. On the reverse side of the coin was her gut feeling that beneath that sophisticated panache, Alistair was perhaps not so much a knight in shining armour but more of a Machiavellian character, playing a very dangerous game. She laughed quietly when she recalled Peter's comments about her 'gut feelings' which invariably turned out to be correct. "We should hire you out to big corporations to suss out their problems. You always get the right answer – you and your gut." But in the final analysis, as far as her feelings for Alistair were concerned, she had to balance facts – as she'd already detailed in her mind – equated with imagination. She knew that facts had to win. There was no place for imaginary doubts when it came to trusting someone she believed she was beginning to fall in love with.

At one stage in the shower, Alistair touched her tummy and his hand slowly travelled downwards. She very gently moved his hand away and noted his erection. She said, "If you keep waving that beautiful weapon of yours about we could well end up with a dozen children. Now behave yourself, Alistair." She gave him a quick kiss on the cheek, stepped out of the shower and went into the body dryer cubicle. She stood at the door of the cubicle for a few moments and watched Alistair shampooing his hair. She admired his strong sculptured body and for one brief moment was tempted to return to the shower and rejoin him in united pleasures. But she quickly discarded the thought and activated the drying button. When thoroughly dried, she then skipped out of the drying cubicle and grabbed a towel which she wrapped around her body. She stood for a few moments watching Alistair in the shower then she turned towards her bedroom to get dressed.

At breakfast Alistair asked, "Are you on the pill?"

"Of course not, Alistair. I haven't had sex for five years until now. I wasn't looking for sex so I didn't go around armed with precautionary measures."

"Sorry," he apologised. "That was silly of me."

"Don't worry," she tried to comfort him with a gentle lie. "Peter and I tried to have a baby without much luck. He maintained there was nothing wrong with his potency and he suspected it was me. So I'm sure it will be OK."

"Didn't you have it properly, medically tested out?" Alistair said.

"We meant to do so. But then it was too late."

After breakfast, Penny said to Alistair that she was popping out to the newsagent and would be a minute or two at most. Alistair asked if she wanted him to accompany her, but she said it was not necessary.

Although she was fairly sure that Alistair had withdrawn each time he ejaculated, she thought it wise for her to invest in some Morning After pills just to be on the safe side. She intended to call in first at the local chemist, before visiting the newsagent's shop.

FORTY-NINE

"She goes out frequently," Green said.

"Shouldn't have to wait here for more than a couple of weeks," Thompson joked.

"You're a real fuckin' comedian," Jordan growled.

"There she is!" Green suddenly shouted, pointing at Penny as she walked out of the pedestrian gate of Knox Court.

Thompson made a move to get out of the van. Jordan snapped, "Stay here."

He drove his van quickly to park it on the same side and outside Knox Court.

They watched her enter the chemist.

"This is what we're going to do," Jordan said. "I'll move up behind the bitch. As she doesn't know me, she won't be suspicious. As she and I near the van, I want you two to have the back doors open. I'll then shove her in. OK? You got that?"

The other two men nodded.

"Now, we'll watch where she goes from the chemist," Jordan said.

They saw her leave the chemist and go in to the newsagent next door. She then came out and began walking back to the apartment block.

"Right, open the back doors," Jordan commanded as he stepped out of his van.

He walked up behind Penny. As they came to the van, Jordan went to push her in but before he could do so he slipped on some ice and fell on his back onto the pavement. Penny heard his shout of surprise. She stopped and turned to look at where he lay. At the same time, Green and Thompson leapt out of the van, grabbed hold of Penny and manhandled her into the rear of the van. Jordan got up, dusted off some of the snowflakes that had clung on to his coat, and jumped into the driving seat. He shot off towards Hounslow, where he had been told the garage was.

Penny sat on the van floor and looked up at the two men who sat on the side bench seat. She recognized Green immediately. She felt very frightened.

"Hello, dahlin," Green said with a wide grin. "Nice to see you again."

"What the hell do you want?" Penny snarled. "Why don't you stop bothering me?"

"Feisty, isn't she?" Thompson commented.

"A real little bruiser," Green said.

No more words were said, and the three passengers at the back of the van as the van made its way to Hounslow. At one stage, the van stopped, Green got out and went to sit in the front passenger seat to direct Jordan to the garage location. It was a long alleyway with garages on either side. Green went up to one of them. He took a key out of his pocket and unlocked the grey shabby door. Jordan drove in. Green followed. Thompson got out of the van. He took with him a couple of kitchen knives which he placed on a small table which was pushed up alongside one of the walls.

"What's those for?" Jordan asked.

"To slash her throat, of course," Thompson said with a smirk.

"Are you fucking thick or what? Knifing someone produces blood all over the bleeding place. Some of it gets sprayed on to your clothes or your shoes. An' if the rozzers get in on the act and trace us, they use DNA and soon establish who did the killing." Jordan walked around in exasperated circles. "Where d'you find this nerd, Phil?" he asked.

Green shrugged.

Jordan walked up to Thompson and poked him in the chest as he spoke to him. "Why d'you think I wanted us to have a tin bath in here? To give you a good bleedin' wash?"

Thompson shrugged and looked over at Green. "Not sure what you wanted it for," he said.

"To drown the bitch, that's what for."

"Ay, that's bloody great," Green cried out. "Bloody fantastic."

Jordan started looking around the garage. He noticed the large square water cistern container in the corner. "Looks good," he remarked as he walked over to it. He stopped and looked inside it.

"Did you check this, Phil, when you rented this dump?"

"Nah. Bloke was in a hurry and it looked alright."

"Looked alright? Full of bleedin' 'oles in bottom? This bugger wouldn't hold a cup full of piss without it leaking out. This is fuckin' useless."

The three men stood around saying nothing. Finally, Jordan said. "Right. Get the bitch out here."

Thompson dragged Penny out of the van.

"Get her clothes off but leave on her bra and pants. An' take her shoes off. Chuck 'em all in the van," Jordan said as he went to the van. He took out from the back a length of rope. "We're going to 'ave to leave you 'ere for a short while, so we'll tie you to that bar until we return."

Penny stood shivering in her underwear. "It's mid-winter. I'll freeze to death like this. Can I have my coat on?" she asked.

"OK, give it her," Jordan instructed Thompson.

Penny put on her coat when she suddenly remembered the yellow button, the tracer alarm that Alistair had given her. She put her hands in the pockets as if to warm them. She felt the button. She quickly squeezed it several times. She prayed it would work as Alistair had said.

"Right," Jordan commanded. "Let's have your hands out and put 'em up like you was facing a gun."

Penny did as ordered. Jordan tied the rope around both her wrists. He then threw the other end of the rope upwards and over the steel bar that run along the roof breadth. He retrieved the loose rope end and tied that around Penny's wrists. Penny now stood with both arms raised and suspended from the rope which lay over the steel roof bar. Jordan then took out from his pocket a dirty handkerchief which he tied across Penny's mouth.

"That'll keep 'er quiet until we return," he said.

"Where we goin'?" Thompson asked.

"To buy a bleedin' tin bath, that's where. I saw a merchant's shop just further down. They should 'ave one."

"Should we leave her here alone?" Green asked.

"She's goin' nowhere with no clothes. An' unless the merchant's got some strong lads around, it's going to take three of us to carry a tin bath large enough to fill to the top with water and drown the bitch."

The three men drove out of the garage and locked the door after them.

FIFTY

At Knox Court, in the garage basement, the tracer box that Alistair had fixed in his car by connecting to the cigarette lighter button automatically went on alert as soon as it received the signal from Penny's button call. A red light flashed on and off and the screen flickered into life. It gradually produced a street outline and in one corner, a flashing green light indicated the location of Penny's yellow button.

Unfortunately, Alistair was not aware of the action taking place in his car as he was heavily absorbed in reading the morning newspaper in his flat.

FIFTY-ONE

Penny tried desperately to free herself but it was proving to be quite impossible. The rope was tightly tied and her arms were beginning to ache. She rolled her shoulders so as to get her circulation moving and that somehow eased her discomfort. She was becoming increasingly terrified at the men's plan to drown her. She could not envisage a worse death. By the time the men returned half an hour later, her head had slumped to her chest and she was quietly weeping from the intense pain in her upraised arms and her fear of being drowned.

"Sorry, we're late, dahlin'," Green said. "but we got us all a coffee. Hope you like regular with milk, 'cos that's what we got you. And no sugar."

Jordan untied Penny's arms and rubbed them vigorously to help her circulation, whilst the other two men put the newly purchased tin bath under the tap and began to fill it.

"What are you going to do to me?" Penny asked quietly.

"Fuck you," Thompson sniggered.

"Nah, bitch. There'll be none of that. We're going to drown you," Jordan said, handing to her her carton of coffee. She pulled off the lid top and took a sip. It was bitter but hot, which was a comfort. For one second she considered splashing her hot coffee into Jordan's face but realized that it would achieve nothing. She wrapped her coat around her and sat on the floor. His threat of drowning her filled her with terror, so much so that she could not stop herself from urinating. She felt the warm flow trickle down her leg and gather in a small pool at her feet.

"It's takin' bleedin' ages to fill," Thompson complained.

"It's bleedin' big, that's why," Jordan snapped back at him.

"Ay!" Thompson exclaimed and laughed out loud. "She's pissing 'erself."

"You would too, if you knew you was goin' to be drowned," Jordan snapped back at him.

FIFTY-TWO

Alistair suddenly realized that Penny had been out for a long time. The newsagent was no more than a five minute walk away. He put down his newspaper and looked at his watch. Penny had been gone for nearly an hour.

Now anxious, Alistair went downstairs. He saw Mac. "'Morning, Mac. Have you seen Mrs. Campbell this morning?"

"She went out a while ago, sir. Everything alright, sir?"

"I'm not sure, Mac. I think I'd best drive around and see if I can find her." With that, Alistair took the elevator down to the garage. He walked up to his car, flicking his automatic door opener. He slid into his car seat and immediately saw the tracer flashing at him. He leaned forward and studied the small map screen. It indicated Penny's location by a small flashing red light as being in Hounslow.

"Bloody hell!" Alistair swore and immediately put the car into gear. He drove out of Knox Court like a maniac. Fortunately, traffic was light and so Alistair made good progress. But he was very worried as the recoded data on the tracer indicated Penny's button having been activated well over one hour ago. He prayed he would not be too late to save her from whatever danger she was in.

FIFTY-THREE

"Bath is full now," Green called out.

Jordan ordered Penny to stand up. "Right, let's 'ave your coat off," he ordered.

"Tell 'er to get stripped," Green called out. "You can't 'ave a bath all dressed up, like with bra and pants."

Jordan raised his eyes heavenwards. "We'll keep the boy 'appy, bitch," he said. "Take the bra and pants off."

Penny hesitated.

"Either you take 'em off or I tear 'em off," Jordan snarled.

Penny stripped.

Green moved towards where she and Jordan stood. He eyed Penny's naked form with undisguised gratification, recalling the time he could have enjoyed her fully until her thuggish rugby-playing boyfriend turned up. "Can't we give 'er a poke before we put 'er in the bath?" he pleaded.

"Your job instructions was to get rid of the bitch," Jordan said. "We're not going to fart around with you wanting a screw and then old daft bugger over there - "he nodded towards Thompson, "wanting his turn. By the time you two 'ave finished we'd 'ave wasted five minutes."

"Ay," Green said angrily. "I'd give 'er a good hours screw. Five minutes? Yeah, that may apply to Alan."

"You know what I mean," Jordan said. "No. Put 'er in the bath. If you're that desperate for a screw I can fix you up with another bitch after we've finished this job."

They forced Penny to step into the tin bath. She screamed loudly. "No! , no! Please, no! Please! , please!"

"Listen bitch, quit farting about and lie down in that bath," Jordan ordered.

"I... I can't!" Penny protested. She struggled violently. "Please don't! Please, no, no, no, no!"

"Push the bitch in," Jordan instructed Green and Thompson.

The men went to her and took hold of her arms but she fought them off. "I ... I can't! No! No! No!" she screamed. She kept kicking out and the men had difficulty keeping hold of her.

"Listen 'ere," Jordan snarled. "You either lie down in that water by yourself or I can punch your lights out and you'll be unconscious and lyin' in the water. What's it to be, bitch?"

Jordan nodded to the two men. They grabbed hold of her again and pushed her down in the bath so she sat in the water that reached her breasts. She screamed from the shock. Her screams reverberated within the small garage.

"Shut the fuck up!" Jordan shouted at Penny. "You," Jordan pointed at Thompson. "Hold 'er down by the 'ead till she drowns."

Thompson rolled up the sleeves of his shirt and put his hands on Penny's head. She struggled wildly, her legs kicking water all over Thompson and the floor.

FIFTY-FOUR

At Hammersmith, Alistair decided to take the Alice motorway. He knew he could go much faster on the motorway. At times his speedometer registered his speed as 150 mph. He shot past other traffic whose much slower speeds were regulated by Central Computer. He turned off at Junction 3 along Parkway and on to the A306 Bath Road towards Hounslow West. He was driving fast on the A306 when he heard the police car siren. It caught up with him at a junction and the driver waved him to stop. Alistair ignored the request, shot past the police panda and careered on. The Panda car could not compete with the performance of Alistair's McLaren.

The small tracker screen showed Alistair's car as a pulsing arrow moving along a broad grey line. Alistair now followed the route indicated by the tracker. The minor side roads were indicated by thin grey lines. He drove down an alleyway and as he did so he heard a woman's loud screams coming from one of the garages.

Just then, the police car pulled up behind Alistair. Two policemen got out and walked determinedly towards him.

"Right," one of them said. "I don't know how you circumvented Centre Computer speed control but we clocked you doing over 150 miles an hour on the motorway and being well in excess of ..."

"D'you hear those screams?" Alistair shouted. "There's someone being hurt in that garage. They work for the Government. As do I." Alistair produced his M15 identification. "Help me break down this door."

The policemen looked at the identification card, then turned towards the garage door behind which Penny' screams had now ended.

"We'll do this, sir," one of the policemen said as he and his partner rushed at the garage door. Their sturdy shoulders shattered the cheap wood.

Alistair quickly took in the scene. Three men stood there with opened mouthed surprise. There was no sign of Penny. Alistair rushed in, followed by the policemen. "Arrest those men," Alistair ordered. Jordan, Green and Thompson were too surprised to fight against the policemen. They were quickly cuffed.

Alistair looked around frantically for some sign of Penny. Then he saw the tin bath.

"You're too late, mate," Jordan said with a smirk. "The bitch is drowned."

Alistair looked in the bath and saw Penny lying at the bottom, her unseeing eyes open. Small bubbles of air trickled from her partly opened mouth.

FIFTY-FIVE

"Call an ambulance quickly," Alistair shouted at the policemen.

Alistair pulled Penny out of the water and began to give her CPR. There was no response from her. "Pass me that coat," he ordered, pointing at Penny's coat. One of the policemen brought it to him. He covered Penny's naked body with it.

He gave her mouth to mouth and pressed down on her chest, but she still did not respond. Within a few minutes, they heard the siren of an approaching ambulance.

Alistair worked on trying to resuscitate Penny. He was suddenly aware of a pair of green trouser legs next to him. He looked up. He saw a middle-aged man of strong and sturdy build and a kind face looking down at him. "We'll take over from here, sir," he said gently, moving Alistair aside and kneeling besides Penny. He then asked, "For about how long was she in the water?"

"You mean like this? We heard her screams and burst in about five minutes ago."

The ambulance attendant nodded.

Alistair stood up. He noticed that the ambulance attendant's companion was a young woman who smiled at him. Alistair went up to the two policemen. "You can take these men in and charge them with kidnap and attempted murder, but they will be questioned by officers from MI5 in due course. These men are not to contact any solicitor or anyone else until MI5 officers arrive at your station. Where are you based? Hounslow?"

One of the policemen nodded. "Yes. That's right, sir."

"I'll need your names and number for the record. You are…?" Alistair asked the policeman who had just answered him.

"P.C. Fisher, 544."

"And you…?" to the other policeman.

"P.C. Chatwin. Number 573, sir."

Alistair typed into his EID the relevant details. He then called MI5 on his mobile and spoke to someone, instructing them to have some officers go to Hounslow police station to interview three suspects. He said he would call back shortly with full details of the charges.

He heard a coughing sound behind him. He whipped round to see Penny sitting sideways and being supported by the ambulance attendant. She had spewed up a quantity of water and frothy pink sputum was around her mouth. She was coughing and gasping for breath but she was alive.

The ambulance attendant gave her an oxygen mask. The girl assistant had prepared some injections and the man gave her intravenous fluids.

"OK, Sonia," he said to his colleague. "Stretcher and blankets love. We'll take her to West Mid."

The girl ambulance attendant had already prepared the stretcher and blankets and moved them to where Penny sat.

"Has she any clothes here, sir?" the girl asked Alistair.

Alistair turned to the three arrested men. "Where did you put her clothes?" he demanded.

None replied immediately. When Alistair stepped forward with a clenched fist, Thompson said quickly, "They're in the van."

The ambulance girl dashed to the van. She looked in and emerged holding Penny's clothes. "Got 'em!" she called out.

Alistair waited until the police and ambulance had left. He was shaking from pent up tension. He got into his car and drove towards West Middlesex Hospital where he had heard the ambulance people say they were taking Penny.

FIFTY-SIX

Several hundred Rathings had been transported to Scotland. Their minders noted the pleasure shown by the clones. The dark, damp caves provided a much more pleasant atmosphere to the Rathings – much more so than the clean, antiseptic smell of the laboratory hospital at Gretorex Hall.

The human minders set about instructing the Rathings which parts of the cave network were designated as sleeping areas, which were for the provision of latrines, and which were for consumption of food. Whilst the humans and Rathings got down to sorting out bedding, furnishings and other complementary placements, two Rathings were instructed to stand at the cave entrance and act as guards. They were told that under no circumstances were any strangers to be permitted to enter, although they were advised that such a visit would be highly unlikely. The human minders knew full well that if anyone did venture to this area they would be dealt with in the cruelest way; that was the Rathing's way.

The two Rathings stood silently in the shadows of the cave entrance and listened to the sounds coming from just below the precipice. It was obvious that there was more than one person climbing towards the caves. After a short time, one head peeped over the escarpment. The man's eyes swivelled around, surveying the scene. "Seems all clear," he whispered and shortly afterwards another man's head poked its way above the cliff edge. Two men now hauled themselves onto the plateau and sat there, with their feet dangling over the edge, in order to regain their breath. "That was a bloody tough climb, Jack," one man gasped. "Too fucking right, Sam," Jack replied.

The Rathings now stepped out of the shadows. "Good evening," one of them said in a deep, rough voice.

The two men were startled. Both suddenly jumped to their feet.

"May we ask what you are doing trespassing here?" a Rathing asked.

"Trespassing?" the man called Jack pretended to be surprised at the allegation of trespass. "We weren't aware this was a prohibited area. If it is, we're sorry to have troubled you."

"Yes, yes," Sam echoed. "Very sorry. We'll make our way down immediately."

"There is no need for that," one of the Rathings said. He turned to Sam and told him to sit down. "There," he pointed. "Against the rock face."

Meanwhile the other Rathing had taken hold of Jack and pushed him against another part of the rock face. He towered over the man. With his left hand only, the Rathing pinned jack's arms above his head. He then pulled down his trousers with his other hand and grabbed hold of Jack's genitals. He gripped them hard and then, using his massive strength, he tore off the penis and testicles and tossed them over the cliff edge. Jack's screams resounded around the hills. The Rathing then quickly drew a short sword from his waistband. He stuck the point savagely into Jack's groin and in one swift movement cut him open to his breastbone. He let go of Jack's arms and Jack fell to the ground. The Rathing then quickly grabbed both sides of the man's body and pulled them apart. Jack's innards spilled onto the ground. Jack's agonized screams were unbearable to hear and Sam vomited violently from terror and shock. The Rathing bent over Jack, took hold of his head with both hands and then twisted it a couple of times before wrenching it off and throwing it into the cave entrance. Sam watched in horror as Jack's body and legs contorted in his death throes. Sam knew it would now be his turn to undergo such unmitigated torture. Rather than experience the same horrible death as that of his friend, Sam did not hesitate to draw the small dirk he carried in his waistband and quickly draw it across his throat. He cut hard and deep and watched the blood spurt out in a long sweeping arc from his slashed windpipe. The Rathing who had ordered him to sit now moved towards him. He bent over the dying Sam who was desperately fighting for breath. "You did not need to do that to yourself. We planned to return you to your people to tell them what you had just witnessed and warn them not to come here. You have killed yourself needlessly."

Both Rathings walked up to each other. They congratulated themselves by a high five hand smack, this action being copied from what they had witnessed their human trainers sometimes doing at the end of a successful test.

FIFTY-SEVEN

Clarence Jarvis had a set routine each morning when he arrived at his office. After he had hanged up his hat, coat and scarf he went to the cupboard in his office and took out a small white kettle, a jar of Espresso ground coffee and a small white toaster. He opened his tiny fridge and took out a packet of French semi-salted butter (usually bought from Harrods or Fortnum and Mason) and two slices of bread from the package of sliced bread in the fridge.

After he had filled the kettle with fresh water and put it on the boil, he spooned one teaspoon of coffee grounds into his cup. Only after he'd poured the water over his coffee grounds and flicked in one sweetener, did he switch on the toaster; he liked his bread very lightly toasted. When done, he spread butter generously on the hot toast and cut each slice diagonally in half. He then placed the four half slices of buttered toast on a small plate and took them and his coffee over to his desk. This was his breakfast each weekday morning. He settled back in his chair and read the Financial Times whilst he breakfasted.

When he had finished, he put the plate and knife on a side table for his secretary to take away and wash when she arrived.

He got up to make himself a further cup of coffee. It had snowed overnight and he looked out of his window at the dull, metal grey sky that hung low over the city like a circus canvas that sagged under the pressure of last night's heavy fall of snow. It had started to snow again, soft flurries of gentle tears falling from the sad-looking grey sky.

Clarence Jarvis had been fast coming to the conclusion that both Green and Thompson were totally inept and that it was probably time he recruited another two people, although in view of what had taken place at the Gretorex Hall meeting, it was more than likely that he would not instigate any further action against the young female detective.

The intercom on Jarvis's desk bleeped. He pushed the switch down. "Yes?"

"Ground floor reception here, sir. I have two gentlemen from Scotland Yard to see you."

"I don't recall having any appointments with the police."

"I don't think an appointment is necessary for this visit, sir. They are quite insistent on seeing you."

Jarvis sighed. "Very well. Send them up."

He made himself his other cup of coffee. He thought the visit was probably to discuss the bank security or something equally unimportant, but was surprised that they were from Scotland Yard. He would be even more surprised when he discovered that they had with them an arrest warrant.

Further visits by other police officers with arrest warrants were made to all those named by Alistair Pellow in his report.

FIFTY-EIGHT

The British Chancellor greeted the American President on the phone and explained the predicament in which the British found themselves.

"Well, I'll be jiggered," the President said on hearing that some Rathings had survived the toxin spread. "I can see your problem, Oskar. I'll talk to the appropriate people here and we will send over some aircraft laden with DTX. We'll saturate the whole goddamn area until the critters turn their tootsies up to heaven. Don't worry, Oskar. It's my pleasure to help you guys out."

"Thank you, Fernando. Your assistance is greatly appreciated," Oskar Brabanti, the British Chancellor replied.

"You just get one of your guys to send over to us the specific areas you want saturated with DTX and we'll take it from there."

"Much obliged, old man. I am really most grateful to you. Goodbye, Fernando" The Chancellor closed the connection and sat back with a satisfied smile.

Everything was going swimmingly well, he decided.

FIFTY-NINE

Shortly after the Chancellor had finished his call to the President of the Americas he issued instructions for the head of MI5 to see him immediately.

Sir Anthony Wollaston now stood in front of Oskar Brabanti in the Chancellor's vast office. Sir Anthony wore his black uniform and black jack boots, which was obligatory dress code when in the presence of the Chancellor. All senior Ministers and heads of departments kept in their office uniform tunics and trousers and jack boots in case they were summoned to see the Chancellor. To visit the Chancellor in any other form of dress was a sure certificate to losing one's job.

The Chancellor sat back in his seat. His little dark eyes – almost black in the soft lighting – studied the head of MI5 and eventually a smile touched his pinched lips. "Your department has done well, Wollaston in apprehending this group of dissidents. I have just conversed with the President of the Americas who has promised to dispatch aircraft loaded with DTX. I am assigning you to contact him as soon as possible with details of the locations where it is necessary for saturation bombardment to take place.

"All the men arrested are to be formally charges with treason and summarily shot. This is to take place within forty eight hours – no later. Is that understood?"

Sir Anthony nodded. "Yes, Chancellor." He then looked over the Chancellor's head, thus avoiding the beady eyes that bore into him, and said, "I should like to mention again that amongst the prisoners is their leader, Sir William Henderson, one of our most senior Ministers. Is there anything specific you wish done in his case?"

Oskar Brabanti quickly rose and walked round his desk to stand opposite the head of MI5. Brabanti was a small, slight man and the top of his head barely reached Sir Anthony's chin. "Wollaston, you surprise me," Brabanti rebuked his officer. "Of course there is something specific in his case. That man's treasonable action demands more than a simple death." The Chancellor's voice now screamed at Sir Anthony. "He betrayed me, his Leader! I shall not tolerate such insolence. I want him to suffer before his life is extinguished." Spittle flew out of Brabanti's thin mouth.

"I see, sir," Sir Anthony said, although he could not see what worse could be done to Sir William other than receiving several bullets.

"You will instruct the officer of the execution squad that none of his men are to aim at Henderson's heart or vital organs. Tell the officer that my instructions are to firstly shoot at that man's legs and shoulders. They are to leave him writhing on the floor in pain for at least ten minutes. They will next shoot off his toes and the officer in charge is to use a blade and cut off his ears and his nose. Henderson is again to be left in agony for another ten minutes. The execution squad may then stand him up and dispatch him with a volley of deadly, fatal fire. Is that understood, Wollaston?"

"It is, Chancellor. You are quite sure you want such a gruesome form of execution, Chancellor?"

"Are you questioning my orders?" Brabanti screamed and stormed around the room, with his arms whirling about him in frenzied agitation like a dervish.

"No, sir. I just wished to be sure I got it right."

"Do as I have commanded. Is that clear?

"Unquestionably."

"Good. Then see to it. That is all."

Sir Anthony Wollaston saluted, turned smartly and marched out of the Chancellor's office.

SIXTY

In his office, Sir William answered his internal phone and spoke to his secretary who had buzzed through to him. "Put him through," he instructed.

"'Morning, Carlton. This is a pleasant surprise," he greeted his caller cheerfully. He listened, his expression growing more serious by the second. "Yes, Carlton, you will obviously have to resign, I'm afraid. Well, thank you for calling and good luck, Carlton."

Sir William put the phone down.

At Scotland Yard, Assistant Chief Constable Carlton Padstone sat quietly at his desk after having spoken with Sir William. He picked up the photograph of his wife in its silver frame and kissed it. He then unlocked and pulled open the bottom drawer of his desk. He brought out his old service revolver. He opened his mouth. He carefully placed the muzzle against his palette. He closed his eyes, held his wife's picture with his other hand against his chest and whispered "Goodbye, darling. I love you." He then gently squeezed the trigger.

*****

Miss Pilgrim gave a brief knock on his door and entered. Her usual calm composure was replaced by one of extreme agitation. "Sir William," she blurted out. "There are two policemen from Scotland Yard out there with an arrest warrant for you. They insist on being admitted immediately."

Sir William got up from his chair and smiled at his secretary. "Please do not concern yourself, Miss Pilgrim. If you would be good enough to show them in I'd be most grateful."

Sir William picked up his phone and keyed in a number. When it was answered, Sir William said "This is Blue Eyes. There is a major problem. We must try and meet."

He then bent down over his desk and began aligning the various items in an orderly fashion whilst waiting for the arrival of the police officers.

SIXTY-ONE

When Penny and Alistair had breakfasted and were drinking their umpteenth cups of coffee, Alistair put down his cup and looked seriously at Penny.

"Penny, I must talk with you."

"I thought that's what we've been doing all this time over our breakfast," she laughed.

"No. This is more serious. It's about the arrests yesterday."

"Oh, you mean those bad men who wanted to bring the Government down. Well, they'll all get thirty years jail and probably serve ten. Isn't that the way things work out in law?"

Alistair shook his head. "No, they won't get thirty year jail terms."

"What? You mean less?"

"They committed a treasonable act. When this government assumed power after the Rathing period, one of the first Acts they introduced was the death penalty for a number of misdemenours. What this group of men embarked on was a treasonous act, and treason is punishable by death."

"Gosh! You mean they'll kill them?"

"They'll be sentenced to death by firing squad."

"Shot!?" Penny exclaimed.

"I'm afraid so."

"Oh Golly!"

"I want to ask you how fond you are of your uncle William."

"What a strange question. Of course I am fond of him. He is after all my uncle."

"Well, I think you should prepare yourself for some bad news. Your uncle is actually the leader of this group of dissidents. He and all of them are held in prison at this very moment."

"What!?" Penny exclaimed.

"I'm afraid so."

"No! There must be a mistake about this? Uncle William was in the Government. He was a Minister. How could he be accused of being against himself? Is he being found guilty because this treasonous act took place on his watch, you know, I mean because he is Minister of Internal Affairs and this is an internal affair, he is being painted with the same brush?"

"I'm afraid not, Penny. Your uncle led this group. And the case against him is even stronger as he is accused of ordering the death of two people, your Scottish detective lady friend and Kilroy, the American newspaper man. He is also held responsible for ordering the deaths of those people who first discovered the Rathings – three policemen, a Scottish parliamentarian, three rock climbers and the disappearance of about twelve members of the search and rescue team involved in the discovery. He is also accused of abusing his position by using the services of Special Branch officers to question certain people. All in all, I'm afraid the evidence is really stacked up against your uncle. I am really sorry, Penny.

"Believe me. I worked in your uncle's office. I did so for many years before he felt he could trust me and over time he eventually introduced me into the group of dissidents. To be on the safe side, I used the first part of my hyphenated surname when I signed up. I am sorry to say that I was duplicitous in my dealings with Sir William. He trusted me and I betrayed him."

Penny took hold of Alistair's hand. "No, Alistair. You did not betray my uncle. I can understand how you must feel but if what you say is right, and I believe you, then my uncle betrayed himself and he betrayed all of us. You were only doing your job. An honorable job. But I hate the thought of Uncle William being shot. I must see him. Can I do so?"

"I can arrange it with my contacts," Alistair said.

Penny leant over and kissed his cheek. "Thank you, darling." She then asked, "Have you seen my uncle at all since his imprisonment?"

Alistair nodded. "Briefly on one earlier occasion."

"How is her? How did you find him?"

"He is bearing up very well. I shall arrange for you to see your uncle."

Alistair spoke to his boss at MI5 who put the wheels in motion and Penny, accompanied by Alistair, was permitted to see her uncle in prison. She entered the interview room, accompanied by a prison guard and saw her uncle sitting at a table waiting for her. He stood up when she entered. Ever the gentleman, she thought, even in these dire circumstances. The guard stationed himself by the door.

Penny sat opposite her uncle. "Hello, Uncle," she said quietly.

He smiled at her. "Hello Penelope. I'm sorry. Penny. How are you?"

"Oh, uncle. More to the point is how you are?"

"As well as can be expected. They're treating me exceedingly well in here. Most polite. If I wasn't obliged to wear this outfit, well, I could almost be in my office in Whitehall."

Penny noted his prison uniform which is normally far from flattering but which her uncle wore with aplomb.

"You look quite fetching in that," she said to lighten the mood.

"Flattery and deception never sit well together, Penelope," her uncle said sternly. "Look my dear," Uncle William continued. "I don't think they're going to give us much time, so I'd like to tell you what I've organized."

"Yes, uncle."

"As you know, I have no immediate family so I have given great consideration as to what I should do with my not inconsiderable assets on my death. Apart from my house in Eaton Place in London there's my weekend retreat in Rye and a cottage in Cornwall. I also have sizeable stocks and shares, so all told we're probably talking about close on nine million pounds. I am leaving them all to you."

"Oh, Uncle! You can't! exclaimed Penny.

"I beg your pardon? You are hardly in a position to tell me what I can or what I cannot do, Penelope."

"Uncle, I didn't mean it like that. I meant that you, you just can't."

"Penelope. I am going to be shot, possibly tomorrow or the day after."

Penny burst into tears. "Oh, Uncle," she sobbed gently.

"Hush there, my dear. Death does not unduly worry me. In fact, I rather imagine I will find it most welcome – certainly the finalization of my existence on this plane will remove me from the daily coruscations of life. I am in many ways quite looking forward to my departure. So my final gesture to you is to give you my Estate. Fortunately this dictatorship that we live under have not seen fit to sequester my assets. So I am at liberty to give them to whomsoever I want."

"Uncle. I can't think of you being shot. It feels terrible."

Sir William patted her hand. "Yes, yes," he said trying hard not to sound irritable. "Now, tell me. I understand that Pellow brought you here. Is he waiting for you outside this room?"

Penny Nodded.

Sir William turned to the guard standing at the door. "Guard!" he called out. The man stepped forward. "Yes, Sir William?"

"George, outside this room is a young man who accompanied my niece here. I should be most grateful if you allowed him entry as I wish to speak with him."

"Yes, certainly sir," the guard called George said and walked to the door.

Penny was struck by the courtesy being shown to her uncle, but she was not surprised. Uncle William had always commanded respect.

The door opened and Alistair and the guard entered. The guard returned to his watch by the door. Alistair walked to the table. "Good day to you, Sir William," he said politely.

"Pellow," Sir William acknowledged. "I have something to ask of you."

"Yes, sir?"

"Oh, do sit down on that extra chair, Pellow. You make the place look untidy standing there."

Alistair smiled and sat down next to Penny and opposite Sir William.

"I'm sorry about this entire business sir," Alistair said.

"Nonsense! You were only doing your job. I hold no grudge against you, Pellow."

"Thank you, sir."

"Now look here. I can't instruct you on this – in fact I can't do so on anything now. Therefore take this as a request."

"Of course, sir."

"I understand that I face execution within the next few days. I have left in my will all my assets to young Penelope here. I would ask that you look after her. At least until either of you get fed up with the other, because there is no guarantee of any long term continuation in anything. Until that time, help her use her new assets sensibly," He then looked at Penny. "You can safely rely on young Pellow here. I know he cares for you."

"Thank you, uncle," Penny said and started to weep silently again.

"Listen, Penelope. Please stop crying," Sir William said gently. "When I heard that you asked to see me, I made a special request to the Warden, which he granted." Sir William waved the guard over. "George. Do you have the bottle I ordered suitably chilled?"

The guard nodded. "Yes, Sir William."

"Then be a good chap and kindly bring it in. I thought it would be pleasant for us to share a last drink together. And especially nice that you are also here, Pellow to share the moment," Penny's uncle said when the guard had gone out of the cell. Sir William leaned back in his chair. "The human psyche is very strange, you know," he said, staring up at the ceiling. "One's train of thought alters radically depending on the circumstances prevailing at the time. Take now, for instance. As I said to you before, Penelope, dying does not frighten me. Yet when I was younger, the representative of death was some far distant shadowy image. Because life was so precious to me then, I believed that the soul could not die, that it would continue to exist through the media of reincarnation; it would be the whole basis of evolutionary development. Surely God would not create souls and grant them such an infinitesimally short life span? No. I firmly believed that when one died, one's soul was directed to another plane to await a rebirth in due time.

"Do you know that there are sects who believe that the soul is a light? And when it leaves its earthly body, it ascends into the heavens and is immortalized as a star. They maintain that the stars in this galaxy of ours, and in the hundreds of other galaxies that abound, are all departed souls waiting for their allotted time to be reincarnated." Sir William shrugged and laughed. "Well, if such pipe dreams help them resolutely face their impending end, then why should we pooh pooh the idea? But I do not believe that that is so. In fact, I am firmly of the opinion that death happens as soon as you step into the dark portal to oblivion; a long black as sin tunnel. Then, the soul is no more. The light goes out. A black curtain descends," here, Sir William chopped down hard on the table with the side of his open hand. "And there is no more. No feeling, no awareness, nothing. Just blackness. A complete and utter void. So that is why I have no fear of death, my dears. Because there is absolutely nothing there to fear. And even if there were, I would be unaware of its presence because I would no longer exist."

The guard returned bearing a tray with a bottle of champagne and three glasses.

"Ah, Dom Perignon, as I asked. Nicely chilled, George?"

The guard smiled and nodded. "Yes, sir. Just as you ordered."

Sir William busied himself opening the bottle. He poured champagne into the glasses. "Only three, George? Are you not joining us in a toast?"

"I don't think that the Governor would be happy to learn I've been slurping champers with the likes of you honorable people."

"Then, take this bottle – there's plenty of champagne left – and enjoy it with your friends. And if you feel so inclined, perhaps raise a farewell toast to me."

The guard took the bottle, thanked Sir William, and went and stood by the cell door.

Sir William raised his glass. As did Penny and Alistair. "To a life well led, and a death well deserved and welcomed," he said.

Penny whispered, "To you, Uncle," and Alistair mumbled, "To you, Sir William."

Sir William gave Penny one of his rare smiles. "Penelope. I'm sorry, Penny. Would you possibly allow me to have a quiet word with young Pellow here without your presence? If you do not mind?"

"Of course not, uncle. Shall I wait outside?"

"If you will. We won't be long."

After Penny had left, Sir William leaned across to Alistair and whispered, "Have you managed to bring what I asked?"

Alistair nodded. "Yes, Sir William. There are two in a small match box in my pocket."

"Hide the box in your hand and pass it to me when we shake goodbye."

Alistair bent down as if to tie his shoe lace. He whispered, "Are you quite sure you want to do this?"

Sir William smiled and whispered back. "Most definitely. I know the Chancellor. He will want to gain the greatest possible satisfaction in seeing me suffer. He is undoubtedly of the opinion that my involvement in planning to overthrow him and his regime is a personal slight against him - a kick in the teeth. He will want me to pay for my perfidious action, and to pay for it in a painful way. His sadistic tendencies are legion amongst his peers. I am quite sure that he has planned some very cruel treatment for me at the time of my

282

execution. As I said before, I do not fear death. Yet part of me feels that what I intend to do might well be regarded as somewhat cowardly. But I am averse to enduring torture so as to satisfy the whims of that monster of a Chancellor. And by taking this action, I shall thoroughly spoil our Glorious Leader's intended satisfactory fun. It will be my final kick in his teeth.

"I shall now prepare to leave you. Pass me the box as we shake hands. And Alistair? I am most grateful to you. Thank you."

Alistair was aware that Sir William had addressed him by his first name; something he had never done before. Alistair was pleased at this.

As the two men shook hands in a farewell gesture, Alistair held in his right hand the small match box. Sir William palmed it into his hand. He then casually put the box into his prison tunic pocket. He nodded to the guard who opened the door to permit Sir William to sweep out.

Sir William intended taking the two pea-sized potassium cyanide pills contained in the box with his hot cup of cocoa that night.

SIXTY-TWO

In the car on the way back to Pimlico Penny said. "Uncle William didn't seem to mind at all that you betrayed him."

Alistair thumped the steering wheel, clearly upset and angry at Penny's words. "I did not betray your uncle. I did my job to protect the status quo of the country and avoid the most horrendous repercussions if the Rathings were let loose by my uncle and his misguided friends."

"I'm sorry, Alistair. I didn't mean that unkindly."

"It still hurts to hear me accused of such underhand action."

Penny reached over and caressed Alistair's hand. "I know you did what you believed is best and I do agree with what you did, no matter how painful it is for me to say that."

Alistair just uttered the word"Hmm," and continued to concentrate on his driving.

"What did uncle want to talk to you without my being there?"

"Oh, he urged me to look after you and make sure that you came to no harm."

"That was so sweet of him. D'you know that uncle's left me as his sole beneficiary? It's a real fortune."

"I'm pleased for you," Alistair said. He even managed a smile.

"Alistair?" Penny said.

"Yep."

"You said something about having a hyphenated name. What is your full name?"

"I never use it, but I did the first part when I got recruited into that group."

"So what is it?"

"It's Featherstonehaugh-Pellow."

"Gosh! That's a mouthful."

"Thank you. I've heard it described in less flattering terms."

After a while Penny said, "Alistair. I've always wondered why Featherstonehaugh – spelt FEATHERSTONEHAUGH - is pronounced Fanshaw. I guess as you hold that name, you'd know."

"I don't, Penny. It's an English peculiarity which has been in force for zillions of years. I really don't know why."

"Is it because people with that name are usually very upper class and they like to feel different from the hoi polloi? Oh, I don't mean your family," Penny added quickly, "because as you said, it's been pronounced that way for zillions of years."

"I guess you might be right," Alistair acknowledged. "But I really don't know."

"As I'm a very wealthy girl now, may I treat us to a dinner somewhere tonight? I think I'll be very miserable sitting in your flat, thinking about Uncle William. It will take my mind off his predicament."

"You're not fabulously wealthy yet. But dinner somewhere special would be nice."

"Any ideas?" Penny asked.

"How about Quanticos?" Alistair said with a grin.

"Quanticos? Gosh, Alistair. I thought you just said I'm not fabulously wealthy yet. You need to own umpteen oil wells to eat there."

"I'm buying – and I don't own any oil wells."

"That would be fabulous, Alistair. It would take us out of ourselves."

"Good, that's settled then. I'll make a reservation when we get home."

"Thank you, Mr. Featherstonehaugh-Pellow. You are very kind."

"Any more sarcasm, Mrs. Penelope Campbell. Note, I said Penelope, and you can come tonight but have only one bread roll with no butter."

"OK, Mr. Meany-Featherstonehaugh-Pellow. Noted."

They both laughed, but each carried at the back of their respective mind some sad regret at the situation of Sir William Henderson. They travelled the rest of the way in quiet, contemplative silence.

EPILOGUE

They were just about to leave the apartment to go to dinner when Front Reception phoned Alistair's flat. It wasn't Mac but one of the evening staff.

"Mr. Pellow, sir. I have Sir Anthony Wollaston down here wishing to come up and see you."

"Sir Anthony? Have someone show him up please."

Alistair replaced the house phone and turned to Penny. He said in a very puzzled voice, "My boss, the head of MI5 is downstairs. He's on his way up."

"Does he normally pop in to see you?" Penny asked.

"Unheard of. He never visits anybody. This is very unusual."

A minute or so later, the front doorbell rang. Alistair strode to the door and opened it. Penny thought Alistair movements were very agitated.

"Sir Anthony!" Alistair exclaimed. "An unusual surprise, sir."

"May I come in?" Sir Anthony Wollaston asked.

"Of course, sir," Alistair stepped aside to allow his visitor entry.

"Sir Anthony. May I introduce Mrs. Penny Campbell," Alistair announced. "She was assigned to investigate the rumours …"

"Yes," Sir Anthony cut in. "I am aware of her role. Good evening, Mrs. Campbell. I am terribly sorry to interrupt your evening."

Penny thought that Alistair seemed to fluff around; he was certainly nervous. She could not imagine why. His boss seemed to be a very pleasant man in his early fifties, of medium height and with well trimmed brown hair. He looked like he carried just a little bit more weight than he should have, but he had a nice face and smiling eyes.

"Can I offer you a drink, Sir Anthony?"

"Thank you, no. I need to talk with you and perhaps…?" he looked over at Penny and raised an eyebrow.

"Oh, please, don't worry about Mrs. Campbell. She knows everything about this case," Alistair said then added, "I assume you are here because of, er, recent events?"

Sir Anthony's smiling eyes now turned a little bit colder. "Pellow, you have been on my staff for what? Two years?"

"Nearly three, Sir Anthony."

"During this time we have got to know each other, I would say, reasonably well. As you are well aware, I never make visits to staff, but this is an exception. If you don't mind my talking in front of Mrs. Campbell, then I'll come straight to the point. Waiting on the other side of this door are three officers from my department with a warrant for your arrest. Because of our close association over the last few years, I thought I should give you the courtesy of prior warning before they cuff you and escort you away."

Alistair's face went very white. "I, I don't understand," he mumbled. "Arrest me? For what?"

"Treason, Mr. Pellow."

"You've got this all wrong," Alistair protested. "You damn well know I've been pretending to support the group of dissidents only in order to out them. You've got them all, including their ring leader, Sir William Henderson."

"You've tried a nice double bluff, but it's been seen through. We have irrefutable evidence that whilst what

288

you have just said might have been your initial objective, your thinking changed over time. You became quite an ardent believer in the group's end purpose, the overthrow of the government.

"It would seem that towards the end, you decided to take over the reins and run the enterprise with you at its head. Although, how you expected to succeed without an army of Rathings is difficult to reconcile. To do so, you had to sacrifice your fellow conspirators, yet at the same time of your doing so, you believed that you strengthened your hand with us, bluffing us into believing that you were truly operating on the Government's behalf. A nice double bluff – which unfortunately for you hasn't come off."

"But, look here..." Alistair began to object but his boss interrupted him.

"I would rather we did not discuss this here. You may, of course, put your case when you are questioned at headquarters but I must tell you that the evidence we have is incontrovertible. My visit here to tell you why you are being arrested is only out of my consideration of you and your parents who are friends of my wife and me. I now propose to allow the arresting officers entry, but I am prepared to give you a couple of minutes in the event that Mrs. Campbell and you wish to discuss any matters." Sir Anthony walked towards the door and left Penny and Alistair alone.

Penny sidled up to Alistair. "Oh, Alistair. This must be some terrible mistake," she whispered.

Alistair's shoulders slumped. "Of course it is, Penny. It's now a known fact by the public at large that I was a member of the dissident group. What is not known is that I was put there by the Government in a spying role and to report on what was being planned. Without that knowledge, the public would want to know why I have not also been arrested as after all, I was a member of the dissident group. The big bosses in Government are now nervous about having to explain their decision to have a mole put in the group by them. I think they believe that it would be difficult to explain the ins and outs of the exercise. Therefore, it is more expedient to get rid of me than have to mount a campaign of justification."

"Oh, Alistair, my poor, poor Alistair. Is there nothing you can do?" Penny asked.

"Oh, I won't be executed. There'll be a low-key trial held in camera. There'll be a clampdown on publicity. I shall receive a reprimand then be released. Obviously, I won't get an OBE or anything like that but I'll be home before you know it."

"Gosh! That would be fantastic." Penny went up to Alistair. She caressed his cheek and kissed him gently.

"You might as well stay here until then," Alistair said and kissed her back.

They had just parted when the door opened and three men followed Sir Anthony and walked up to Alistair and informed him of his arrest and his rights.

Sir Anthony bowed to Penny. "Good night, Mrs. Campbell. I am sorry to have disturbed your planned evening."

"Good night, Sir Anthony," Penny replied.

Sir Anthony and the men escorted Alistair out of the flat.

Penny felt as if her world had shattered. In the space of hours, she had lost her uncle, and now the man she had begun to love and believe in. But she gave a small smile at the thought that Alistair would be home again soon. In a small corner of her heart she felt there remained a chance of future happiness with Alistair.

She considered that it would be wrong for her to stay at Knox Court without Alistair. She decided that it would be best for her to return to her flat in Teddington and await news from there. Reluctantly, she walked out of the apartment door and out of the apartment block. It was snowing quite heavily and soft flakes kissed her face. She decided to walk to the tube station in Sloane Square. As she walked, she wiped off her cheek the mixture of melting snow and tears that she could not control. She felt very empty and very sad.

EXTRACT FROM THE GLOBE NEWSPAPER

MISSING RATHINGS

Following the saturation of DTX toxin by American aircraft, a body count of the dead Rathings in the caves at Uamh an Claonaite in Scotland, showed a shortfall of forty eight creatures, based on the records of the organization that controlled them. Also missing are a dozen of their instructors/ trainers who police were unable to locate when seeking them with arrest warrants. Intensive searches continue.

Experts say that the Rathings could not survive unless they were sheltered in deep locations and provided with some means of suitable breathing equipment so as to ensure the toxin did not affect them.

After this news was publicized, a dealer in air oxygenators and respirators, based in Durham, came forward and stated that about a year before he had sold fifty head covers and hoods and associated equipment to a gentleman whose name was Featherstonehaugh-Pellow. The items were not found at the given delivery address.

Alistair Featherstonehaugh-Pellow was executed two months ago on a charge of treason.

John de Relya von Kesmark lives with his wife, Diane by the River Thames near Richmond, Surrey. This is his fourth published book. He is a member of the Society of Authors and of the Authors' Licensing and Collecting Society (ALCS).

www.ingramcontent.com/pod-product-compliance
Lightning Source LLC
Chambersburg PA
CBHW020946260626
47169CB00006B/1843